"It's as if Xander from *Buffy the Vampire Slayer* wandered into a place a lot scarier than Sunnydale and Buffy wasn't there to save him. This is a horror novel for smart people—brave, smart people. I could hear the audience screaming, "*Don't go in there!*" as I turned the pages, but I had to open the door and go through. *Age of Consent* is too fun and creepy to resist."—Stacy Horn, author of *The Restless Sleep*

Did people make noises like that?

From his sister's room came a whimpering.

Peter stepped to the door, and he was sure he heard voices from behind it, indistinct but more than one. Male voices, gibbering, whispering, rising into an insane giggle and falling again.

He called out her name in the dark of the hallway.

"Virginia?"

He put his hand to the doorknob and it all stopped dead.

He tried to turn the knob, but the door wouldn't open. He put his shoulder to it. Nothing.

Footsteps, crossing the room to the door. Slow, heavy footsteps. Virginia never made that much noise walking across a room.

He pressed his ear to the door, tried the doorknob again. Another set of footsteps, faster, scurrying across the room. He could hear breathing on the other side of the door now, he thought, coming from right where his ear was, too high up for Virginia, unless she was standing on something. There was something right there, inches away from him, inches from his face. Panting. Peter could feel it listening through the door, just like he was.

AGE OF CONSENT

Howard Mittelmark

A SIGNET BOOK

SIGNET
Published by New American Library, a division of
Penguin Group (USA) Inc., 375 Hudson Street,
New York, New York 10014, USA
Penguin Group (Canada), 90 Eglinton Avenue East, Suite 700, Toronto,
Ontario M4P 2Y3, Canada (a division of Pearson Penguin Canada Inc.)
Penguin Books Ltd., 80 Strand, London WC2R 0RL, England
Penguin Ireland, 25 St. Stephen's Green, Dublin 2,
Ireland (a division of Penguin Books Ltd.)
Penguin Group (Australia), 250 Camberwell Road, Camberwell, Victoria 3124,
Australia (a division of Pearson Australia Group Pty. Ltd.)
Penguin Books India Pvt. Ltd., 11 Community Centre, Panchsheel Park,
New Delhi - 110 017, India
Penguin Group (NZ), cnr Airborne and Rosedale Roads, Albany,
Auckland 1310, New Zealand (a division of Pearson New Zealand Ltd.)
Penguin Books (South Africa) (Pty.) Ltd., 24 Sturdee Avenue,
Rosebank, Johannesburg 2196, South Africa

Penguin Books Ltd., Registered Offices:
80 Strand, London WC2R 0RL, England

First published by Signet, an imprint of New American Library,
a division of Penguin Group (USA) Inc.

First Printing, February 2007
10 9 8 7 6 5 4 3 2 1

ACKNOWLEDGMENTS

Thanks go to my editor, Tracy Bernstein (more loyal a friend than can reasonably be expected), and my landlord, Roman Bohdanowycz (inadvertent patron of the arts).

It was the sort of place you'd expect to find littered with crushed, empty beer cans and discarded condoms, with crumpled Marlboro hard packs and Bic lighters tossed away. It was the sort of place where you knew what the graffiti on the walls would say before you saw it, the faded red and black words spray-painted two feet high, chronicling multiple generations of teenage parties and teenage gropings, drunken humpings and stoned fumblings, variations of KEVIN RULES and STACY BLOWS and CLASS OF 84 ROCKS in every room, recording each wave of high school kids who had sought a place to get high and get laid and feel like adults or just not feel, one after the other, year after year.

Oneida House was the sort of place where you'd expect all that, so much that when you walked in and found none of it—not a matchbook on the floor nor one crude word scrawled on the walls, nothing to indicate that a single teenager had ever lit a single joint here—the absence came so abruptly that all that detritus, all those discarded artifacts of traditional American youth, all that *stuff*, seemed to actually exist in the space between what should have been and what was; a history that never happened seemed to break through for just a second, and then it was gone.

No one had lived in the house for years, not officially, not since 1971, when the college shut it down. Even so, it looked worse than that. The weather off the lake had stripped the back of the house down to wood, without a hint that it had ever been painted, and the pier back there was off-kilter and missing planks. The porch in front, facing the trees that stood between the house and Route 9, had caved in, as had the veranda above it, and dense, moist mosses had emerged from the darkness beneath the house and spread across the rotting wood and halfway up the columns that framed the doorway.

The contractor who did the renovation had moved to Seneca a few years earlier from Rochester, an hour's drive north; he was doing pretty well fixing up summer houses along the lake, and didn't have to take the job. But when he met the buyer and his wife—he was the one with the money, a writer, and she was an architect, it turned out, but not the pushy, know-it-all kind, at least—to do a walk-through and come up with an estimate to make the old Greek Revival house habitable, it was the first time he'd seen the property, and he saw no reason not to.

He took the job, and the job got done, because that was the kind of man he was, but if there was ever a job he wanted to walk away from, this was it. He just could not keep a crew. He'd never seen anything like it. Workers kept quitting, and the ones that stayed wanted to leave as soon as the sun started going down, wouldn't work past dark even for overtime pay.

There were noises upstairs, one of them would say in newly acquired English, over the excited Spanish of the other day laborers, and some of them had seen things. Nobody wanted to disappoint the new *jefe*, but they hadn't traveled so far from their homes and families and churches for this.

He'd heard the noises, too, and he'd gone up there looking, but he never told any of them about it.

The first time, he'd followed the thumpings and indistinct voices to the first bedroom right by the stairs. Bracing himself with the thought that he was a practical man who did not believe in superstitious nonsense, he'd thrown the door open. In the bright light of the full moon that shined in on the bare white walls and newly polyurethaned floor, it took him a moment to see the spill of water. It wasn't until he played his flashlight over it—the electrician hadn't gotten to the bedrooms yet—that he saw the wet footprints that led from the puddle straight into a wall.

The time after that, the thumping was louder, and when he followed it upstairs to the master bedroom he was almost certain that he heard a girl crying, too. There was no moon that night, but the wiring was done and the lights were on, at least until the moment he opened the door. Something blew and the whole house went dark. He froze in the doorway, blinking, his retinas turned camera by the abrupt darkness, a negative afterimage floating in front of him. A mound of bodies, naked, long-haired, the blank and uncurious faces of the young men on top turned to look his way.

He backed away, fumbling for the Maglite on his tool belt, tripped and landed on his ass, and when he'd finally turned it on, he found nothing there but another pool of water.

After that, he left before the sun set, too.

It took three months longer than planned and went

over budget, and the client had been calling weekly from New York, self-important and demanding, to whine and grouse the entire time, but the job finally got done. On the last day he'd painted all the trim on the first floor himself. From then on, though, he always drove down the other side of the lake, even when he was jammed up in a hurry, and it was going to make him late.

1

The thin sounds of music bleeding from two sets of headphones in the backseat were very clear in the sudden silence of the car. Outside, the only sound was the slow tick of the cooling engine. Tall grass led to woods on either side of the house, and through the open windows, after a hesitant pause, the whir and chirp of crickets and cicadas washed back over them.

"We're home," Phil Coulter said, willfully chipper, not really expecting a response. His son, Peter, sixteen and still wearing his almost man-sized body uncomfortably and self-consciously, like a rented tux a size too large, opened his door and stepped out, head bobbing to Led Zeppelin. Peter's sister, Virginia, three years younger, closed her *Gossip Girl* novel after fastidiously placing her bookmark. She shut off whichever bare-bellied girl singer she was currently looking to for hints of how to grow up and exited from the other side. They'd been here before, earlier in the summer, and once last year, but the trees and the calm and the clean lake air remained as alien to the Brooklyn neighborhood they had grown up in as a Pacific island, and they stood, blinking, in front of their new home, momentarily stilled.

Phil emerged from the front seat, went around to the rear of his new black Lexus, and started unloading. Virginia sneezed, then began to walk toward the lake, tramping down a path in the waist-high grass. The sound of sporadic sneezing trailed behind her.

"Can I get a hand here?" Phil said, lifting two bags and a carton from the trunk. "Peter?"

Peter took his headphones off, stuffed them in a pocket of his baggy cargo shorts, and stepped over to help. There were only the few things in the trunk; most of the family's possessions had been brought up by movers and, with Julia, Phil's wife, directing, situated through the house days ago.

Peter hefted onto his shoulder a cardboard carton filled with things they were using in their Brooklyn kitchen right up until that morning. His mother, who'd be staying down in the city until she finished up a couple of projects, never ate breakfast and seldom cooked unless it was for her family; they'd left behind little more than a coffeemaker and a microwave oven. He grabbed a duffel bag with his other hand and followed his father up the dirt path that ran through the tall grass to the front door of the house.

"Dad?"

"Ginny!" his father yelled at the same time. She had walked halfway to the water. "Be careful!" The girl looked their way and waved, continued toward the shoreline.

"I'm sorry, Peter. What?" They stopped in front of the house before stepping up onto the porch, their shadows reaching out behind them in the late afternoon sun, misshapen where they fell across the irregular plane formed by the tops of long-unmowed grass.

"This was a good idea, right?" Peter did his best to

keep his feelings within some abstract shell of cool, but he wasn't very good at it yet, and the slight anxiety was obvious in his voice. He'd been the only one who had backed his father in the move. The house had split along gender lines, and though his father joked about boys versus girls, Peter knew it was more like nothing-to-lose versus already-have-a-life. His father did nothing but work, and Peter sure wasn't leaving anything behind in Brooklyn. He felt bad about uprooting his mother and his sister, pulling them away from their friends, but what really worried him was whether it might be even worse for him up here.

"Of course it was," his father said with characteristic certainty. "They'll be thanking me by Christmas."

Phil mounted the two steps up onto the porch, switched the two bags into one hand, and balanced the carton between the doorframe and the upper curve of his substantial gut to unlock the door. Peter followed him into the house, a few paces behind.

"Dad?" Peter said, as he stepped through the door, but his father had already followed the hallway to the kitchen in the back of the house. He peered into the dim living room to his left, half the furniture things he'd grown up with, the rest brand-new. Peter stepped into the room and put down the things he was carrying, and went to the tall, narrow windows to open the curtains and let in some light.

"*Ginny!*" his father yelled from the kitchen, in the back of the house.

"Dad?" Peter called.

"Ginny!" he heard him yell again, out the kitchen window, as Peter followed the dark hallway back to see what was up. "Get off of there now!"

Peter went to his father's side, leaned over the

newly installed stainless steel sink. Out the window he could see his sister, halfway down the ramshackle pier, outlined against the blue of the lake stretching into the distance. His sister stood oblivious, looking down into the water.

His father shouted again. Virginia stood, unmoving. It wasn't like her. She wasn't far enough away that she could possibly not hear, and she was always obedient. So routinely good and annoyingly obedient, in fact, that Peter sometimes wanted to smack her for it.

"Peter, go down to the pier and get your sister in here, okay? Before she falls in and hurts herself or something."

"Sure thing, Dad," he said. Peter left the kitchen and headed down the hall that led to the back of the house. A bright new key was fitted into the newly installed brass lock on the heavy wooden door, and he let himself out onto the screened-in back porch that ran the length of the house, and then through the screen door and down the steps.

Peter hurried down to the pier, feeling his father's eyes on him through the kitchen window. Grass whipped against his bare legs.

"Hey, moron," he said when he got there.

Virginia was crouching now, leaning over, still staring down into the water. Her hair fell forward, hiding her face. She didn't look up.

"Hey, c'mon. Dad says to get off the pier and come up to the house."

"Peter!" he heard his father call behind him, impatient, letting him know that, once again, he'd like Peter to do a better job of what he sent him off to do. It's not as if it's my fault she's out here, Peter thought, and took it out on his sister.

"I'm gonna push you in if you don't come now," he said, and stepped out onto the pier. He immediately felt how weak the plank he stood on was, the shakiness of the whole thing. It was a simple structure of weathered planks, at least a third of them missing, and it looked and felt like it should have collapsed long ago.

Virginia stood up straight, turned to look at him. The smile on her face was as familiar to him as it was easily interpreted. *She* hadn't hesitated to walk out on the rickety pier. One of them was acting like a girl, and it wasn't her.

"Stop being a jerk, you little shit," he said, and continued toward her, crossing the remaining space in three quick strides. He looked down into the water where she'd been staring. There was nothing there, just his own face staring up at him from the still surface and the murky darkness beneath it in the shadow of the pier. He couldn't help asking. "What were you looking at, lame ass?"

"Drop dead, loser," Virginia said, and walked past him.

He controlled an impulse to hit her—no way his father wouldn't see—and followed her back up to the house.

They drove into town for dinner at nine, into downtown Seneca, Seneca proper. There were three restaurants on Main Street, but the Main Street Café and the Seneca Lunch Nook were already closed, and the third was Chez du Lac, tiny and candlelit, not what they were looking for. At the end of Main Street, after passing the bank, the two churches facing each other across the street, Roman Catholic and Pentecostal, and the darkened plate-glass windows of a dozen small stores—with no pull-down gates protecting them, Peter finally realized, after wondering what made these stores look like something out of an old movie—Phil turned right, following High Street north away from downtown, heading to where the high school was.

"Not to worry! The diner's probably open," he said, as he drove past the well-kept houses on either side of the street. "You kids just think about what you want for your first dinner in your new hometown."

The first three-block stretch of High Street was the best real estate in town. The houses were from roughly the same early-nineteenth-century period as their new home, but these had been kept up, instead of being worn down by passing time. A number of them had been featured in magazines that concerned themselves with fine Americana.

Peter and Virginia slumped against the doors in the backseat and stared out silently from opposite sides at the glowing windows they passed, some tableaux of family life, others still lifes, waiting to be inhabited. They went on past the high school, and out of town to the Seneca Diner, located to serve the traffic passing on Route 20, the local alternate to Interstate 90 connecting Albany to Buffalo, but used just as much to get from Cazenovia to Seneca and Geneva to Canandaigua.

"It's open twenty-four hours, I think," said Peter, offhandedly.

"Duh," Virginia said as the car turned the corner and they both saw the bright neon sign atop the railroad car diner: *24 Hour Diner.*

"You didn't know that, dumb ass."

Whatever Virginia might have said in response was

lost as the car pulled into the parking lot on the far side of the diner, next to the Shell station. Peter and Virginia saw the pack of kids hanging out by the battered metal guardrail between the two properties at the same time, and their desultory bickering was instantly dropped.

In the pool of dim yellow light cast by one tall streetlamp, half a dozen or so teenagers stood about. Lots of lank, unwashed-looking hair—Strokes hair, except you could tell they didn't spend hours getting it to look that way, the way you'd just assume they did back home. The glow of cigarettes adorned the group like jewelry, and they were almost all wearing uniformly faded jeans.

One of the girls wore cutoffs with quite a bit of leg exposed, which caught Phil's eye when his headlights swept over the crowd, almost making him too late on the sharp right to pull into a parking space. Other than that one arresting glimpse of skin, though, to Phil it was an undifferentiated mass of teenager, but Virginia and Peter, with a sense as specific and accurate as a migrating bird's feel for south, read meaning in every detail of stance and inclination. It needed to be sorted out, adjustments made for local style and custom once they understood it, but they immediately began to process the details. Everything was different here, they could both tell at a glance. Virginia didn't recognize a single clothing brand, except . . . could those possibly be *Levi's*? No one in her crowd would be caught *dead* in Levi's. At the same time, though, they both knew everything was exactly the same.

Phil was already halfway to the diner's entrance when Peter and Virginia exited the car in an unspoken truce, both of them forcedly casual. In the light spilling from the diner across the parking lot, it felt as if they were walking across a stage. They had almost made it safely off without tripping or blowing their lines when their father called out from the doorway.

"Come on, kids!"

The burst of laughter that reached them from across the parking lot made both their faces hot, but they continued on with barely a hitch in their step.

Inside, Phil was already seated in a booth. Virginia shot past Peter to get the seat by the window opposite her father; when Peter realized what she was doing, he tried to trip her, but he wasn't fast enough.

He slid in after her.

"Ow!"

Their father looked up at him from his menu, didn't see Virginia surreptitiously place her fork back on the table. Peter rubbed his thigh where she'd jabbed him.

"Leave your sister alone," Phil said.

"But she—"

The waitress, a bored-looking woman in her forties, dropped three glasses of water on the table, spilling just a bit, then pulled out her pad, addressed Phil.

"Know what you're having?"

They ordered burgers all around. Phil unfolded *The New York Review of Books* and disappeared behind it, scanning the table of contents. Somebody'd told him that his book was mentioned in two different essays. Only the top of his head, dark hair brushed straight back from high forehead, was visible above the paper.

Peter tried not to be too obvious about staring out the window, in case somebody looked over, but Virginia had no such compunction, and just about pressed her face right up against the glass. Before a minute passed, two girls separated from the crowd and headed toward them across the parking lot to the diner. Peter watched them as they passed under the window, and one of them, the really cute one with curly brown hair—did she just smile at him?

Peter could hear them come in the door, and next to him, his sister got up on her knees and turned around to look behind them. Peter peered around the edge of the booth, and . . . Virginia sneezed, and the two girls turned to look at them. He yanked his head back in. His sister looked down at him and laughed, turned back to look again.

"I told you kids a hundred times you can't use the bathroom unless you buy something. Go use the bathroom at the gas station."

Peter looked again. An old guy in a dirty white apron had come out from behind the counter, where he'd been attending the grill. Peter had an idea. It terrified him and thrilled him at the same time. Was he really thinking of doing that?

"C'mon, Mr. Calabrese. It's so gross over there. Just, please?" It was the other girl talking, the blonde.

Nobody knew him here, Peter thought. He could be different, starting now. He started to get up. No, he couldn't. He sat back down. Virginia turned and slid back down into the seat.

"Yeah, right. I dare you to talk to them." She smiled at him, taunting.

I could be a different person, he thought, starting *right now.* He slid to the edge of the booth and stood up. Nobody's ever beat me up here. Nobody's ever laughed at me here. Nobody's even heard of me here. I don't have to be that person anymore, he told himself.

A girl could like me.

He turned and looked at the girls, but before he

could take a step, Virginia reached out and grabbed a handful of his shirt. "No, wait, I didn't mean it. Don't."

In the end, Virginia was neither heartless nor without affection for her brother, and she couldn't let this happen. She'd heard about the time he'd asked out Diane Harris, last year: it had made it all the way down to the seventh grade. Kids still called him "Juicebox." Peter pulled away from her.

"What are you gonna say?" Virginia asked him in a thick whisper, seriously alarmed now.

"You two settle down, okay? We're out in public," Phil said, without looking up from his journal. They ignored him.

"Yeah, and what do I do when your friends come in here after you? I end up with a parade a you kids in and outta here, bothering my customers," Mr. Calabrese said.

You can do this, Peter thought, and walked toward them. His sister was up on her knees again, watching. Pretend it's a movie, he told himself. You're the hero. You're not afraid of anything. Just like a movie. Ohgod ohgod ohgod. He could feel his heart thudding in his chest as he opened his mouth.

"Hi," he said to the girl who had smiled at him.

She wasn't smiling anymore. She was confused. She didn't know how to react. He wasn't supposed to do this. Sure, she'd smiled at him, he was kind of cute, but one smile did not mean he could walk right up to her in front of people.

The conversation stopped, and all three of them looked at him, clearly wondering what the hell he was doing.

You're in a movie, he told himself, and you are

cooler than cool. He pulled his wallet out of his back pocket, reached in with two fingers and took out the five-dollar bill he kept in there. You are James Fucking Bond.

"Here. I'd like to buy them a soda," he said, and gave the money to the counterman. "Now they're customers."

"Bye," he said to the girl, then turned carefully and walked the half dozen steps back to the booth, quickly slid in. His wallet was still in his now-trembling hand.

Voice didn't crack? Check.

Didn't trip over anything? Check.

Didn't wet myself? He glanced down quickly. Thank god.

He let out his breath.

"That was *so* lame," Virginia said. "You don't even *know* them." Her heart wasn't in it, though, Peter could tell, and behind her words he heard something like admiration. He slumped down into the booth.

They'd just started eating—their plates set down roughly, and with a glare from the waitress at Peter— a few minutes later, when the girls left the diner. Peter heard their hushed giggling voices and then the door swinging shut behind them. He swallowed quickly and put down his hamburger so as not to be caught with a mouthful of food if she looked his way again.

He looked out the window and they were walking away, without a look back.

That's okay, he thought, you still did pretty good, and then she turned around and walked backward for a few steps, waved at Peter, a take-out Coke in her other hand. She held up the soda and mouthed "Thanks," before spinning around to catch up with her friend.

2

Half asleep, roused by and immersed in a vivid half dream of the girl from the diner, at five a.m. Peter lay in his darkened room, right hand moving steadily. Maybe because he wasn't in the cramped apartment he'd grown up in, where'd he always been afraid of discovery, he was for the first time free to lose himself in fantasy. Maybe because his sister wasn't one thin wall away from him on one side, his parents on the other, he even found himself making noises deep in his throat in response to what he was feeling.

Whatever it was, he was vaguely aware that this didn't just feel better than it ever had before, it felt different, a whole other thing. On some level, in a small observing part of his mind, he knew that something was not right, but in the end he didn't care. It was too good, too real, to interrupt.

He thought of the girl's face, and it was like she was right there, looking at him. He imagined what she looked like without her clothes on, and he could see her, clear as a downloaded picture. He imagined what it would be like if she touched him, and suddenly—*oh!* he sucked in his breath—it didn't even feel like his own hand anymore. He sunk deeper into the fantasy, and that small observing part of him drowned in sensation. He could feel her touch all over him, her hands here, and there, and there. Peter's hands, both of them, splayed out to either side, grasping, clenching the blanket.

Peter would have been alarmed, horrified even, if he had any idea how loud the noises coming from his room had become, how it maybe even sounded like there might be more than one person in there. He would have been even more alarmed, though, if he could hear the very similar sounds coming from his little sister's room.

Usually, their father would awaken to much less noise than this, put out and snappish. But in his half sleep, Phil felt his wife's arms around him, felt her pressing herself against him, and the sounds were a part of it, and he let them envelop him as he added to them.

Even this far below the surface of consciousness, he knew Julia didn't touch him like this anymore, but he pulled her closer, nonetheless, and his hips began moving with hers.

Julia jolted up out of sleep, abruptly awakened by— what was it? A noise? She listened intently, straining against the silence of her apartment. She raised herself up on her elbows, looked around the bedroom. The light coming in from the street showed the room starkly, disconcertingly empty, the big chair missing from the corner, an empty stretch of wall where Phil's dresser should be. Then she remembered that her family was gone.

That's what woke her up: her first night alone here, her children hundreds of miles away. Not a noise. No noise.

She checked the time—five A.M.—and decided to get up. She'd been sleeping since just after ten, when the kids called to say good night, and she had multiple drawings to print out and go over anyway. She started to pull on her robe, then tossed it back across the foot of the bed and walked naked to the kitchen to start coffee.

It had been a long time since she last walked naked through this apartment. It had seemed like a big apartment back then, too, empty and echoey, like it was now.

"The cramped years," she said out loud. They're over. She felt guilty and a little exhilarated at the same time.

Since they'd moved in here, her family had expanded to fill the big apartment, and her responsibilities had grown to occupy her thoughts nearly nonstop. Mostly, though, what had made her life increasingly claustrophobic, a straightjacket of a life, was Phil. His book, his ambition, his ego, had pressed in on her, taking over everything, making it the central fact of their lives.

In the kitchen, she didn't turn the light on. It was so peaceful being in an empty apartment in the dark. She drank grapefruit juice from the carton, scooped coffee by the light of the open refrigerator door.

But what could she have said? What could she have done? She had thought about leaving and taking the kids, but as bad as it was, that would probably have been worse. And, besides, when Phil insisted that his work was important, she'd known he was right. It was his intensity that had made him so attractive to her to begin with, that he was passionate about something. That passion never flagged, but it was also never extended to anything beyond his work.

She walked to the computer in the living room while she waited for the coffee to brew. The leather chair was cool against her skin.

The work she did as an architect—the boring retail

spaces, all the same; the vapid interiors for vapid stockbrokers and their vapid wives; the banal Tribeca office spaces, each one with the same obvious bohemian touches to show that this company was different—nobody would remember them. They made no real difference in anybody's life. Even she didn't care. She looked forward to the end of each project almost as soon as it started.

But *Taking the Measure of Heaven*—you couldn't argue with that sort of success. Phil's book would be around long after they were gone. It was an important book, just like he'd said it would be, a major work of scholarship.

The computer booted, and she called up the drawings she'd been working on. Compare that to this crap. She couldn't argue with him and the priorities he set for the family.

You couldn't argue with the money from the Whittaker Prize, either. Which made it even harder to argue with Phil's insistence that they all move upstate, closer to his research for the next book when he got a job offer from Harcourt College. She'd tried, but her voice had grown even smaller in their decisions since the book had come out and everything changed. In the end, she had given in. Phil didn't seem to think it was that much of a problem that she'd have to stay in New York for the foreseeable future.

She heard the whine of the printer as it started turning out pages, and went back to the kitchen for her coffee. She turned on the light and filled a large mug, leaned back against the counter and sipped. From there, she could see the nearly empty living room.

This really was a pretty nice apartment, now that it wasn't so crowded. You could do a lot with it.

3

Every year the beginning of school held for Peter the promise of a fresh start. September was a clean crisp scent piercing the thick hot air that had pressed down on Brooklyn all summer. Every year, the feel on his fingertips of the smooth, white paper in a new notebook, light blue lines like veins; the pens all in a row, unchewed, not a tooth mark anywhere; the new clothes he wore, unfamiliar against his skin, it was all part of the feeling he always had that this was the year when everything would change. And every year, somebody came up behind him in the hall and pushed his notebooks onto the floor from under his arm, or stole his pens, or mocked his new clothes, which he'd somehow gotten wrong yet again.

Every year, Peter thought, I fell for it, but this time it was different. This really was the year everything could change, he told himself as he walked through the loud, crowded, fluorescent-lit halls of Seneca High School. Lockers slammed as he walked past unfamiliar faces, clumps of teenagers talking, kids rushing through the halls to their next class. He was halfway through his first day and nobody had given him a hard time yet. Of course, nobody had talked to him either.

He thought he'd recognized a couple of kids from the other night in his first few classes, but he still felt safely anonymous.

Peter checked the printout of his classes he'd picked up in the office that morning. The bell rang just as he walked into his history class, and there she was, the girl from the diner, brown curls falling over her shoulders, the tip of a pen held against her lips. She was sitting halfway back, third row over. There was a seat open in the next row, one forward, in front of a big, muscular, shaggy-haired guy. He was wearing a long-sleeve waffle-knit under a black T-shirt, but two layers were not enough to even begin to hide the size of his shoulders and arms, and his jaw was dark with a day's stubble.

Great, Peter thought, it must be that special program where they mix the inmate population in with the high school kids. He quickly took a seat. He glanced over at the girl, but she was looking away from him, talking to a girl in the next row. "Patricia? Allison? I'm sure it's important, but could it wait until after class?"

The two of them shut up, as the teacher, whose name, Ms. Bourne, was written on the blackboard, began to speak. She was in her fifties, with short gray hair, and a compact body beginning to thicken at the waist.

"This is a regents history class. If you have already taken the regents exam in New York history, or do not intend to take a history regents, you should not be here. Between now and December we will be discussing the social, economic, and religious history of New York State. . . ."

Peter paid as much attention as he could, making a note now and then, until he saw a bit of white flutter to the floor beside him. He picked up the folded piece of paper, and opened it to read,

> *Hi! Welcome to Seneca High School!*
> *Write back what bands you like.*
>
>   *Trish Willits*

He looked back over his shoulder and got a big smile from Trish, whom he now realized he would almost certainly someday marry. He bent to his task, confident about at least this one thing. He'd spent many, many weekends cruising the used music stores of Williamsburg, and the hard drive of his laptop was running short of space due to downloaded MP3s.

Velvet Underground, he wrote. The coolest band ever. *Lou Reed. Nico. Bowie. Eno. Zeppelin. Radiohead.* Hip cred covered, he had to add some stuff everyone knows, some bands from the radio. *Hives, White Stripes, Interpol,* the *Strokes.* Those were happening. Nothing too emo. But maybe something a little emo wouldn't hurt. Bright Eyes? Death Cab for Cutie? Would she think that was too gay?

Peter was deep in thought, contemplating the virtues of each band he wrote down, the picture they together painted of him, when he became aware that, first, somebody, and then, specifically Ms. Bourne, was standing over him. She held out her hand.

Sheepishly, with a glance back at Trish, he handed her the note.

"Peter, is it? Our new student from New York City?" she said, after a quick glance. "You have good taste in music, but this is not the place to exercise it."

Peter sunk into his seat, the laughter around him so familiar he didn't really need to hear it. The laughter died out as Ms. Bourne began to speak again, and Peter listened to the extent that the sinking feeling in his stomach and the heat radiating from his cheeks allowed him to.

The finger poking him in the shoulder from behind was completely unexpected, and hurt a little, too; fortunately, the embarrassingly high-pitched sound that came out of him involuntarily was not loud enough to draw the eyes of the *entire* class. With cheeks freshly inflamed, he heard a whisper from over his shoulder.

"After school. Behind the annex."

Of course. The Hulk's her boyfriend. I should have known.

Peter had been hearing some variation on those words at school since he'd been tall enough to get knocked down.

Well, nice knowing you, New Peter, he thought. As imaginary people go, you were the best. Good times.

It's just as well. If he were to become a new person, there'd be all kinds of decisions to make, all sorts of choices. What would New Peter wear? How would he walk? Would he still like science fiction? Would he talk to his new friends on the phone, or meet them somewhere to hang out? Would he tell his new friends he used to be fat, so they could all have a laugh about it? Actually, he could probably count on Virginia to do that.

But if he were to suddenly find himself a person with a social life, he'd have to figure out how to do all the mysterious things he'd been watching other kids do, like talk to girls. Who needed the grief? Now the only choice he'd have to make was whether to get the first beating of the year out of the way today, or slink away home after school wondering when it would catch up with him.

*   *   *

Tray in hand, Virginia scoped out the geography of
the cafeteria with the sharp eye of an Indian scout
surveying unknown terrain. She was in a bad spot,
just a few feet off from the cash register, where
plenty of kids were sure to notice her indecision if
she waited too long. If Virginia had been just some
kid on her first day of school, that would be okay;
then it would even have been okay if she let some
sympathetic loser who'd seen her in class rescue her,
and invite her to her table . . . like the pimply girl in
the red sweater she saw headed toward her, a stupid,
friendly smile on her face. But that would not do for
what she had planned.

There! She spotted them. At a table in the rear of the
cafeteria, near the doors. Just in time, too. In the am-
bient noise of a hundred kids talking all at once, she
began walking confidently forward, just before the girl
in the red sweater reached her, which wasn't really
snubbing her because how was Virginia supposed to
know what she wanted?

Virginia had been planning this moment for weeks,
every detail, down to the color of her socks. She
crossed the cafeteria with as casual an air as she could
muster, her Benetton skirt swishing against her thighs,
passing the various lower-ranking cliques at their tables on her way. She'd had to get the feel of the room
before she could figure out where the most popular
girls sat; fortunately, like steel filings, the other kids in
the cafeteria were subtly arrayed around them as if
they were magnetic north. The main jock group, the
most popular boys, were right next to them, ranking on
each other just loudly enough to be heard by the popular girls. On the other side, the second-string girls
surreptitiously studied them, copying their gestures,

memorizing their outfits, preparing and practicing for when it was their time to move up.

As she got closer and her intent became clear, she could feel the eyes of those other girls turn to her, and at the last minute she almost veered, almost took a seat with them, where the stakes wouldn't be so high, but *no,* she'd been the most popular girl at Brooklyn Prep Middle School two years in a row, and she knew where she belonged.

"Hi. Okay if I sit here?" Virginia asked the table, and flipped her hair. Unlike their lesser satellites, the five girls sitting here hadn't until now looked her way. Now the table fell silent, and they all looked at her. One of them, a pretty blond girl, said noncommittally, "Sure."

"I'm Virginia," she said as she sat, and then, "I love that top," to the girl who had spoken. "J. Crew, right?"

The girl looked down at her shirt, a pale blue polo shirt, and then back up at Virginia. "No. Sears."

Virginia laughed. "Right, Sears."

Nobody else laughed. They were staring at her. Virginia felt it all start to fall apart right then. The girl hadn't been joking. It was really from Sears, wasn't it? She moved quickly onward to cover her confusion.

"I just moved here from New York."

"I'm Melanie," said the pretty girl who shopped at Sears. She seemed friendly enough as she introduced the other four girls at the table, and Virginia started to think it might still be okay.

"I know I'm really going to love it here, but I'm going to miss New York."

"I went to New York once," one of the other girls, another prim blonde, said. "We got to see them do *TRL.* I waited for hours."

"Oh, *TRL.* I did that when I was little," Virginia said.

"Oh. . . . Well, Bobby Donohue was there. I got his autograph after."

"He was supposed to be at the big peace march last summer. He didn't show up. Tim Robbins was there, though. And Elvis Costello and Gwen Stefani. And everyone in Green Day. I walked next to Bono for a while."

"You were in that big peace march that was on TV?" Melanie asked, impressed, it seemed, just as Virginia had hoped.

"Yeah," Virginia said, warming to the subject; she had more names to drop, more status points to lay out. "I went to that one, and the one the summer before. . . . "

"So you hate America?" Melanie asked her.

"I was . . . what?"

"You don't support our troops?" Melanie asked, innocently, almost sweetly.

Although both Brooklyn and Seneca are technically part of New York State, one was as red as the other was blue, and while the political stance of adolescents was generally as shallow as it was fervent, it was no less effective a means of defining who belonged and who didn't as, say, who thought they were too good to shop at Sears.

Virginia, of course, didn't understand the red and the blue of it, and certainly didn't understand the socioeconomic factors that made her new home the sort of place soldiers came from, and there was no way she could possibly have known that two of the girls at that table had brothers overseas. Virginia came from a place where being antiwar was as much a given as being pro-shopping for new clothes. All Virginia knew was that she'd walked into a trap, and she couldn't see a way out.

"But . . . I was just saying . . . ," Virginia began, when Melanie stood up and picked up her tray. The other girls aped her, a heartbeat behind.

Melanie leaned over, brought her face closer to Virginia's, her eyes focused on Virginia's forehead.

"You should do something about your skin, Virginia," she said loudly, before she and her friends walked away, laughing.

As she sat there, eyes down, going through the motions of eating the food on her tray, not even looking up until after the bell rang and the clamor of students getting up, talking, laughing, heading on to their next class, had already faded from the room, Virginia thought about the patch of skin across her forehead that had broken out a couple of weeks ago and just wouldn't clear up. She thought about how ugly it was, how nobody could look at her without seeing that first. They'd probably been staring at it the whole time.

Virginia thought, too, about how her body had softened and bulged over this last summer and how she'd had to squeeze into the outfit she'd chosen for today. What could she have been thinking, dressing like that? She probably looked like some gross, obese thing, like Miss Piggy, trying to wear clothing half her size.

How could she ever have thought this was a good idea? No wonder Melanie had been like that.

She wondered how she'd ever show her fat, pimply, loser face in school again. And, for just a second, she wondered if this was what Peter had felt like back in Brooklyn.

After school, Peter had hung by his locker for as long as he could, spinning the combination, opening and shutting the slightly off-kilter gray metal door, then examining the lock, the hinges, the top and bottom, as if he had a mechanic's interest in how it all worked. When the sound of the last echoing footsteps were gone, leaving him alone in the dim four o'clock hallway, he briefly considered going to Ms. Bourne's classroom to discuss bands with her. In the end, though, he knew there was nothing for it but to get it over with. He'd been beaten up before. Hell, he might even be good at it by now.

Peter pulled on his denim jacket and hefted his new backpack—no less absurdly heavy with textbooks here than back home—onto his shoulder, and headed out of the building. Peter saw a few students in some of the classrooms, for detention or extracurriculars, as he glanced left and right, but when he stepped out of the middle pair of doors—the set on either side chained shut—to the front steps of the school, he stood alone in the sudden sunlight. Blinking, he walked through the nearly empty parking lot, around the side of the building, past the athletic field to his right where the football team scrimmaged, past the school proper and across the stretch of buckled black asphalt, weeds growing from its cracks, that led to the annex.

The annex was a corrugated prefab building that stood alone about fifty yards beyond the school. Beyond it were empty fields that were no longer farmed, stretching back almost as far as Peter could see, to a scrim of tiny trees. The annex had once been painted white, but its paint had faded to a pale gray that almost matched the gray of the metal it covered, and the whole thing was spotted with patches of rust.

Peter thought it looked like a construction shack, which is what it would have been had the school not bought it in the early eighties, when a sudden boom in the student population had—briefly, it turned out—required extra classrooms. It had served various purposes since then. It had been a detention hall, a place for student organizations to meet, a storage locker for all sorts of athletic gear, but its most important purpose for almost a decade now had been to block the view of any teachers looking in that direction.

As Peter rounded the corner into the shadow of the structure, the first thing he saw was the big guy from class, who stood with his head back and a beer upturned, three other guys nearby. Peter stopped and waited to be noticed. Trish was there, too, sitting with two other girls on the concrete steps that led up to one of the annex doors. They were giggling as they wrote things on the sides of the white soles of their sneakers with a blue Bic pen.

Trish and the guy noticed him at the same time. The guy tossed his can aside and started walking toward him as Trish stood up, then the whole crowd, the four boys and three girls, advanced on him across the stretch of unpaved ground. Their feet threw up small puffs of fine, buff-colored dirt.

Trish was smiling, but Peter found it impossible under the circumstances to smile back. They all stood there, and then the big guy took one more step toward him.

Here it comes, thought Peter, but the guy made him wait. Lit a cigarette. Took a drag before speaking.

"You're from New York?"

"Yeah. So?" Peter said.

"So you're probably a homo then, right?"

His friends chuckled, and Peter thought that if he were any kind of man, which he wasn't, he would maybe throw the first punch, ineffectual as it was sure to be. At least make a stand in front of Trish. He could feel his face being pushed down into the dirt already. Before he could react, though, Trish pushed the guy from behind so hard that he stumbled forward a step and dropped his smoke.

"*God,* Buddy. You are *such* a dick," she said. "Ignore him," she said to Peter, walking toward him, "he knows you're not a homo."

"Ow," Buddy said, rubbing his shoulder. "Bitch."

"You're the bitch," she said, and kicked some dirt his way. The rest of the group started to crowd around Peter.

"You ever see anyone famous?" one of the girls who wasn't Trish asked him.

"Well, sure, lots of—"

"I bet you get some kick-ass drugs in New York, right?" one of the guys who wasn't Buddy said.

"Yeah, sometimes I—"

"We get some pretty wack drugs here," Buddy said. "Here, try this," and he held out a joint. Peter took it, processor working double time to reunderstand his circumstance. Buddy flicked open a Zippo adorned with a Guns n' Roses skull and bandana.

"Do you live near the Hard Rock Café?" a girl asked him. "I went there once."

"No," Peter said, squeaking and squinting as he held in a hit of pot. "I live, I mean I lived in Brooklyn." He exhaled.

"Brooklyn! That is *righteous*, dude," a long-haired guy in a leather jacket festooned with chains said, and then started singing "No sleep till Brooklyn! No sleep till Brooklyn!" The guy held up his hand and Buddy high-fived him. "Beastie Boys!" Buddy yelped.

With Trish's shoulder touching his as he passed her the joint, just starting to feel the soft shimmer of the pot on the borders of his awareness, Peter understood that, somehow, it had happened. He had become somebody else.

"Party!" Buddy shouted, for no apparent reason, throwing his fist in the air.

Somebody who hangs out with people like that, Peter couldn't help, even now, noting. Still, beats being me, he thought, and shouted "Party!" himself, holding up his hand and receiving a high five. He didn't even look to see who from.

"Dude," Buddy said, as he hit the joint and passed it along, "did you see the Towers go down? I wish I coulda seen that. I heard some guy totally *surfed* down the side when they fell. Oh, man, I wish I coulda seen that."

1971

"Shhh!"

Alex grabbed Ellen's arm and pulled her back behind the mausoleum, where they couldn't be seen from the path. Ellen leaned back against the wall, out of breath and laughing, and slid down until she was sitting with her hip-hugger-jean-clad butt on the cold, damp grass, the small of her back bare against the smooth cold granite. She had to put her hand over her mouth to stifle her giggles. Alex peered around the corner, then she took a step back and sat down next to Ellen. From here in the cemetery, they could see out over the lake, all the way across to campus. The buildings were vague darknesses in the darkness, suggestions of shapes; the few lighted windows stood out as sharp and clear as the north star in the cold night sky above, and reflected in the water below so perfectly

that you couldn't tell where the land ended and the reflection began.

Alex took a pack of Marlboros out of a pocket of her
jean jacket, and held it out to Ellen. They both lit up
off the Zippo Alex carried in the back pocket of her
Levi's.

"Did you see them?" Ellen asked.

"Not a sign. I think they're lost," Alex said, and then
they both started laughing again, at the idea of Seth
and Paul wandering lost in the woods, after all their
talk at dinner about learning to survive and live off the
land, dropping out of the System and going underground to start striking real blows against the Establishment. It was obvious to both of them that the boys
were showing off, trying to out-cool each other in front
of Ellen. They had probably known it, too, but
couldn't seem to stop themselves.

The first time she'd been out to Oneida House, Ellen
had been sort of intimidated. Everyone seemed so
much more serious, so much cooler, so much more
grown up, than her. And Ellen had heard all sorts of rumors about the place when she first came to Harcourt
College: They were manufacturing LSD and distribut-
ing it up and down the East Coast. They were an actual
communist cell, and they were getting funding from
Cuba through the Panthers. A couple of Weathermen
had been spotted coming into the house late at night by
boat off the lake. A couple of Weathermen *and Owsley.*

But Alex had made sure she was comfortable, and
the way the guys acted, it was hard to stay intimidated
for long. Sure, they were all upperclassmen, and really
smart and well-read, and serious about their politics.
Keith and Amy had been to the March on Washington,
and Paul had been in El Salvador with Alex, working

with the peasants during their junior year abroad, and they'd all been involved in organizing the antiwar protest that had shut down the campus at the beginning of the year and turned Harcourt into one of those names, like Berkeley and Columbia and Kent State, that made the Establishment uncomfortable.

But by this point in the school year, the middle of March, Seth and Paul had already tried and failed to get it on with Alex, and it had been a particularly cold and snowy winter, isolating them out here on the lake, making trips back to campus after dinner less frequent than they might otherwise have been, and the fairly constant rutting of Keith and Amy, the house couple, however discreet they tried to be, which was not very, had been making the two boys insane. The appearance among them of an attractive new girl had sent the two of them into an orgy of posturing countercultural male behavior.

Which was not to deny their commitment to the anarcho-Leninist synthesis they had fastened on in their readings of Marx and Proudhon and Fourier and Kropotkin. Everyone in the house was a serious member of the antiwar movement, and they knew Movement people at campuses across the country. Every one of them believed in the Revolution, and felt that they were ready to make whatever sacrifices were asked of them to overthrow the Establishment. But the way Seth and Paul saw it, that could wait until after graduation, and where in *Das Kapital* did it say they couldn't get laid?

"You don't have any grass with you, do you?" Alex asked. She picked up a rock and sidearmed it at a tree not far away.

"Sorry, no," Ellen said. She really wished she'd taken some from her suite mate before she met Alex for the ride out to the house.

"I might have a roach somewhere," Alex said, and started searching her pockets.

There was no denying that Ellen had been flattered by all the male attention, but she was more flattered that Alex had taken an interest in her, taken her up and become her friend.

Alex was the coolest woman she had ever met. She was, first of all, gorgeous, and Ellen had never known a woman so sure of herself before. She seemed to just assume that she would get to do things that Ellen had grown up thinking only men got to do. Alex was involved in half a dozen political groups on campus, and she was one of the founders of the Women's Consciousness Raising Circle—and she'd done that as a freshman. This year, she was coeditor of the school paper, which was where Ellen met her.

It wouldn't be going too far to say that Alex was Ellen's hero. In the six months since they'd met, Ellen had even started growing out her hair to more closely resemble Alex's wild blond curls, and she'd dropped the Fair Isle sweaters and white turtlenecks she'd been wearing since Fairfield Country Day School in favor of the jeans and T-shirts and flannel that Alex always wore. If she could, Ellen would change the color of her dark brown eyes to Alex's precise shade of emerald green, and let people think they were sisters.

What Ellen admired most about Alex, though, what she tried to imitate, and never could quite pull off, was that Alex was the same around men as she was around women. She didn't display that subtle deference to men in social situations that Ellen had grown up thinking of as normal. Harcourt had opened Ellen's eyes to a much larger world; Alex had given Ellen an idea of who she might be in it.

"Fucker," Alex muttered, giving up and then finally remembering to check her cigarette pack. She pulled the pack out, turned it over, and shook out half of a joint. "Got ya," she said and lit it up. She took a hit and passed it to Ellen.

"You know, I can bring up your name to move into the house next fall if you want," Alex said. "They could use more women next year." Because you had to be both approved by your department head and voted in by the previous year's residents, Oneida House was as exclusive as any fraternity on campus; sort of an anti-fraternity, really. That by itself would have been enough to make it a highly desirable residence, but Oneida House had been at the center of Harcourt's radical politics since before radical politics was cool. For the first three years of its existence, while most of the Harcourt student body was off to houses on Lake George and the Vineyard and Cape Hatteras in the summer, everyone living in Oneida House had gone off to march with the Freedom Riders down south.

"That'd be really cool, Alex. Too bad you'll be gone."

"Well, you know, I was thinking about staying in town next—"

"Alex . . . Ellen—"

"Goddamnit, Seth, watch where you're going."

Alex laughed. "Okay, we've let them wander long enough. I have to talk to them about something anyway. Come on."

Alex led Ellen out from behind the mausoleum. In front was an array of cement benches and urns and pedestals, a sort of landscaping in miniature meant to summon both classical antiquity and an English garden where Wordsworth might have contemplated a cloud. Alex sat herself down on a bench and lit another cigarette. "We're over here!" she called out. Ellen sat down next to her, and Seth and Paul soon turned off of the dirt road running by and joined them.

"Hey, guys," Alex said.

"Hey," Seth said, and offered the joint he and Paul had been passing back and forth to Ellen.

"Thanks," Ellen said.

"Listen, I wanted to talk to you guys about something," Alex said, "before we tell Keith and Amy."

Sounded like intrigue. The two of them were instantly attuned.

"You know that trunk I brought out to the house the other day?"

"Yeah. Your stuff from El Salvador, you said."

"Yeah, I did say that."

"So?"

"Well, it isn't. Remember when I got back from Ann Arbor before Thanksgiving, I told you I met this guy?"

"Yeah," Paul said, sounding as if he were losing interest already.

"Remember how I said I invited him to visit, come stay at the house?"

"So he's coming? We're very happy for you, Alex . . . so, Ellen, what do you think of the cemetery? Pretty cool, huh? Great place to trip, if you want to sometime. . . . "

"Seth, pay attention, wouldja? And stop hitting on Ellen. This isn't about me getting laid, okay? It's serious."

"We think that would be pretty serious," Paul said,

and dropped down onto the bench next to Alex. "Tell us all about it."

Alex punched Paul in the arm. "Just stop, okay?"

"Ow." She'd hit him pretty hard. He'd have a purple-brown blotch there tomorrow.

"Yeah, he's coming, Seth, but it's not social. It's business. Movement business."

"Yeah?" Paul said. She had their attention again.

"Yeah. The guy? It's Graham Walker. The trunk, that's his stuff."

" 'Microgram' Walker? No fucking way!" Seth said.

"Graham Walker is coming here? Really?" Paul asked.

"Yeah, we've been planning an action."

"Far out," Seth said.

"So," Paul said, "does that mean that trunk—"

"*Yes*," Alex said, cutting him off and looking toward Ellen significantly. "That's right. Now, look, you know Keith and Amy aren't going to like this, so if it comes to a house vote, I gotta know you guys are in. I can't tell him to turn around and go away when he gets here."

"Fuck, no," Paul said. "You know I'm ready for something real. I'm tired of just talking about doing something. Theory has its place and all, but praxis is where it's at."

"Yeah," Seth said. "Whatever you come up with, I'm ready to do."

"Good," Alex said, satisfied. "I don't know when he's getting here, but I told him it would be good if we could make something happen for graduation. That'll get the most notice. More likely to get in the Rochester paper. I'll tell Keith and Amy tomorrow at dinner, if you two could both be there."

"Abso-fucking-lutely," Seth said. Paul nodded his head enthusiastically while holding in a hit of pot.

Ellen didn't know what they were talking about exactly, but if Alex was planning it, she was sure it was smart and cool, and she knew it was something she wanted to be part of.

4

Friday afternoon at three forty-five, the school disgorged a mass of students out the front doors, Peter right in there with them. He waited as the kids dispersed, saying "Hey" to some of them as they walked by, jutting his chin forward in greeting to others—he was getting to know everybody, it seemed like, and not even two full weeks since school started. The kids headed variously to their cars in the parking lot, to either of the two waiting school buses, or to the bike racks off to the side of the front doors. Peter had locked his bicycle up there this morning, a newish Trek, but he was in no hurry to head home.

Peter waited for his sister, starting to get annoyed at how long she was taking, when he saw her shuffle out into the light and sneeze. The main mass of students had already moved on, and Virginia was walking by herself, behind a couple of teachers Peter didn't know. The teachers looked behind them, and one said, "God bless you," before rejoining the conversation with his colleague and walking off to the teachers' portion of the parking lot.

"Virginia!" Peter called out, from where he waited over by the bike racks.

She looked around and found him, and walked over to where he waited. She was wearing a white cardigan sweater, stretched out a bit and too warm for the day, over a blah kind of skirt and top, and the shirt was coming untucked. A sheen of sweat made her forehead look greasy. "What do you want?" she asked.

Peter wanted to say something about her appearance, but he didn't know what. She used to be annoyingly well put together, but now, well, a little more effort wouldn't be a bad idea.

"When Dad gets home, tell him I'm going to a friend's house and I'm going to be home late, okay?"

"What friend?" Virginia asked.

"You don't need to know what friend. Just tell him, okay?"

"You're going to hang out with those stoners behind the annex, right?"

"What do you care?"

"I don't," she said, and looked away. Then she turned back to him and said, quickly, "Can't you just ride the bus home with me, though?"

"Forget it. I've got my bike, anyway."

"Oh, yeah. Okay. I'll tell him," she said, and then turned and walked away toward the bus.

"See you at home," Peter said, but she didn't look back. He watched her climb up the steps of the yellow school bus, and through the windows he could see her make her way down the aisle to the very rear, ignored by the kids she passed. She wedged herself into the backseat, knees up against the back of the seat in front of her, and seconds later, the bus pulled away.

"Ass, gas, or cash," Buddy said, and held out his hand. Crisp, the guy who wore the leather jacket with all the chains, pulled out his wallet, also on a chain, and extracted two dollars. The three girls came up with four bucks between them. Grunt, another one of the guys, only had some change, and Weaver, a wiry, handsome guy with long, black hair and a generally rough look, looked at Buddy and made kissing noises. "Ass, Buddy. We know you want it."

Karen, a blond girl whose considerable breasts were always prominently displayed—making it nearly impossible not to consider them, if you were a guy, or consider how much guys considered them, if you weren't—standing next to him, laughed. She was Weaver's girlfriend.

"Fuck you, Weaver. You don't wanna drink tonight, that's fine with me."

Peter had found everyone behind the annex, where they had just decided to get a couple of cases of beer for the night. Trish had rolled her eyes at her friend Allison, because that's what the guys decided to do every Friday night.

"What about you, Coulter?" Crisp asked. "You're coming drinking with us, aren't you? Ante up."

"Yeah, sure," Peter said, and kicked in the five dollars he had on him.

Buddy counted up the money, and shook his head in mock disgust.

"This is pathetic. This is barely enough to get *me* drunk," he said, and started to pocket the money.

"I didn't notice you pulling out anything," Weaver said.

"I got the car, I paid for gas, I got the ID. Without me, you got nothing."

"We can just get some grass," Grunt suggested. He was a big, hefty guy, his hair a bushy mess, and his clothes looked like he'd taken apart an engine in them, which he had, but it was a couple of days ago.

"Shut the fuck up, Grunt," Buddy said, and flicked his cigarette at Grunt's work boots. "You're lucky we're even letting you hang out with us."

"C'mon," Allison said to Trish, grabbing her arm, "I've got to tell you something," and the two of them walked away out of earshot, toward the fields. Allison was Trish's best friend, the blond girl he'd seen her with in the diner that first night.

Peter watched them go, and caught Allison and Trish looking back at him while they talked, and then laughing. His cheeks grew warm.

Weaver reached into his back pocket and held out a rolled-up baggie. "Gimme five bucks and we can split this."

"Shoulda known you were holding out on us, you faggot," Buddy said, and tried to snatch the bag, but Weaver pulled it quickly back, and slipped it back into his pocket.

"Nope. That's mine, dude. Unless you're paying for it."

"Fuck that. I wanna get drunk anyway," Buddy said.

"I can get some more money, probably," Peter volunteered. He was pretty sure his father would advance him on his allowance.

"All right!" Buddy said, and clapped him on the shoulder. "Brooklyn comes through. Another fifteen bucks, we're all set."

"I gotta go on campus to get it, though. It'll take a while."

"That's okay," Buddy said. "I'll give you a ride. Maybe pick up some nice hippie pussy from the college. We'll leave these losers here."

"No, I got my bike," Peter said, suddenly aware that the girls were back, and embarrassed at the way Buddy was talking. "I'll go get it and meet you back here."

"Hey," Trish said. "I'll take a ride with you, if you want."

"That'd be okay," Peter said.

"Come on." She touched him on the arm. "Leave your backpack," she said, and slipped hers off her shoulder to the ground. Peter did the same. "We'll meet you all at Wadsworth, okay? Allison, bring them in the car with you?"

She began to walk away, and Peter hurried to follow, leaving Buddy and Weaver to argue about Weaver's bag of grass. As soon as they'd passed around the annex and back into the bright sunshine, out of sight of the others, Peter and Trish each realized that it was the first time they had been alone together. Awkwardness claimed them both.

"Uh . . . ," Peter said, as they walked, and couldn't think of anything else to say.

Trish glanced at him quickly and relaxed a bit. If he was that uncomfortable, she didn't have to be.

To their left, on the other side of the high chain-link fence, the football team scrimmaged, far enough away that the oofs and grunts that carried to them were faint though distinct.

"You going out for any teams?" she asked.

Peter looked at her to see if she was joking. She wasn't. Okay. He could field this one.

"Yeah, I was thinking about going out for soccer."

She looked away, hiding a smile.

"What? I'm pretty good at soccer." It was the only sport he'd ever tried where he could consistently connect with a ball.

"We don't have a soccer team."

"I knew that. That's, uh, why I'm not going to."

"Uh-huh. The jocks are all jerks, anyway."

"Yeah," Peter said.

When they reached the bike racks in front of the school, Peter unlocked his bike and pulled it out.

"Aren't you going to unlock your bike?" he asked, looking around at the few still in the racks.

"I forgot, mine's at home," Trish said. "You're gonna have to ride me, I guess." The earnestly innocent expression on her face, he would eventually learn, was how Trish looked when she was pretending that things weren't going exactly as she had planned them.

Peter was a little wobbly at first, especially when the honk of a car approaching from behind sent him veering to the side of the road, but he had no complaints. Trish sat behind him, her hands on his hips, as he stood over the bar of the bicycle and pedaled.

It wasn't far, a couple of miles down High Street into town, and then across Main Street to the outskirts of Seneca, where the campus started. Trish commented on some of the houses they passed on High Street, pointing out where kids from their school lived, and where she'd been to parties in backyards. Peter looked and listened, but he was mainly aware of her hands, warm against his skin where his T-shirt had pulled up from pedaling, and the sound of her voice, sweet and musical. Everything she said sounded interesting to him, even when he wasn't quite hearing it.

There was a bit more traffic once he turned onto Main Street, and in a few minutes they were past the last block of little stores. He turned up Putncy Street, the unofficial dividing line between the town and the school. There was a long downhill stretch before he turned left onto the campus, and he sat down on the bar to coast. Trish leaned forward into him, her arms stretching up around him to grip the handlebars with him, and he could feel her breasts pressing soft against his back, and he found it difficult to really pay attention to anything else, or not think about what it might be like . . . he started getting hard, and then, suddenly, powerfully, he remembered a dream he'd had last night.

Someone on top of him, pinning him down, her breasts against his chest, her legs straddling his, and he was inside her. There was a feeling of déjà vu inside the dream, stretching back, the feeling that he was returning to somewhere he'd been before, that it had been waiting for him, and he came back again and again.

The feel of the dream enveloped him, a sense of darkness and lust, and of water; his hips straining upward, the feel of her skin, hot and moist, touching every bit of his—and there was just a hint of fear, too, creeping in from the edges. It was dark there, and the walls were too close, the bed was too soft, and he felt himself sinking into it as she drove him deeper with each thrust of her hips. The bed was swallowing them up, and still she pressed him down further, her breasts heavy on his chest, and he knew that if he looked the ceiling would be far far away, above the surface of the water.

She was grinding against him, fluid dripping down out of her, and he realized he was afraid to open his eyes, to see who he was trapped here with, who was holding him down underwater and fucking him. He held his breath because he knew he'd come if he let his breath out, and if he came he'd open his eyes, and if he opened his eyes he'd see who it was as he drowned, and in the dream he started to come, and he tried to stop, but she kept on fucking him, sliding up and down, and he was going to come, and—

"Dude!"

He came back to himself as Trish screamed and jumped from the back of the bike, and he just managed to swerve and miss the parked car, and then stop, without going over.

"What the fuck, dude?" Trish said, walking up to where he stood astride the bicycle, dazed, the last wisps of the remembered dream fading, the feel of it, a taste of something rotten in the back of his throat, just barely there.

"Sorry. I was daydreaming."

"Nice time to daydream, you loser," Trish said. "Glad you're not in my driver's ed class."

"Yeah, sorry. I never did that before . . . you're taking driver's ed already?"

"Yeah, I'm gonna be seventeen in November, and my mom can't wait until she doesn't have to drive me and my sisters around anymore."

"You're lucky. I have to wait until spring."

"I guess you'll have to be nice to me then, if you want a ride."

Peter suddenly had a picture in his head of the two of them in the backseat of a car, parked somewhere at night.

"Where's your dad's office?" Trish asked.

"It's, uh, well, I'm not sure. I've only been there once, to help him move some books. But I'll recognize it," he said, and dismounted. They walked together onto campus, Peter wheeling his bike.

He started looking at the buildings as they walked, and they all looked sort of the same, red brick with white painted eaves, ivy climbing the sides, windows in regular rows marching down the walls. They passed between two of the buildings, which brought them through to the quad, a vast verdant football-field-sized lawn, sunken down, with buildings standing sentry on all four sides. Some of the buildings were dorms, and there were speakers in a few windows of each of those, blasting music out. All of them were tuned to the college station, now playing an elaborate, spacey Phish jam, which served as the soundtrack for the students on the quad, some throwing Frisbees back and forth, others sitting together and talking, or reading, or just baking in the late afternoon sun. The scent of marijuana teased at them as they walked.

"Okay, I don't recognize it. I'll call," Peter said, and pulled his cell phone out of his pocket.

"What does he teach?" Trish asked, before he could dial.

"History."

"Then he's in that building," she said, and pointed to a building across from where they stood. They turned off the sidewalk and walked directly across the grass. "My dad used to work maintenance here when I was a little kid. On the weekends he'd bring me with him sometimes."

"Heads up!" somebody shouted, and they both ducked as a Frisbee sliced through the air a couple of feet away.

"Sorry, man," the guy said, as he ran past them to retrieve it, shirtless and barefoot, tie-dyed bandana over trustafarian dreads.

"I don't remember going through a time warp," Peter said. "Do you?"

"Goddamn hippies," Trish said in a near-perfect imitation of Eric Cartman.

"Oh my god, I wish I could do that," Peter said, a touch of awe in his voice.

"You will respect my authoritay," Trish continued in Cartman's voice, but couldn't finish because they were both laughing.

"I'm a very talented girl," Trish said, a moment later.

"Obviously," Peter said as he wheeled his bike up the slope of the lawn on the far side of the quad, to the entrance of the history department building.

"My dad used to say that all the time, for real, though," Trish said. "He hated the way all the rich kids come here to be hippies."

"Yeah? What about you?" Peter asked, as he laid his bike down on the grass outside the building.

"They're okay. I don't care. Anyway, Weaver always gets excellent drugs here."

"Watch my bike?" Peter asked. "I'll just be a couple of minutes."

"Sure," she said, sitting down next to it, and turning so the sun shone on her face. "Maybe I'll meet a cool hippie guy with good drugs." She leaned back on her elbows and stretched out. The sun outlined her body and sparkled in her hair; in this light, Peter noticed, her curls looked red as much as brown. He felt a pang of jealousy, even though he knew she'd been joking.

"Hey, why don't you come with me? I'll put my bike inside."

"You sure?"

"Yeah, come on. He'll probably just give me the money if you're there. He might give me a hard time if it's just me."

"Okay." Trish got to her feet and Peter walked the bike in the front door.

Inside, they stood blinking as their eyes adjusted to

the dim light of the hallway. The building felt cool and damp, as if the air had been trapped there, away from the sun, a hundred years ago. Once he could see, Peter wheeled his bike into a nook a little way down the hall, where a bank of pay phones obsolesced.

"What floor?" Trish asked, from the stairwell doorway.

"Top."

"Race ya," she called out, and sprinted to the stairs and up, already on the first landing before Peter had his bike propped up and stable against the wall.

Standing by the window in his office, where the canted ceiling of the room dipped lowest, there was only a few inches of clearance for Phil's head. Directly across from the window, his door stood open, the wall on that side of the room almost two feet higher.

When Phil had first been shown to his office by Macaulay Thomas, the head of the history department, each of them carrying a carton of Phil's books and papers, he'd had the forbearance not to express his displeasure. The room was small, the desk was ancient, and even if the ceiling never actually dipped low enough to bump into, he found himself unconsciously ducking his head every time he stood up. Certainly the author of the book that won last year's Whittaker Prize deserved better than this, he'd thought, and stewed about it for days.

Fortunately, before he'd determined to register a complaint with Macaulay—he'd demand a better office; if necessary, he'd threaten to quit if they were going to treat him like some twenty-five-year-old adjunct—he'd puzzled out, from a word dropped here and there by various colleagues introducing themselves, that his claustrophobic space on the fourth floor of Denton Hall was among the most prestigious offices on campus.

The four flights of stairs discouraged disturbances by students, which underlined the importance of the work he was doing, but more centrally, Harcourt College, an Episcopalian institution founded by an Oxford-educated anglophile, was shot through with the understated disdain for showiness characteristic of those born into the long-moneyed classes and those who aspired to be mistaken for them. By the reverse logic of that tradition, and counter to Phil's every instinct as a longtime New Yorker, his cramped quarters, looking much the same as they had in the school's earliest days, apart from two electrical outlets and whatever plugged into them, was highly desirable real estate, a testament to the esteem in which he was held by the history department.

Understanding that, Phil looked out the window and across the quad to Garrick Hall, the administration building. All of that out there, he thought—the students at play on the grass; the bureaucrats at work; the classes taking place; the lesser works of scholarship being compiled by academics who would never be known outside their own departments—existed as a sort of support structure that allowed people like himself to do real work: new research, original analyses, and the presentation of these understandings so that people better understood themselves and their society.

Really—he'd have to be blind not to notice—the structure was not dissimilar to the most common model for Western religions: a select few supplying visions that brought meaning to the lives of those whose work supplied the sustenance for all. And, he noticed now, looking first to his left, and then to his right out the window, being on the fourth floor of this building put him level with the steeple of the chapel, otherwise the tallest structure on campus. He chuckled at the poetry of that while he walked back to his desk, then sat himself down and called up the file of the old newspapers he'd found in the local historical society's archives.

He was just about to begin making some notes when he heard the heavy door to the stairwell bang open, releasing an explosion of sound into the quiet of the hallway. Running feet pounding, laughter, a shriek—students. Well, he couldn't expect them all to stay away, but he could insist that they not disturb him. He stood up and walked to his office door, stepped out into the hallway with a stern look already set on his face. "Excuse me!" he said to the two figures heading toward him at speed.

He might better have stayed where he was, as the girl in the lead was laughing back over her shoulder at her companion, and didn't see Phil in time to stop herself from running right into him. Phil's large and solid body absorbed most of the shock of the impact, but he had to take a step back, and the girl threw up her hands at the same time, pushing off against his chest to stop her forward motion, which was enough to throw him off balance. He threw out an arm and grabbed the doorjamb to keep from going down.

"What do you think—" Phil began yelling at the girl, as he pulled himself upright, realizing that her companion was his son at the same time that Peter, horrified at the circumstance, shouted out, "Dad!"

"I'm really sorry, Mr. Coulter," Trish said, shrinking back from him, as if she were afraid he was going to hit her.

"Dad," Peter said again, urgently, doing his best to

draw his father's attention away from Trish. He didn't mind them meeting, but the idea of Trish—or anyone from his new life, really—seeing anything other than his father's bland, unengaged public face, this flare-up of anger, for instance, made him very uncomfortable.

"Peter! What are you doing here?" A little too loud.

"Oh, we just—" This was obviously not the best time to ask for money. Peter could tell that at the moment the answer would be no.

"Is everything all right, Phil?" Macaulay Thomas asked, poking his head out of his office farther down the hall.

"What? Yes, Mac, of course. Everything's fine," Phil answered, almost as uncomfortable as Peter had been a moment ago. This was very sloppy, unprofessional, not at all the image he sought to maintain. "Sorry to disturb you. My son's just dropped by."

Peter saw his opening.

"Hello, Professor," he said to his father's boss, and then, immediately, "Dad, I wanted to see if I could get an advance on my allowance, maybe twenty bucks?" making sure the other man heard him. His father would not want to seem ungenerous in front of a colleague.

"Heh," Phil said, a sound meant for Macaulay's ears, his false smile meant for both of them, but the nuance of threat meant only for Peter. "Why don't you come inside," he said in a slightly strained voice. He shook his head for Macaulay's benefit, a "Kids! What are you going to do?" gesture, and ushered the two teenagers into his office.

"This is Trish," Peter said, once they were inside.

"I'm really, really sorry," Trish said, apologizing again.

"Well, just be more careful," Phil said, disarmed by the girl, whom he was registering as very attractive, now that his anger was subsiding. Peter was certainly growing up—if he'd seen this girl in another context, if she hadn't come in with Peter, Phil would have assumed she was a student at the college, virtually an adult. "Nice to meet you," he said, grudgingly, and sat himself back down behind his desk.

"What are you working on, Dad?" Peter asked, knowing that talking about his work was likely to put him in a more receptive mood.

"Come look at this," Phil said, getting excited as his thoughts went back to his work. He waved Peter over to look at the computer screen. There were no lights on in the old office, just the sunlight coming in the open, unscreened window, and the glow of the computer monitor.

Peter walked behind the desk and peered over his father's shoulder, where a scan of an ancient-looking newspaper was displayed. Yellowed and crudely printed, it was a page from the *Cayuga Picayune*, with a date in the 1830s.

The first two columns were filled with old-timey-looking advertising, but on top of the third column was the headline "Community Alarmed by Self-Proclaimed Messiah." The first few paragraphs made it clear that the town of Seneca was not pleased at the arrival of Joseph Smith and his handful of early followers.

"Cool, Dad. So the Mormons were here in Seneca, too? That's great. Do you think—"

"Not just in town, son. I believe . . . well, the lot numbers match up. It seems Joseph Smith lived in our house."

"Yeah, Dad, that's great, but—" Peter stopped, having

actually taken in what his father had said. "Wow. That
really *is* cool. You didn't know that when you bought
the place?"

"I had no idea. I was almost certain that John
Humphrey Noyes had lived there at some point, along
with some of the people who joined him at the Oneida
Community. I still haven't documented it conclusively.
But I hadn't been expecting this at all."

"My dad wrote a really great book about the Mormons," Peter explained to Trish, something he hadn't
had reason to bring up before.

"Wow," Trish said, from where she was standing on
the other side of the desk. "I never met anybody who
wrote a book before."

Phil looked up at her, couldn't help but smile at her
admiration. "It's not unusual, really. Most historians
publish, you know. Not as successfully, of course. . . . "
Phil caught himself trying to impress his son's girlfriend and changed the subject. "What did you want
that money for, Peter?" he said, suddenly stern, more
the way he thought a father should sound in front of
his teenage son's girlfriend.

"We were going to . . . " Peter realized he couldn't
tell his father what the money was for, and he hadn't
prepared a lie. He had failed to think ahead.

"A movie," Trish said, when she realized Peter
needed help.

Phil heard the pause and the save, and looked from
one of them to the other. He held her eyes for a moment,
but she didn't look away. She was a bold young thing.
They weren't going to a movie and they all knew it.

"Very well," he said, and took a twenty from his
pocket and passed it to Peter.

"You won't be home for dinner, I assume?"

"Yeah, I told Gin to tell you. . . . " And then Peter thought of his sister alone in the house, and all the time she was spending by herself in her room, and the dream came back to him for just an instant, and those two things together made him vaguely uneasy. He consciously pushed the thought away.

"That's fine. I'll pick something up for the two of us," Phil said. He stood. "Do you two want a ride to the movie theater?"

"Uh, no, thanks," Peter said. "I've got my bike. C'mon, Trish. Thanks for the money, Dad."·

Phil watched them leave, thought that the girl didn't look like a child from behind, either. He walked back to the window and looked down on the quad. There were dozens of girls like Trish out there, young women, all around, every time he walked across campus, and they all had boys sniffing after them. Now even his own son . . . were they having sex? he wondered. What an absurd thought. Little Peter, his son, having sex with somebody like that.

He sat back down at his desk, glanced at the headline again and thought about Joseph Smith and his dozens of wives, about how some fundamentalist Mormons threw dozens of teenage boys out of their community, so that they wouldn't interfere with the older men taking the young girls for wives.

Maybe they have the right idea, he thought, and smiled at his own joke.

In her room, Virginia sat on her bed, legs crossed beneath her, laptop open and waiting. Her hair fell, lank, around her face, covering some of the pimples that had spread across her forehead and now spotted her cheeks. It had grown dark outside while she sat

there, and only the slightest twilight remained to come
in the two windows in the wall behind her bed. The
furniture in her room, her dresser, the ladder-back
chair against the wall, covered with dirty clothing,
even the bed she sat on, had grown indistinct, their
outlines fading into the darkness around them. She sat,
unmoving, as the aquarium screensaver sent the same
three fish swimming across her screen, again and
again, the same jet of bubbles released from the bright
gravel, over and over. She was waiting for somebody
to instant message her, and she was prepared to sit
waiting until morning.

She had given up on hearing from her old friends in
Brooklyn. She hadn't received an IM from any of them
since she'd moved. She didn't know how, but she was
sure they'd heard what a loser she'd become and had
all changed their screennames so they wouldn't ever
have to talk to her. Maybe Peter told them.

There was somebody new, though. A new friend.
Somebody who she thought maybe didn't hate her.
Somebody who understood what it was like to be her.

The computer bleeped the arrival of an instant message, and Virginia touched her finger to the touchpad,
making the screensaver vanish, revealing the little
window from her new friend flashing on her screen.

Hi, Virginia. You're alone like you promised, right?
it asked.

"Yeah. Hi. Of course," she said aloud as she typed
the words.

I can't visit if you're not alone.

"You don't have to worry about that. I'm always
alone."

School's still that bad?

"The usual. Like the worst. Do you know who Anne Frank is?" she said and typed.

The Jewish girl? Sure.

"She had more friends than me."

That's funny, Virginia. And smart. Not many girls could make that joke.

"Whatever. We studied her last year . . . so, you gonna tell me more stuff?"

Sure thing. I told you I would. Did you get those things I asked you to?

" . . ."

Did you? We made a deal.

"Yeah, I got them."

Okay, good. Now, let's see. You know that girl in your homeroom, Karen Santamero, hasn't been in all week?

"Yeah, the teacher said she was in the hospital with a bad flu."

Since when do they treat a flu by scraping out your insides?

"No! She got an abortion?"

Killed her baby, yeah. You know Ms. Evanson? The gym teacher?

"Yeah?"

Remember how she left you all alone to play dodge-ball last week?

"I didn't play."

You want to know where she went?

"Okay."

She was giving the vice principal a blow job in his office.

"Really?"

Yeah. Sneak out after her next time. You can watch them from the secretary's office. And you know that really fat girl in your math class? And how she's always late?

"If you say so."

Math's right after lunch. What do you think she's doing?

"She's throwing up?"

And it's not helping much, is it?

"I don't want to talk about her."

Because you think you're too fat, too, right? And you think nobody at school's ever going to be your friend, right?

"Yeah."

Why don't you take out those things now?

"Do you really think it's gonna help me, knowing all these secrets about people?"

I promise. You can make people do all sorts of things if you know their secrets. And you can get even with them if they're mean to you.

"When are you gonna tell me stuff about Melanie and the rest of them? And my brother?"

First you have to do things for me.

". . ."

Don't you think you should be punished?

"I told you. No. I didn't do anything. Why do you have to talk like that?"

But you've gotten so fat, and you're not pretty anymore. You used to be so pretty.

And then the IM window faded out, and then the rest of the desktop, and the screen showed Virginia's picture from her eighth-grade yearbook, taken last winter, and it was true, she used to look like that. Her hair was smooth and perfect. And her face, it was so thin, and pretty.

Then the screen changed and it was like she had a

webcam, aimed right at her, and she saw what she looked like now, her rounded cheeks, her pudgy chin, her hair hanging around her face like rats' tails. And as she looked, it got worse, but truer, she could tell, always looking more and more like she *really* looked, her nose flattening a little, her eyes getting smaller and squintier, her skin getting shinier with oils, pimples rising all over, and it was so gross, and she *hated* the way she looked, and she wanted to take her fist and punch the screen, punch that face, she hated that girl. . . .

That's right, and now Virginia heard the voice in her head as she stared at the picture, and it was all she could do not to rip at her cheeks with her nails, she was so fat and ugly. *Don't you want to hurt her, Virginia? You'll feel better if you hurt her. Why don't you take out a razor now?*

He was right, Virginia knew, it would make her feel better. She reached back under her pillow where she'd hidden all the sharp things she'd assembled. She pulled out the razor and pressed its sharp edge, a corner of it, into her cheek, right below where her cheekbone would be, if she weren't so fat.

No, not your face, darlin'. Not yet. Pull up your shirt.

She reached down and lifted her shirt, folded it up so it would leave her stomach exposed. She looked at her midsection, all around a roll of pale, soft flesh, lying there like something you'd find growing deep in a cave, some gross giant blind white worm, that wouldn't even make a noise when you hit it with a stick again and again until it was dead. In the glow of the laptop screen her skin had a grayish pallor, as if it were already dead and rotting.

Good, the voice in her head said. *Let's begin.*

*   *   *

Peter was lying on his back, the concrete bench cold through his shirt, looking up at a sky dense with stars. The sky never looked like this back home. He'd never realized that stars could be so beautiful. He sat up, and picked up the half-empty bottle of Genny Cream Ale, which would be his second, and drained it. This was fun.

They were outside the Wadsworth Mausoleum, the most elaborate structure in a cemetery that had seen its last burial sometime before World War I. Set on a gentle slope overlooking Lake Seneca, it was down the shore a few miles south from Peter's new home, through the stretch of woods that started right next door.

Route 9 had cut it in half, and the stones and monuments of the cemetery spread out for acres, but the Wadsworth Mausoleum, with its faux-Grecian benches and pillars and urns laid out in front of it, was the kids' favorite spot to hang out. Except for hippies from the college, nobody ever came to the cemetery, Buddy had explained to Peter, and half the time they were tripping. "And nobody's easier to scare away than a hippie on acid," he'd said.

Buddy had taken the money from Peter and returned with two cases of Genesee Cream Ale, a new taste for Peter, but it wasn't bad at all. While Buddy was gone, Weaver had passed around a couple of joints and they'd watched the sun set and played music on Grunt's big portable radio.

Now, an hour or two later, Weaver and Karen were making out, leaning up against the wall of the mausoleum, just out of sight. Buddy, Crisp, and Grunt were standing not far away, loudly arguing the merits of various types of automatic weaponry, their arguments informed solely by a decade of action movies and video games. Their voices were periodically interrupted by a crash of broken glass as they threw their empties at a nearby headstone, which was, going by the foot-high mound of shards surrounding it, a traditional target.

Trish and Allison sat on the ground by Peter, leaning back against the bench. He was half listening to their conversation, until they'd gotten to the part about "doing it," which got his full attention.

"Of course they are," Trish said. She was talking about Karen and Weaver.

"You don't know that," Allison said. "Did she tell you she let him?"

"No. I'm still not talking to her."

"Well, then, you don't know they're doing it."

"Just believe me. Weaver wouldn't be going out with her if they weren't doing it, even if she does have boobs for three. Why do you think I broke up with him?"

"I know," Allison said. "But didn't Karen say—"

What Karen said remained unspoken, because Peter couldn't keep himself from interrupting.

"You were going out with Weaver?" Weaver was cool, cooler than Peter could ever hope to be. He seemed to know all about things Peter was just barely aware of, aspects of "doing it," Peter suspected, primary among them.

Allison and Trish both looked up at him.

"Yeah," Trish said. "So?"

"But a long time ago, right?" Peter asked. After all, Weaver and Karen, they acted like they'd been together quite a while.

Allison laughed and Trish smacked her on the shoulder.

"No. Not really that long."

"Well, how long ago, then?" Peter insisted on asking.

"I'm gonna go see what the guys are doing," Allison said, laughing. She stood up, brushed the dirt off the rear of her jeans and walked away, making tsking noises at Trish.

Trish and Peter stood up, too. Trish looked up at him, and said in a rising voice, "Two weeks?" She scrunched her face up, miming fear of Peter's response.

"Two weeks?" he said, and thought back. That was just before school started. That night at the diner, she was still going out with Weaver. He found this somehow upsetting, just like she had known he would, because, well, boys are just like that, even the really sweet ones.

"Come on," Trish said. "Let's take a walk," and she took his hand and he followed her, walking away from the others through the rows of hundred-year-old gravestones, some leaning over, others fallen and almost completely reclaimed by the earth. The moon was bright enough that their way was clear all the way to a smaller, less elaborate mausoleum out of sight of the others.

She turned around to face him.

"You know, I'm not going out with Weaver *now*."

"I know, but . . ."

"And you're not going out with anyone now, are you?"

"No, of course not."

"And I don't care about who *you* went out with before." She stepped forward, closing the distance between them. "So you shouldn't care who *I* went out with before, right?"

But I never went out with anyone before, Peter thought, looking down at Trish's face in the moonlight . . . and then it struck him. I'm supposed to kiss her now, aren't I? He forgot any concerns about Weaver, or Trish's past.

She looked up at him, her eyes big, her lips slightly parted. The silver light of the moon made her look like a girl in a movie, like they were in one together.

Yep, he thought, I'm definitely supposed to kiss her now.

He looked down into her face—she was *so* beautiful—and she closed her eyes.

Okay, yeah. At this point, no question, kissing should be taking place.

And then, what the hell, so what if he didn't know what he was doing, he lowered his lips to hers.

He needn't have worried, he quickly found out. Kissing came naturally, and if it didn't, Trish knew how to kiss. She had some kind of special powers or something, because it wasn't possible that every girl could make a soft shimmering cloud come down over their heads together, and make his body come alive in some entirely new way that involved melting. Trish knew how to kiss so that time disappeared, and he had no idea if they'd been gone together into their softly glowing private world for two minutes or half an hour when he heard Buddy shout.

"Hey! Newlyweds! You two over there?" and then a flung bottle smashed against a headstone ten feet away from them. There was laughter, Buddy and Crisp, and the clap of a high five. Trish and Peter were just stepping apart when Buddy and Crisp found them.

"I don't know why you need outta-town talent when you coulda had me," Buddy said to Trish.

"Yeah, right, dude," Trish said. "Just what I've always wanted. My very own venereal disease."

A look passed across Buddy's face just then that

made Peter think something bad was about to happen,
but it could have just been the shadows.

Was he supposed to say something?

Buddy took a step toward Trish, and Peter was suddenly once again aware of Buddy's size, the bulk of his
shoulders and his arms, and he started to move to step
in between them, when Buddy reached out toward
Trish with a joint. "Here," he said.

"Thanks, Buddy," Trish said, and took it from him,
completely at ease.

She hit it and passed it to Peter, and slipped her arm
around his waist at the same time. Peter took it, put an
arm over Trish's shoulder.

"You know, Buddy," he said, and took a hit,
"women just prefer imported to domestic. What are
you gonna do?"

"Good one!" Crisp said, and Peter passed him the
joint.

"Yeah," Buddy said. "Good one." He didn't sound
that enthused. "Come on, I'm leaving. Anybody wants
a ride gotta go now."

"So," Peter asked, as they all walked toward
Buddy's car, "doesn't anybody think it's, you know,
just a little weird, hanging out in a cemetery?"

"No," Crisp and Trish said, at the same time. The
question had never occurred to them. It's what they'd
always done.

"Whatsa matter?" Buddy asked. "You afraid of
ghosts? You been watching *Night of the Living Dead*
or something?"

"Cool movie," Crisp said. "You know what's even
cooler, though? You ever see *Faces of Death*? It's this
bootleg video of all these, like, dead bodies and shit,
and all the different ways you can die."

Peter felt it was his turn to ante up a cool, gross movie.

"Yeah, but did you ever see a video of Survival Research Laboratories? They make all these cool robots, and then blow things up. It's, like, art. This guy, the main guy, Mark Pauline? He only has one hand now because he blew off the other one in an explosion."

"Really?" Crisp asked. "That's cool. I blew some stuff up. Right, Buddy? Back in junior high—"

"But seriously, dude," Buddy said to Peter, cutting Crisp off. "You believe in ghosts?"

They'd reached his car now, parked on the small gravel road that led past Wadsworth Mausoleum. Weaver and Karen were already in the backseat, making out. Allison and Grunt were sitting on the hood passing a joint back and forth. Trees lined the other side of the road, and the moon threw shadows of their interwoven branches over the car, like a net.

Buddy leaned down and untwisted a length of wire to open the trunk.

"No, of course not," Peter said. He wheeled his bike over from where it was leaning against a headstone, and put it in the trunk of the car.

"Well, good thing, dude. Because you know what? Your house is haunted."

"Get out," Peter said, as he got into the backseat. "There's no such thing."

"No, seriously," Buddy said as he got in behind the wheel. Allison, Crisp, and Grunt slid into the front seat from the other side, Grunt in the middle, Allison on Crisp's lap. "That's why nobody was living there. You moved into a haunted house."

Weaver stopped making out with Karen long enough to say, "Don't listen to that bullshit, dude." He turned to Peter. "A bunch of people died there, back in the sixties or something, so the college closed down the house. The rest of it is crap. Buddy just likes scary stories." He turned his attention back to Karen.

"Fuck you, Weaver. Crisp, tell him, man."

"You got some ghosts, dude. People have seen things out there."

"Supremely fucking haunted, dude," Buddy said.

Trish got in with Peter, sitting on his lap.

"I'd know if something was up with my own house," Peter said.

"I'm telling you, dude," Buddy said, turning in his seat to look at him. He looked completely serious, a little frustrated, even.

"Trish?" Peter asked. "You believe that, too?"

She squirmed around on his lap to look him in the face. "I don't know," she said, and gave him a quick kiss. "But I'll come over and play Ghostbusters with you anytime you want." The whole car laughed, except for Buddy, who shook his head as he turned the key in the ignition.

"You should listen to me, dude. You really fucking should," he muttered, shaking his head, but more to himself than anyone else. They drove back down the narrow rutted road, and Buddy swung wide once, to knock over a tilted headstone he'd noticed on the way in.

Late that night, Peter lay in bed, waiting to fall asleep again after having gotten up as an inevitable consequence of consuming his new favorite beverage. There was a sleepy, goofy smile on his face as he re-lived in his head his first kisses with Trish, undeniably the all-time best event of his life so far. As he got closer to sleep, the movie playing out in his head grew more and more real; as he let go of consciousness, instead of just pictures he could feel her lips press against his, feel the way her arms had gone around his waist to rest on the small of his back, and he could feel himself growing hard against her warm soft belly.

That small part of his mind that was still awake, watching his fantasy instead of experiencing it, willed it further, tried to imagine himself into actually doing it, but the pleasure of real kisses kept him anchored to that memory, until the last part of his conscious mind let go of the world and slipped away into the fantasy, where suddenly, instead of lingering kisses and curious tongues gently exploring, he felt himself shoved roughly down onto his own bed, felt the focus of the world move from Trish's lips to his own pulsing dick, felt hands grasping him, stroking him.

It felt good, and his hips started moving, and he starting moaning, but as good as it felt, it was a different kind of good, it was a rough, hot good, an outside good, not the glowing warmth of Trish in his arms that reached all the way inside of him, and he started to struggle up from the depths of his unconsciousness, toward where he'd left her, and he had almost pulled himself out of the dream, he could look up from where he was and see the surface, and the sounds that were out there in his house, the ones he'd hear if he were awake, the grunting from his father's room, the whimpering from his sister's, almost reached him, but then he felt himself slipping into the hot, moist flesh, felt soft skin in his hands, skin against his own, and he was pulled back down to where he went every night in the new house.

5

1971

It was the first really warm day of the spring, one of those misplaced summer days that fall right out of nowhere into the wrong part of the calendar and throw everything off; flowers thinking they should blossom; animals thinking they should leave their burrows and mate; students, well, also thinking they should leave their burrows and mate.

From where Ellen was sitting on the redbrick steps of the student union building, during a break between her 10:30 French Lit class and Classical Econ at noon, it looked like classrooms were probably not filled to capacity; at least half the student body seemed to be out on the quad taking advantage of the sun and the clear blue sky. There was motion all over; lean, shirtless young men, their smooth, hairless torsos somehow a satisfying contrast to all those scraggly beards and disheveled mops of bouncing hair as they leaped after Frisbees, caught them and turned in the air to fire them off to where another boy was already in motion, racing to where the Frisbee would be at the moment of intersection.

The displays of athleticism did not go unappreciated by the girls among them, sitting in the sun in twos and threes, one with a guitar, another blowing bubbles from a plastic wand, enough tie-dye and peasant shirts among them that with "Uncle John's Band" floating out of a dorm window to join the sweet wafting cloud of pot smoke hovering over the whole scene, it put you in mind of a medieval market on a festival day.

Ellen had noticed Alex sitting out on the grass, supporting herself with arms thrust out behind her, and was considering blowing off economics to join her when Alex got up and, with a wave, walked toward her, backpack slung over her shoulder.

"Happy St. Frabjous Day," Alex said, when she reached the steps.

"I didn't know it was an official holiday."

Alex mounted the steps and sat beside her. "You didn't know it was St. Frabjous Day?"

"Completely slipped my mind. And how does the indigenous population celebrate?"

Alex smiled. "Traditionally, it involves a pilgrimage. Which is why *we* are going to take a little trip."

"You got some acid?" Ellen asked, jerking forward, excited and scared at the same time, the self-consciously clever tone gone from her voice. When she'd told Alex she'd never tripped, Alex had offered to find some acid so they could do it together for Ellen's first time. That had been weeks ago, though.

"I did," Alex said, and patted her backpack, slung around into her lap.

"I thought there was nothing around."

"There wasn't. But we have a visitor at the house. He brought a bunch."

"Yeah? That guy you were talking about?"

"Yeah. You'll meet him next time you come out to the house. Right now, though"—Alex reached into her backpack and took out a small envelope—"stick out your tongue."

"Okay, now I'm sort of scared."

"Don't worry. It'll be great. I've done this lots. It can change your whole life. You'll see things you never saw before. It makes everything different. It's like a religious experience, except really fun. You just have to be open to whatever speaks to you."

Ellen stuck her tongue out and Alex put her finger in the envelope and withdrew it with a tiny amber square of windowpane acid on her fingertip. She touched the tip of her finger to Ellen's tongue, then took a hit herself.

"Now let's get out of here. I want to be away from campus before we start to get off."

They got Ellen's yellow Beetle from the parking lot behind the student union and headed off campus. Windows cranked open, the college station playing a set of Dylan on the radio—*I saw a* newborn *baby with wild wolves all around it*—they drove through town, to Route 9, and down the other side of the lake. Ellen automatically started to turn off when they reached Oneida House, but Alex reached over and put her hand on the steering wheel, and kept her driving straight.

"I don't want to deal with those guys now. They're on their own trip. Anyway, I know a better place to go."

Ellen kept driving for another couple of miles, nothing but trees on either side of the road, in places putting the whole road in cool shadow. The only vehicle they passed was an old red pickup with the name of a local orchard hand-painted in white on the door. Alex pointed to a wide shoulder on their side of the road, a stretch of brown dirt and weeds pressed smooth by many tires.

Getting out of the car, Ellen became aware of a strange electricity in her body, a physical sensation of expectation, a thought as much as a feeling, like the excitement that fills the air of a theater before the curtain rises. She stood with her hand still on the door, and looked at the trees, and saw that they were becoming more . . . there. They were really, really there, every detail. It struck her that she'd never really seen a tree before, on its own terms, that she'd always imposed her own ideas on it, instead of simply accepting its treeness. . . .

Ellen looked back at the road, the way they'd come. It occurred to her that it was very important they get out of view of the road before anybody saw them.

"Come on," Alex said, on the other side of the car. "I want to get out to Kashong before we're too fucked up." Could Alex read her mind? Why hadn't she ever said so?

"What's Kashong?" Ellen asked.

"You'll see, just come on," Alex said and started into the woods, down a trail that you couldn't tell was there until you were on it.

They walked for almost half an hour, weaving between trees, getting deeper into their trip as they got deeper into the woods. With each passing moment, Ellen could feel an unfolding of things, an opening up of layers of meaning to trees, leaves, clouds, that she realized she had somehow always known was there, but just hadn't known to know it. You know? Even now, the meaning, the actual message she could see written all around, eluded her, just. It was as though everything was just about to speak to her, as if a

message was already traveling toward her, just about
to reach her ears.

She knew, as she followed Alex farther into the
woods, that they were getting closer and closer to
something important. She could sense it ahead of
them, waiting for them, and the trees were like heralds,
almost arranged in such a way to lead them to where
they were going, like the woods themselves knew
where they would start and where they would end up.
She started to explain it to Alex, and Alex said, "You
mean like a path?" and well, yeah, that was what she
meant, but it wasn't as simple as that, now that she
really understood what a path really *was*, so she was
going to try to explain it better when the presence,
whatever it was—and whatever it was, it was huge—
got closer, she could sense, and then that sense of presence resolved into sound, the sound of water, tons of
it, flowing, falling.

And then they were out of the woods and across a
field of grass, and then standing on an expanse of flat
gray rock, boulders and jagged chunks of slate all
around, walls of rock rising on three sides. They stood
at the edge of a deep pool in the rock, looking up at a
roaring, rushing waterfall pouring down. The surface
of the water was alive where the waterfall poured in,
but the rest of the pool was calm and clear. Sunlight
shone down on them, heating the rock beneath their
feet—Ellen could feel the heat from above and below,
enfolding her—and making the surface of the waterfall
dance with glimmering light, like a living thing carved
out of some exquisite animate quartz.

"Alex, it's beautiful," Ellen said, so beautiful she almost couldn't wrap her mind around it, had to sit down
just to take it in, and they both sat down where they

were to stare at the waterfall for a while, and then they laid back on the warm smooth stone to stare at the sky. A flock of birds, small, dense, darting, flew overhead and they both forgot what they were saying and watched.

Ellen was telling Alex how she'd never realized before, but then she couldn't remember what she'd realized because Alex said, "Wanna go swimming?" and they were both out of their clothes in a flash, Ellen's body sleek and compact, the curves of ass and belly slight and perfect, almost precise, her breasts just big enough to curve below; Alex all flesh and bounce, big brown nipples on big soft breasts, hips swelling out. Ellen stared, startled by the sudden nakedness, couldn't take her eyes off of Alex, but Alex grabbed her hand and they walked across the rock, hot under their bare feet, to the water, and in they went, Alex jumping feetfirst, Ellen doing the same right after, still holding hands, and then they popped back out as if launched, like seals leaping, the water was so cold, frigid, shocking. The water was so cold that they would have screamed if they could have caught their breath, so cold that the rippling veil of acid was torn right from them, stripped right out of their brains for the brief seconds it took to switch them back from doing anything but register the cold, to getting them the fuck out of there.

They scrambled up out of the water, scraping their skin as they dragged themselves out, so cold and numb they didn't notice. They lay there gasping until they could breathe again.

"I've never been so cold," Ellen said.

"I'm sorry, I'm so sorry, I didn't think. All this water is ice melt, from the mountains," Alex said.

"It was so cold," Ellen said.

"It was really really cold," Alex said.

"I'll never be warm again," Ellen said, and then, "Where are our clothes?"

"Over there," Alex said, and pointed, and they got up and ran there, leaving dark footprints on the rock, their wet skin glossy in the sun.

Ellen grabbed her jeans and started to pull them on, but her skin was wet and her jeans were tight and she was hopping around getting nowhere when Alex stopped her.

"Wait, we're still wet, we'll dry off in the sun in a few minutes."

"But I'm so cold!"

"Come here, then," Alex said, and held her arms open, and Ellen threw herself into Alex's arms without hesitation, and then realized what she was doing, but Alex pulled her in against her, and Ellen's arms went around her, and her hands followed the curve of Alex's back, down to the swell of her ass, and then she pulled back and looked at Alex, and then Alex leaned in and kissed her.

I'm kissing a girl! Ellen thought, and then she thought, but what could make more sense? *She* was a girl, too! Why would she ever kiss anybody else? It was a joy as unexpected and warm as the water's icy chill had been unexpected and punishing, and they both forgot about being cold, stopped being cold, as their bodies pressed against each other, the acid making every point of contact all points of contact, every inch of skin alive to the other, a numinous glow to everything, and then they were down on the ground, their clothes spread out underneath them with no intervening moment, and Alex was touching her, her hands running over her skin, touching her arms, her breasts, her legs, then between her legs, and no boy had ever been so gentle with her, had known to touch her right there—and Ellen laughed out loud: how could a boy possibly know?

And Alex stopped what she was doing and laughed, too—obviously, Alex really could hear what she was thinking—and then Ellen kissed Alex's neck, and down to her breasts, and thought, Oh, that's what it feels like, that's what *I* feel like, and then they were rolling over each other, and a fire was kindling down low in her, and she could feel it in Alex, too, answering. They were connected through their bodies, it was one fire growing between them, as if they didn't end where skin met skin, but merged there, a blurring together, one woman with two manifestations and it was growing even more and Ellen was saying "Oh, oh," and the warmth of the stone was glowing up through her back, up through her body into Alex, and she opened her eyes and saw standing off among the black branches of the trees a guy with long dark hair, watching them, like something feral emerged from the woods, so she closed her eyes again to make him disappear because she didn't want him to be there, and then she opened her eyes, and it had worked.

6

"Hey, guys," Molly called out cheerfully from the kitchen, when she heard Peter and Virginia come in the front door. Phil had hired Molly Dellinger, a tall, slim history major with close-cropped red hair, through the student employment office at the college. She came in twice a week to clean, and spent another day doing the grocery shopping and assorted errands.

Outside, the engine of the old school bus growled as the driver shifted gears and pulled away from the house.

"Hi, Molly." Peter went directly into the kitchen, his sister following more slowly behind. "You make us dinner?"

Molly bent over to open the oven and check the lasagna she'd put together after cleaning. "Yep. Come see."

Peter came over to stand beside her. When they were lucky, Molly had time to make dinner. Otherwise, it was sandwiches, or something from the freezer microwaved. Occasionally, Peter tried to cook, which usually led back to sandwiches or something from the freezer.

"Smells great," he said. Molly closed the oven door and stood up.

"I'm gonna go. Shut it off in half an hour, okay?"

"Is dad here?" Virginia asked.

They both turned to where she stood by the sink, looking out the window. The sun was starting to sink lower in the sky, beyond the lake, the shadows of the hills on the opposite shore just starting to incline in their direction, reaching out toward them.

"Nope, he's on campus today. He said he'd be home to have dinner with you, though."

"Oh." Virginia took a jar of peanut butter from the cabinet, and clattered a drawer open to get a spoon, then left the room.

"I'll be back on Monday," Molly said, Peter following her out of the kitchen to the front door. "You do your homework, Peter. And no partying," she said, in a semi-ironic way, wagging a finger at him. This was her first experience as anything like an authority figure, and she had trouble taking it quite seriously, particularly since she was just a few years older than Peter.

"Yes, ma'am," Peter said, playing along. He had a bit of a crush on Molly, and if it weren't for Trish, and his newfound comfort in the presence of girls, he'd be too self-conscious to joke around like that. Still, he almost tripped himself rushing to open the door for her before she could reach out and do it herself. Sometimes New Peter got a reminder that awkward, fumbling Old Peter wasn't quite completely gone.

"Hey, Molly?" Peter asked, before she stepped off the porch. "You're not from around here, right?"

"No, I'm from Vermont."

"Oh. But since you came to Harcourt College, have you ever heard anything weird about this house?"

"You're pretty weird," Molly said, "but nobody had to tell me that."

Peter smiled. "So you never heard that this house was maybe . . . haunted?"

Molly laughed. "Nice try, Peter. But whatever trick it is you have planned, you might want to check with the boys of Putney, Vermont, first. I am the reigning Queen of Revenge."

"Okay," Peter said a little sheepishly. He'd felt sort of foolish asking in the first place. He stood in the open door and watched Molly drive away in her battered white Honda.

He did have some homework to do, but he hadn't talked to Trish since lunchtime. He called from the kitchen, and was still on the phone more than an hour later when he simultaneously heard his father coming in the front door and noticed that the once savory smell of lasagna that had filled the kitchen had acquired an additional burnt note.

"Shit!" he said to Trish as his father came into the kitchen. "The lasagna's burning. I gotta go. Talk to you later, okay?"

Phil looked up from the journal he had folded open on top of the stack of books he carried. "What's that?"

Peter had his back turned to him, shutting off the oven and pulling out the lasagna. The top was burned, and probably the bottom, too, but he could scoop out the rest, maybe put more sauce on it.

"Nothing, Dad. Dinner's ready."

"Where's your sister?"

"She's, uh . . . " He realized he didn't know. Was she out on the pier again? He'd spotted her out there a few times since they'd arrived, for no reason he could figure out. He glanced quickly, but there was nothing by the pier but a handful of birds darting about in the air, feasting on the cloud of midges that appeared at the water's edge every day at dusk.

"I don't know. She's probably in her room. I'll get her."

"Fine, I'll be in my study," Phil said, and turned back to his journal, reading as he walked out of the kitchen and through the dining room.

"Virginia!" Peter called up the stairs. When there was no response, he climbed the stairs, turning on the light in the hallway, which had grown dark, the small clerestory window on the landing letting in enough light to see only till early afternoon, when the sun tilted directly in.

"Gin!" he said, and knocked on her door. Did he hear voices in there? He leaned in closer to the door, and if he had heard something, it had stopped.

"What?" Virginia said. "Come in."

He opened the door and found her sitting on her bed in the dark, her laptop opened on her lap. In the gray glow from the screen, her face looked even more sallow and blotchy than it had lately become.

"What are you doing?" he asked.

"Nothing." Virginia looked up from the laptop and stared at him.

"Talking to Courtney and them?" Good, Peter thought. If she had no friends here, at least she was still IMing with her friends back home.

Virginia waited, impatient to get back to her computer.

He stepped into the room and was immediately struck by the smell; musky, oddly sweet, not really pleasant at all.

"Dude, why don't you open a window once in a while?" he said, and stepped in to do so himself.

" 'Dude'?" Virginia said, and snorted.

"Fuck you," he said, but he felt caught out and embarrassed.

As his eyes adjusted to the light, he saw the half-empty jar of peanut butter sitting on the night table beside her, and the spoon dropped carelessly on the bed. He hadn't been in her room since they first moved in, and now he saw an accumulation of plates on various surfaces, bits of dried food on them, and half-eaten pieces of fruit. There were more than a few flies flitting around. There were empty cookie boxes on the floor, a bag of pretzels; even, he noticed, a piece of a sandwich in a corner on the floor. There was a wrinkled heap of clothing at the foot of the bed, clothes on the floor, and on the floor of the open closet, another pile of clothing, wire hangers tangled in with them.

"Jesus," he said. "What's wrong with you? Doesn't Molly clean in here?"

"I asked her not to. I don't want anybody coming in my room when I'm not here. You better not either."

"Well, then you gotta clean in here, Gin. This is just gross."

"Okay, fine, big deal, I'll clean the room," she said. She typed something quickly, and then slammed her laptop closed. She stood up and started picking up pieces of clothing from the floor, sloppily folding them and tossing them on the bed. "What do you want, anyway?"

"Come help me get dinner out," Peter said. "Or else you can do all the dishes after. Including these," he said, gesturing around him.

"Yeah, okay. I'll be right down," she said.

Virginia was dressed in sweatpants and a shapeless gray sweater. Peter could remember when she wouldn't have dressed like that even if she wasn't leaving the house. Even when she was home sick she paid more attention than that to her appearance. The sweatpants looked dirty, and the sweater . . . "Hey! Is that my sweater?" She'd stretched it all out of shape.

She looked down at herself. "Yeah."

He looked more closely.

"And you got peanut butter on it."

"Oh, big deal," she said. "You want it back?"

"Forget it," he started to say, but before he could she had reached down and lifted it up to take it off, pulling it up over her head. She wasn't wearing anything underneath.

"Put that back on," he blurted, immediately and immensely uncomfortable.

Peter had seen his little sister shirtless dozens of times growing up, of course, there'd even been a while when they got baths together, but it had been a long time ago and, anyway, this was different.

First of all, she had developed real breasts since then, which he had of course sort of known, but it wasn't like he'd really thought about it. In his head, they didn't quite go together, *sister* and *breasts*; it was like trying to jam together two magnets with the same polarity, and the resistant force they generated was his discomfort; the closer they got, the stronger it became. Right now, it was very very strong.

The rest of her was different, too. She'd always been slim, boy-hipped, but his sweater had hidden folds that bulged out over the elastic waistband of her sweatpants, and extra flesh padded her all around her waist.

Peter moved to her side, almost leaped, to yank her sweater back down, because she wasn't moving anywhere near fast enough for him.

Altogether, she couldn't have been exposed to him more than a handful of seconds, and even with the light from the hallway, it was still pretty dark in her bedroom, so it would have been pretty hard for Peter to notice the red lines crisscrossing the soft flesh of her belly, the cuts running down the tops and sides of her breasts. But if he hadn't been trying so hard not to see his sister's body, while he might have missed the shallower cuts a week or two old, the pink ones that were even now becoming scars as the scabs peeled away from them, he might at least have noticed the cuts that were fresh and raw, with dark beads of blood still welling from them, making the thin incisions swell to thick strokes of red on her pale, white skin.

"Jesus," he said. "Keep the sweater. I don't need to see that, thanks."

"Whatever," she said, and settled the sweater back onto her.

"Just come downstairs," he said, and left.

"Mom!" he said, halfway down the stairs, and his mother turned a big smile his way.

"Surprise!" she said, and he walked down the stairs and let her hug him. She roughed his hair and pushed his head back and said, "Let me see my big grown-up boy."

He stepped back, stuffed his hands in his pockets, embarrassed. "Hey, Mom. It's great to see you. I thought you weren't coming up till tomorrow."

"I got some work out of the way and thought I'd—"

"Mommy!" Virginia screamed and ran down the rest of the stairs faster than Peter had seen her move in a long time. She almost knocked Peter down getting to Julia, and she threw her arms around her. "I missed you so much, Mom, can you move up here with us? You can work from here and take care of us like you always do, can't you?"

"Baby, what's wrong?" Julia said, and held Virginia tight.

Virginia pulled back enough that Julia could see there were tears in her eyes.

"Nothing. I just missed you is all," she said and tightened her arms around her mother again, and buried her face in her chest. Julia looked toward Phil, who had joined them, and the alarm in her face at the change in her daughter was plain to anyone who wanted to see it.

7

Julia woke up squinting against the sunlight, brought her arm up to cover her eyes. A few seconds later she sat up, blinking. She was surprised to realize she was naked.

She pulled the sheet from the bed to cover herself, and in so doing discovered that Phil, still sleeping on the other side of the bed, was naked, too, which surprised her even more.

It's not that she wasn't comfortable with her body, or that she disapproved; it's just that she hadn't been naked in bed with her husband for years. They always wore something: she a T-shirt, he pajama pants, an outward sign of the emotional state they brought with them to bed.

With the sheet wrapped over her shoulders, she stood to walk across the floor and look out the window—it was a beautiful room, white walls bright with the sunlight, the floor bare wood with a silky finish, and the window looked out over miles of hills and trees—but she almost immediately stepped on what she thought at first was a dead mouse. She yanked her foot back, without thinking, before she'd stepped all the way down, so fast that she almost fell back into the bed. But it wasn't a mouse at all.

It was her bloody tampon, which she was starting to remember had been flung from the bed, pulled out of her and tossed aside; she was starting to remember that, and she remembered more looking down at herself, when she saw the blood on her thighs, handprints dried into it, and she looked up into the mirror on top of the dresser, and saw the blood on her mouth, on her cheeks and jaw, where he'd pressed his face to hers, and then she did sit back down on the bed, had to, as she remembered it all.

They'd made love . . . no, they'd fucked. No, that wasn't even it. He'd *taken* her. That was the only word for it, taken, the way they talked about these things in historical romances. Phil had *taken* her, he had *had* her. Which, politically correct or not, she wouldn't have thought him capable of.

There had been no sex between them for, well, a really long time, and even when there had been, it was perfunctory at best. Phil had never been inspired, and he certainly wasn't inspiring. But last night, she thought, as details came and went in her mind, each one so clear it felt like it was happening again, last night he'd been like another person.

She'd been sleeping. They'd all had dinner, while the kids had caught her up on things and she shared news from the neighborhood. Virginia had been clinging to her the whole time. She hadn't acted like that since the time she got lost on a fourth-grade field trip, convinced herself that she'd never see her mother again until Julia, one of the class parents for the day, had found her sitting on the steps outside the Museum of Natural History.

With Virginia beside her like that, Julia hadn't had a chance to express her concern about the girl, and then, what? Peter had told them that there were rumors the house was haunted, and Phil said it was nonsense. Then he'd gone into a lecture about Joseph Smith, and John Humphrey Noyes, and how he was now sure that they'd both occupied this house with their followers at different times. The presence of great men, he said, made the small-minded people of this town demonize them, and the house by extension. They'd driven them away before, and they were still uncomfortable with the memory.

Peter had felt dismissed, which he had been, and went up to his room, and Virginia started falling asleep and went to bed. She'd tried to talk about Ginny with Phil, about the change in her, but he just went on and on about how remarkable it all was, how fortunate they were to have moved into such a special place, and then he'd tried to show Julia all the documentation he was accumulating, and she'd gotten fed up and gone to bed herself.

She woken up in the dark a little later with his hands on her, and for a minute she couldn't even believe it, couldn't imagine, really, what he was doing, it seemed so unlikely. By the time she'd woken up enough to object, Phil was handling her, turning her, pawing and grabbing and squeezing, his hands, his mouth everywhere: He *took* her.

Julia's hoarse whispers of "Stop it!" and "What are you doing!" slowed him down not at all, and she hesitated to shout and have the kids run in and find their parents like this, and he was just too strong for her to stop him, and then she had felt herself responding to him, and she'd forgotten about objecting.

It was almost like it wasn't her. It was her body responding; she was reacting to him in a way that had never been a part of their marriage, because the way he was touching her never had been a part of their marriage. It didn't even *feel* like him, the wiry strength in his hands and arms when he pinned her down, the bones of his pelvis against hers when he was pushing himself into her again and again. In the end she'd come and she'd come, and she'd thrown her arms around him and tried to pull him even deeper into herself.

She glanced over at the man she had woken up next to, and started to reach out to touch him, so she could look him in the eyes and try to understand what this meant, whether there was something left in their marriage that she hadn't realized, when Ginny knocked on the door.

"Mom? Are you up? When are you coming out? I'm making you breakfast."

She thought briefly about pretending to still be asleep so that she could wake Phil and spend a few minutes with him here, alone, in bed, but she knew that Virginia would just come in. Instead she called out that she'd be there in a minute and went through the door to their bathroom to clean herself up and get dressed.

Julia sat at the kitchen table in shorts and a T-shirt, blond hair gathered in a loose ponytail. Virginia flitted about her like a hummingbird, coming at her from all sides, bringing her more coffee, offering more eggs, pouring more juice.

"Enough," she'd had to say, laughing at Virginia's eagerness to please her. "Sit down with me."

They'd been sitting together when Phil had joined them. He sat down with his coffee and Julia waited, sought his eyes, ready to exchange a private smile, but he had picked up the newspaper and begun to read.

"Did you sleep well, Phil?" she asked.

"Hmmm." Little more than a grunt.

"That really is a lovely room to sleep in," Julia said. Phil looked up at her.

"Yes, I suppose it is," he said and returned to his reading.

There was nothing there. It was as if he didn't care that it had happened at all.

Julia's stomach flipped, and she suddenly felt exposed and used. The way he'd touched her, the way she'd let him. A surge of anger. How could she have thought he'd changed? After all this time. Damn him and damn her for thinking that last night had meant something. It occurred to her that he was probably fucking a student; and never mind what she'd been doing herself since Phil had been gone, she would never have done that if he'd shown any sign of interest in her. But no, it wasn't her. He'd been having sex with some young girl, and that's why his engine had been all revved. It made a lot more sense than to believe that the sexual dynamic between them had changed so thoroughly at this late date. Her grip on her coffee cup tightened, and the question in her eyes when he had entered the room was now more like a death ray as she glared at him.

". . . and then we could go into town. I could show you—Mom, are you listening? I could show you around the town, okay?" Virginia was saying.

Peter walked into the room, just out of bed, mumbling his good morning.

"I was thinking," Julia said, putting aside her feelings about her husband, something she was as practiced at as she was tired of, "we could all do something together, as a family. Don't you think, Phil?"

"I can't today, Mom. Sorry," Peter said. Leaning back against the counter with his coffee, shirtless, long and rangy in a pair of jeans, his hair still in the shape the pillow had given it, he looked like one of those lifestyle ads for young people, Julia thought.

"I haven't seen you in a month and you can't spend one day with your family?" Julia asked, wincing internally at her guilt-inducing mother reflex.

"Mom, I told the guys I'd hang out with them today," Peter said, almost whining, and the illusion was broken. It was just her son, elongated and slimmed down, but the same boy.

"I didn't make any plans for this weekend, Mom," Virginia said.

"Well," Julia said, holding back the sigh and smiling at Virginia instead. "I had a look at your room. Maybe we could start with that."

Around noon, Peter was showered and waiting on the front porch, his hair still wet, when Buddy's car screeched off of Route 9 and into the dirt drive up to the house. Crisp rode in the front seat with him. Peter stood up to leave, yelling good-bye through the screen door behind him, but his mother stepped out before he even got off the porch.

"Am I going to meet your new friends, Peter?" Julia asked.

Peter tensed himself against the myriad possibilities for embarrassment that this situation presented.

"Nah, you don't need to meet them, Mom," he said, but Buddy and Crisp had emerged from the car on their own, and were already walking through the grass toward the house.

"Hey, Peter didn't say he had another sister," Crisp

said, as he stepped up onto the porch. "And such a beautiful sister, too." He held out his hand.

Julia narrowed her eyes at him and tried to be stern, but in the end she couldn't help laughing. She shook her head.

"And Peter didn't tell me he was hanging out with Eddie Haskell," she said, as she shook his hand. "I'm Peter's mother. You can call me Julia."

"It's very nice to meet you, Julia," Crisp said. He shook her hand with a fingerless leather glove, and the many small chains looped variously about his black leather jacket swung when he turned to Buddy. "I'm Crispin D'Angelo, and this is our friend Buddy Lahey."

Buddy, much less the courtier around parents, looked up from where he stood, a step away from the porch, his fists stuffed in the pockets of his sleeveless denim jacket, his biceps large and flexed under his T-shirt. "Hey," he said. For a friend, he didn't sound particularly friendly.

"We're gonna go now, Mom," Peter said, and even though his mother had the grace not to kiss him good-bye in front of his friends, she was still his mother.

"When are you going to be back, Peter? Are you having dinner with us?"

"I don't know," he said. "I'll call you, okay?"

"Mom," Virginia said from just inside the screen door, "are you coming back in now? I need you to help me."

"I'll be right in, Ginny."

"It was very nice to meet you, Julia," Crisp said, and then he and Buddy turned and walked back to the car. Peter clearly itched to join them.

"Okay? I'll call you?" he said.

"It would be nice if we could all sit down to dinner

together, Peter," Julia said, the emphasis in her voice
letting him know that she did not mean this casually.

"Okay!" he protested, already resenting her expectation and implied disappointment. He hopped down
off the porch and hurried to the car.

"Your mom is fucking hot," Crisp said, watching
her through the windshield, when Peter got into the
backseat. "For somebody her age, I mean. M.I. fucking L.F."

"I'd do her," Buddy added.

"Jesus!" Peter said. "That's my mother! You're
fucking gross." He looked at her watching them from
the porch, in, okay, pretty short denim cutoffs, and
yeah, it had never occurred to him before, but maybe
it would be better if she wore a bra under the T-shirt,
and he could almost see it, but it wasn't something he
was willing to go along with. "Can we talk about
something else, please?"

"Hell, yeah," Crisp said, and turned around to face
Peter as Buddy backed the car out of the drive, and
then out onto the road as soon as it was clear. Crisp
pulled a folded-up envelope from an inner pocket.
"Let's talk about crank. Nabbed it from my father. He
just cooked up a fresh batch."

Crisp's father was a mechanic at the Libby's can-
ning plant just outside of town, and had lately supple-
mented his income by providing his colleagues with
the means to pull double shifts. Crisp had, in the same
time frame, suddenly realized the need for a paternal
presence in his life, and started dropping by his father's trailer to visit. Oddly, his father was almost
never home on those occasions.

"Let's go get fucked up," Buddy said, and turned the
local rock station on loud as he hit the gas.

"Fuck, yeah!" Crisp said and started drumming on the dashboard with his hands. "Dude," he added, over his shoulder, "who's Freddie Haskell?"

Phil had planted himself in his study with a box of papers he'd brought home from the college right after breakfast. Julia got to work with Virginia on cleaning up her room, and even drove her forty miles to the nearest Wal-Mart, outside of Canandaigua, so they could buy some things to decorate with. Peter sat in the backseat of Buddy's car while Buddy drove all the way around the lake three times, fast, thirty miles on a side, pulling over approximately every twenty minutes so they could all do some more lines of crystal meth.

Peter had always imagined that methamphetamine, crystal meth, would be just that: crystalline, an icy arrow into your brain that made you sharp, fast, full of energy. This was a much more savage brew. It went in harsh, felt like it was shredding his nasal passages all the way down, like he'd snorted something that wasn't meant to go in the human body.

He was nonetheless jaw-clenchingly, teeth-grindingly tweaked from the first line, and he couldn't wait for each pit stop to do some more.

The three of them were jabbering at each other about rock and roll bands, all at the same time, when Crisp's cell phone rang, and a second later, Peter's did, too.

"Hey," Crisp said.

"Hello?" Peter said.

"Dude," Crisp said.

"Hi," Peter said.

Buddy continued telling them about this one concert. When they both ended their calls a minute later,

Crisp said, "Let's go to Wadsworth. Weaver scored some ludes and he's gonna meet us there."

"Yeah," Peter said, "Trish and them are already there."

"No such thing as ludes," Buddy said. "You can't get 'em anymore."

"Yeah, right, we know that, Buddy. These are bootleg ludes. Fake ludes. You eat them, pretend they're ludes, and you get fucked up just like they're ludes."

"Yeah, okay," Buddy said. "We could do that."

"Ludes," Peter said from the back, just enjoying the sound of it.

They got to Wadsworth twenty minutes later, and the first thing they noticed was the black SUV parked in the gravel road, where Buddy's car usually sat. There was still dust settling around the tires. Compared to the SUV, Buddy's once-white, fourteen-year-old Camaro looked like a piece of shit.

Standing over in front of the mausoleum were Weaver and Grunt, facing off four guys Peter recognized as jocks from their school, three of them from the football team. They were each of them half again as big as Weaver, and Grunt, though he was big, was fat and out of shape. Karen stood just a little behind Weaver, and Trish and Allison were sitting on a bench off to the side, glaring at the jocks.

Seneca High School was too small for there to be any real ongoing overt intra-clique hostility; these kids had all gone to school together since kindergarten, mostly. Every once in a while, though, the jocks, who sat at the apex of the school's social order, and Peter's new friends, who alone among the student body did not pay them fealty, would go at it, a skirmish over territory or somebody's new girlfriend, or simply because each group thought of the other as a set of people the world would be a better place without.

Buddy shut off the ignition, got out of the car, and leaned over on the roof. Crisp, closer to them on his side of the car, stepped out and stood there, arms crossed. Peter got out on Buddy's side.

There was a large smile of relief on Weaver's face.

"Hey, guys," he said through his grin. "Look who's here. The varsity cheerleaders say we should go somewhere else so they can drink here today."

"Well, that's just fucking rude, isn't it? Chuck," Crisp said, addressing one of the football players, "didn't your coach ever make you stop jerking each other off in the locker room long enough to learn how to behave in public?"

"Fuck you, D'Angelo," Chuck said.

"No, fuck you, fucktard," Trish said, propelling herself up off the bench.

One of the other guys, Brandon, Peter thought it was, picked up a stray piece of gravel from the ground and winged it at Trish, sidearm. She was standing at an angle to him, and he hit her square in the middle of the rear pocket of her jeans, as he'd meant to. He was second-string quarterback, after all.

"*Ow!* You asshole, that hurt."

The jocks laughed. It wasn't real laughter, but it served its purpose.

Crisp started walking toward the intruders. Peter saw him reach up under the back of his jacket and pull something out.

"Reach under the seat," Buddy said to Peter as he passed him, moving to the rear of the car in three quick steps.

"What?" Peter said.

Buddy opened the trunk and reached in. "Under the backseat. Reach under there."

He slammed the trunk shut and stood holding a baseball bat.

Peter bent down and brushed past the empty bags, Big Mac boxes and beer bottles. The bottles clinked when he pulled out a wooden club like a miniature baseball bat, the kind fishermen use to bash in the heads of the spikier, nonedible fish they reeled in, the ones that were all bones and spines.

Club in hand, he walked over to where Buddy was, as Crisp advanced on the jocks. Now that backup was here, Weaver and Grunt started moving in, too. The thing in Crisp's hand flicked open into a knife.

Buddy looked at the miniature club in Peter's hand and shook his head. "Ah, fuck it. Here, take this," and he swapped him for the baseball bat, now a serious weight in Peter's hand. Then Buddy considered the little club he was now holding and tossed it aside. "C'mon, dude. This'll be fun," he said to Peter and started forward.

Evolutionary psychologists have suggested that the way we respond to violence is programmed in, and the evidence of the latest genetic mapping seems to suggest that there is actually a specific set of genetic switches that incline us toward violence. Those who exhibit one specific configuration become the brutal men responsible for most of the immediate pain in the world. They will initiate violence with little or no provocation, because hurting others does not bother them. When faced with violence they react with violence, without any doubt or hesitation. They think violence is fun. Buddy would be an example of this sort.

Others, with a different combination of switches and

triggers in their genetic makeup, were perfectly capable of violence, but it was a choice they made more than it was a blind instinct. They had to look at the circumstance, think through the consequences one way or the other, and then, if it made sense strategically, they would respond with as much violence as they thought necessary. Crisp, whose constant posturing included the idea that there was the whiff of danger about him, would have liked others to think he was like Buddy, but he would more properly be understood as this second type, which was, in fact, ultimately the more formidable of the two, but he was too young to understand that.

Then there are those who simply do not have violence in them. These are people who freeze when confronted with violence, like a Tennessee Fainting Goat. They lack the capacity for violence, and therefore pursue a different strategy for survival, avoiding physical confrontations as best they can, or when they encounter it, going down with the first blow and staying there, hoping it will pass. Peter's history with confrontation, according to this thinking, would clearly place him within this category.

There are many criticisms leveled at the field of evolutionary psychology, but one that is not heard nearly often enough is that evolutionary psychologists always fail to take into account the effect of fast cars, heavy metal rock and roll, and consuming enough crystal meth to power the space shuttle.

Those ev psych dudes always leave out the crank.

Peter lifted the bat above his head and ran screaming toward the guy who had hurt his girlfriend. Even Buddy blinked as Peter flashed past him waving the baseball bat in the air, murder in his eyes.

8

There had been six Adirondack chairs, at least fifty years old, scattered across the sloping lawn leading down to the lake when they'd bought the house. Three had been salvageable, and had been repainted white. Julia and Phil were sitting in two of them, drinking the iced tea that Virginia had made. It wasn't very good, but they drank it anyway.

Julia had taken her glass of iced tea from Virginia and left her in the kitchen putting together a salad for dinner, and walked through the back part of the house to the backyard. Phil had joined her after she'd been sitting and staring out over the water for fifteen minutes, pulled up another chair and plunked himself down. The silence that ensued was a familiar silence, but not a comfortable one.

"Shouldn't you be working on something?" Julia finally asked.

Phil didn't hear, or ignored, her bitterness.

"I've done enough for today. I'm much further in my research than I expected to be by now. I didn't think I would find so much so quickly." He looked at his wife. "I was right to move us up here, Julia. There's something about this place."

Julia didn't answer.

"John Humphrey Noyes might have sat in this very spot, Julia, imagining a classless, moneyless, completely equitable society before he founded the Oneida Community. In fact, I have reason to believe that he worked out his theories of group marriage in this very house. He was attempting to create a society without sexual jealousy. Something right here moved him to take a whole new approach to relations between men and women."

How ironic, Julia thought, and sipped her tea. Do you explain that to the students you fuck?

"And Joseph Smith, a man who communicated with angels, slept under this roof. Can you imagine? Perhaps the angel Moroni appeared to him in *our* bedroom."

Julia gave him a sideways look. "You know, Phil, you're starting to sound like you believe these things actually happen."

"Don't be silly, it's all metaphor. But metaphors of such incredible power that they changed history. You can't brush that aside. Their effects in the world were real. Whether or not Smith actually dug up a set of gold tablets, whether or not the angel Moroni appeared to him and told him where to dig, he founded the most important religious movement of the last two hundred years."

"Phil, would you listen to yourself?"

He cocked his head, considered what he'd said.

"Well, yes, you have a point, Julia. The argument could be made that Pentecostalism had the greater effect on the established denominations, but I'd still hold out for the predominance of Mormonism, if only because of the wealth and political influence the LDS has accumulated since then."

Julia closed her eyes and sighed audibly.

Phil ignored her. "The only thing that puzzles me is that there seems to be some common element, and I can't pin down what it was. Did they share some experience? Some influence? It couldn't be purely coincidence that it happens here . . ." His voice trailed off as he thought about this further. What had they both encountered here? Could it just be the nature of the land itself? It might not be a bad idea to look into regional Native American religious traditions. Iroquois myth. He sipped his tea.

"I really want to talk about Virginia, Phil."

"So you've said." He pulled his attention back and focused on his wife. "Fine. Let's talk about Virginia."

"Why do you even have to say it like that? Like it's imposing on you to talk about your daughter? Haven't you noticed the change in her? There's something wrong, Phil. She's not taking care of herself. Haven't you even noticed the way she dresses now? She's always covered up, and she looks like crap. She's sounded so depressed when I talk to her on the phone."

"She doesn't seem depressed now."

Something jumped in the lake, a splash, and they were both silent for a moment, looking down by the pier to see what it was.

"Yes, I know. Since I got here. But there's something weird about that, too. She's been sort of manic around me. She's trying too hard. Don't you remember how she was back home, Phil? The Queen of Everything? You know, I didn't like the way she was getting to be, with the clothes, and the way she ordered her friends around. I thought being up here would be good for her. . . ."

"I'm sure this is all completely normal, Julia. Adolescent girls, their bodies change, they get self-conscious and moody. Didn't you ever go through anything like that? She just has to adjust to being here. Make some friends. I'm sure this will all pass."

What Phil said made sense, but it still didn't feel right.

"I don't know—"

The phone rang inside, in the kitchen. They could hear Virginia answer it, but it was too far away to hear her words. A second later she came to the window. "Peter's not coming home for dinner," she said.

"Okay, thanks, Ginny," Julia said.

"So come inside and let's finish making dinner together, okay, Mom?"

"I'll be right in," she said. This was obviously all Phil had to say about his daughter. Maybe he was even right. But there were other issues they had to deal with. "There's something else I want to talk to you about, later, when the kids aren't around." If he could treat her the way he did, and have affairs with students, maybe it was time to talk about divorce.

They never did get to talk about it that night, or anything else, because Phil went to bed early. Julia sat up watching television with Virginia, growing increasingly concerned about Peter as time passed. At ten she called his cell phone, and he didn't answer, and at eleven she tried again and left another message. She was telling herself everything was fine, and thinking about waking Phil up, because she was sure everything wasn't fine, when she heard a car pull up to the front of the house, a car door slam, and Peter's footsteps on the porch.

She was there to open the door before he could get his keys out. He stepped into the light of the hallway and Julia gasped. There was dried blood on his chin, his forearms were scraped raw, and through tears in his jeans she could see that his knees were just as bad.

"What happened to you!" She tried to keep the fear from her voice.

"Nothing," Peter said, looking down at himself. "I fell."

Which was true, as far as it went.

Running with the bat waving in the air, Peter had stumbled and gone sprawling forward, landing painfully facedown on cement. Everyone stopped what they were doing to look. Trish ran to him to see if he was okay, and Buddy stepped over him and picked up the bat.

The time-out gave everyone a moment to think, and the jocks considered Crisp's knife, and Buddy with the bat—they were big, the football players, but so was Buddy, and they all knew he was meaner, and a dirty fighter besides—and they even took the guy on the ground into account, the new kid in school. He might be skinny, and he might be out of it for the moment, but he was clearly some kind of madman, which made sense when you thought about it, him being from New York. They thought about all the new factors in the situation and decided they'd just as soon drink their beers elsewhere.

"Why didn't you answer your phone? We don't pay for your cell phone so you can ignore it when I want to get in touch with you."

"Sorry, Mom. Jeez. It broke when I fell." He took it from his pocket and showed her.

Peter had called home on Karen's phone, and spent the rest of the evening getting fucked up in the very excellent company of his new friends.

Julia looked at him standing there, noticed that he was swaying slightly, and the redness of his eyes.

"You're high, aren't you?"

"C'mon, Mom. Lay off. I had a couple of beers. It's not a big deal."

Julia actually agreed with him—she'd done her share of drinking at sixteen, and a great deal more than that—but knew that she was not supposed to, and did her best.

"Until you're old enough to drink, it is a big deal. And staying out until midnight without letting me know where you are is a big deal, too." She made the point about drinking with as much conviction as she could muster, but was afraid that Peter could tell that she had her doubts. Great, she thought. Not only am I now being a hypocrite with my own child, I'm not even doing it well enough to meet minimum parental requirements.

Peter, for his part, having successfully diverted her from the narcotics and focused her on the beer—which he had in fact been drinking, and many more than a couple; crystal meth, besides everything else, he had discovered, made you really good at drinking beer— understood at that moment that his mother really knew nothing about the world.

"You don't know where I am *ever.* You don't even *live* here." The disdain in his voice was so thick and obvious that it remained there in the hallway with her long after he had turned and walked away up the stairs.

Peter woke, or rather came to, sometime after three a.m.

When he left his mother to that particular tangle of anger and guilt that teenagers are so adept at inspiring in their parents, he had gone upstairs, turned on his iPod, and opened his laptop. He still couldn't get the wireless to connect, and the characters on the screen were vibrating and blurring a bit too much for him to make a real effort to figure out why. Instead, he put the computer aside, leaned back in his bed and closed his eyes. He soon passed out.

A couple of hours later, the remaining crystal methedrine in his bloodstream won out over the combined effects of marijuana, alcohol, and fake Quaalude, all fading, and he was roused back to consciousness.

He was greeted by the strange, angular rhythms of a Modest Mouse song, the slightly lunatic sound of Isaac Brock's singing. *These walls are paper-thin and everyone hears every little sound.* The song seemed to him thin and strained. He'd heard it a hundred times; how could he not have noticed that before?

The bright light from the overhead fixture seemed to isolate him with the music; his room was a bubble of light in an empty, lifeless world. It was too bright in there, uncomfortably bright; he was washed in a stark fluorescence, harsh and cold, making everything in the room look shoddy, every imperfection in the walls and furniture standing out. The two windows and the one in the top of the door out onto the veranda revealed a featureless dark, the light inside making them mirrors, showing him nothing outside of the room. It occurred to him that if someone had been watching him through the window, if there were a face just on the other side of the glass, he wouldn't know until he shut out the light.

The music shuffled to the next song, a warmer, more human sounding Rilo Kiley. He stuffed the iPod in his pocket when he got up to pee, but first he went to the door and stepped out onto the veranda. It was, of course, empty. The cool night air made him feel a little more normal. He looked out over the lake, completely still, a mirror moon floating on its surface. He could save himself a trip to the bathroom if he just peed over the railing. He looked to his left, toward the door to his sister's bedroom; if she caught him peeing over the balcony, his parents would know the second they woke up.

He walked the few steps that brought him to his sister's door and looked in the glass in the upper part of the door. No sign she was awake. He stepped to the railing and looked down. Damn. They'd moved the chairs up toward the house. No way he'd miss all of them.

He turned and walked back through his room. The light from the overhead spilled out into the dark hallway when he opened the door. It was probably just the remaining crank, but he felt a tightening in his chest as he stepped out of his room, his heart speeding up.

He walked to the bathroom between his room and his sister's, and quickly turned the light on and shut the door behind him. After flushing, he stepped over to the old-fashioned freestanding sink and turned on the water to splash his face before going back to bed. Actually washing his face seemed like too much effort.

Fortunately, he remembered to take off his earphones before he got them wet, but it was still not until after he had toweled his face dry and then shut off the water that he heard the sounds.

Through the closed door of the bathroom, he could almost tell himself that he was imagining them.

Peter opened the door slowly, and the noises were immediately louder and clearer. The light spilling out of the door to his room seemed weaker than it had minutes before, surrendering the hallway to indistinct shadow.

They were animal noises, he thought at first, and they were coming from his parents' bedroom. Grunting, moaning, banging. He stood there looking across at the door. Did he hear a voice? Was that his mother? He heard a steady babbling, "nonononono," it could have been, but maybe not; it sounded mindless, like it was not intended to communicate information.

Warring in his mind were two ideas, both too unpleasant to really consider. The first was that he was simply hearing his parents having sex, and the other was that even with his limited experience, he knew that this is not what people having sex sounded like. It was the sound of insane people flailing at each other, maybe, subhuman, prehuman sounds, sounds before speech.

But maybe that's what *his* parents sounded like when they were having sex.

He shuddered at the images forming in his mind. He shook his head, physically trying to get rid of the idea, like a dog trying to shake off a sharp-toothed burr sunk deep into the tender flesh of its snout.

Peter sincerely did not want to think about his parents having sex, and he didn't want to have heard the noises they made together, and if he could admit to himself that what he was hearing behind their door could not possibly be them, he would be relieved of that burden, but he really really did not want to think about what that would mean, either.

I'm telling you, man. You got some ghosts.

He didn't believe in ghosts.

He stood frozen there, pushing away the pictures in

his head; whichever way his mind went, nothing it confronted was anything less than awful. It would veer away, and then get pulled back.

He heard another sound, now, to his right, a muffled scream. From his sister's room.

"Ginny?"

Nothing.

He definitely could have imagined that.

And if he didn't, she could just be having a nightmare.

There was a series of bangs, like a piece of furniture thudding into a wall, over and over, and then the sounds from his parents' room stopped.

From his sister's room came a whimpering.

He stepped to the door, and he was sure he heard voices from behind it, indistinct but more than one. Male voices, gibbering, whispering, rising into an insane giggle and falling again.

He called out her name in the dark of the hallway.

"Virginia?"

He put his hand to the doorknob and it all stopped dead.

He tried to turn the knob, but the door wouldn't open. He put his shoulder to it. Nothing.

Footsteps, crossing the room to the door. Slow, heavy footsteps. Virginia never made that much noise walking across a room.

He pressed his ear to the door, tried the doorknob again. Another set of footsteps, faster, scurrying across the room. He could hear breathing on the other side of the door now, he thought, coming from right where his ear was, too high up for Virginia, unless she was standing on something. There was something right there, inches away from him, inches from his face. Panting. Peter could feel it listening through the door, just like he was.

Supremely fucking haunted, dude.

"Ginny?" he asked, just barely able to choke out the words. "Is that you?"

In his hand, he felt the doorknob start to turn.

Peter bolted for his room, flying down the hall in what felt like one leap, and slammed the door shut behind him. He sat down on the floor with his back to the door, his feet planted in front of him, ready to brace himself and push if he had to. He put his headphones back on and turned the sound up loud.

1971

They'd ended up spending that first night together in Ellen's dorm room, which nobody would even think to comment on, Alex from off campus getting fucked up and crashing with a friend. They had driven back to campus as the sun went down, creeping along, hugging the side of the road, circling north of the town of Seneca and driving back onto campus from the back to avoid seeing anybody. They'd slept together in Ellen's narrow single bed, what little sleep they got, smoking pot as they came down to draw out the high, cushioning themselves as they crashed, talking all night.

Alex had known since she was a kid, and she didn't keep it a secret, but she didn't advertise it either. Ellen, she'd never even thought of it, though she'd read this trashy paperback that was getting passed around in the seventh grade, about women who drove trucks, and found herself getting a bit too turned on, and made a point not to think about it again, because what kind of people do that? But now she knew what kind of people—people like Alex, and could you believe it? People like her.

In the morning, Alex borrowed her car to go home and change and get her books for class, and left Ellen almost bursting with her secret, wandering through her day, to classes, to the library, a smile stealing over her face when she didn't know it. Her friend Beth even asked her if she was okay when they met for lunch to go over French notes. It all went together, Ellen thought, the tripping and her and Alex, the revelations, the revealings, and she really couldn't wait to do it again, all of it.

Alex had called and said to meet her at the Oaks, a bar almost right on campus, at five. It was a student favorite, but it had to be the convenience, because the interior was no different from the two dim, worn, beer-soaked bars downtown, where the old World War II vets, unshaven and dank with body odor, would pour out their life stories if you sat down next to them. Ellen, not much of a drinker, sat on a stool at the battered, drink-stained bar and managed to make a beer last the full forty-five minutes that Alex was late.

"Sorry," Alex said, slipping onto the stool next to Ellen. Getting close to six, the bar was filling up with kids, ordering pitchers and burgers. On the jukebox, Neil Young was singing "Southern Man."

"That's okay. Is something wrong?" Ellen asked. Just in the way Alex held herself, Ellen could sense something different.

"No," Alex said, and shook her head. "Yes. I should have been at the house last night. There's some stuff going on." She ordered a beer and another one for Ellen.

"What do you mean? What kind of stuff?"

"Okay, look, you can't tell anybody about this,

okay? The guy I said? He's sort of a political organizer. He used to be with the SDS, but since Chicago," by which she meant the 1969 convention of the Students for a Democratic Society, when the group had exploded into more and less radical factions, "he's been underground and—"

"You mean he's in *the Weather Underground*?" Ellen whispered, looking around to make sure nobody was listening in. The Weathermen, they seemed as unreal and far from her life as Richard Nixon or Dick Cavett or Chairman Mao.

"Something like that, yeah."

"*Alex!* Those people, they're all gonna get killed, or go to jail for the rest of their lives. What does 'something like that' mean?"

Alex gave her a measuring look that seemed leagues from how she'd looked at her yesterday. Like Ellen was a different person. Or Alex was. "Forget it. I thought you'd want to get involved."

"No, I do. Tell me. I was just worried about you, that's all."

"Okay," and Alex leaned over to speak to her more closely, "yeah, he was with the Weather Underground, but he's on his own now. He has some ideas that they weren't willing to go along with."

"Okay, but why is he here?"

Alex gave her a long stare.

"Ellen, I don't know if this is really for you. I thought you'd be into it, but maybe I was wrong about you."

Ellen felt her heart do something funny, maybe stop for a second before going on perfectly normally. "Don't say that, Alex."

"Ellen, everything's political. When we trip, we're saying no to the consensual reality, and what we did, that was saying no to the patriarchy. There's a war going on, and it's our responsibility to stop it. Doing nothing, that's almost as bad as being the guy dropping bombs on Cambodia. He's just following orders, and if we don't fight back, if we just do what society tells us to, we're doing the same thing.

"If you're just playing around, having some fun while you're in college, fine, we can do that, but this is something I'm serious about, and I'm going to be serious about whatever comes next."

Ellen took hold of her arm. "No, I'm serious, too, Alex. I'm just, you know, I don't want you to get hurt. If you tell me it's the right thing to do, I'll do it with you, but don't act like I can't have an opinion about it, too."

"Yeah, sorry, you're right. I'm just always . . . Ellen, you know what's weird? Those guys at the house, they look up to me. They respect me. You know how hard it is for women to get respect in the Movement? Remember what Stokely Carmichael said? 'The only position for women in the Movement is prone.' When I first got here, the guys I was talking to, they'd hear me talking, and all they'd think is, 'Hey! Libber! Easy lay!'

"Now, nobody organizes at the house, on the campus, without talking to me. And they only do that because they realized I was as tough as they were, and they only think that because I'm tougher. Whatever they do, I have to do a little more. Why's Microgram Walker here? He's here because I got in touch with him and told him we wanted to work with him. Yeah, okay, this is going to be a little dangerous. The guy blows things up. We all know that, but things need to be blown up, and I can't back down just because it's dangerous."

Ellen listened, nodding her head. "Okay, Alex."

"Listen, I've got to get back to the house. Why don't you come out tomorrow after classes, and you can meet him."

"You can't stay tonight?" The disappointment in her voice was as plain as it was sincere.

Alex looked at her and the sternness melted away. Now she looked to Ellen like she had yesterday. Alex reached over to Ellen's lap, and below the bar, she took her hand.

"I'd like that, I really would, but this is important. You'll see tomorrow, okay? And you can stay over with me."

9

Peter slept until well after noon. He woke up on the floor, brain fuzzy, mouth gluey, the events from yesterday afternoon on removed and out of focus, as if he'd watched them happen to somebody else and hadn't been paying enough attention. A cramp in his side pulled when he stood up, and when he breathed his nasal passages felt painfully raw from his nostrils all the way to the back of his throat.

After going into the bathroom and scooping up water with his hand, slurping up palmful after palmful, he aimed himself downstairs. His mother sat alone at the kitchen table drinking coffee, fuel for the six-hour drive back to Brooklyn.

"Good morning, Peter," she said.

Peter had poured himself a cup of coffee, and sat down at the table with his mother, before her formal and slightly chilly greeting helped him recall coming home the night before, the things he said to her when he'd walked in the door.

He wanted to ask about the noises he'd heard, but felt somewhat sheepish about his drug-fueled outburst.

"Morning. Where is everybody?" he asked.

"Your father's in his study working, and your sister

shut herself in her room when I told her I'm not staying and she can't come back to Brooklyn with me."
She didn't look at Peter when she spoke; she lifted the
coffee cup with two hands and sipped. From her tone,
she was clearly disgruntled with her entire nuclear
family. At least it wasn't just him.

"Listen, Mom. . . . " He hesitated, thought about
what he was, in essence, going to be asking her, even if
he didn't say it directly. *Were you and Dad having
really loud sex last night?* He grew flustered before he
could even start to ask. Sex was just not something
he was comfortable bringing up with his mother. He
hadn't forgotten the intensely uncomfortable half hour
shortly after his fourteenth birthday when, tired of waiting for his father to step in, she'd taken it upon herself
to explain sex to him. Forget that he could learn—had
learned—anything he'd need to know on the Internet,
complete with pictures, diagrams, and illustrative
videos, the one word you never wanted to hear your
mother say to you was "erection," particularly if you
wanted to be having one again anytime soon.

To her credit, she had seemed almost as uncomfortable as he was, and she'd said what she felt had to be
said as quickly as possible, but he still shrunk at the
memory. Literally. Still, he had to ask, somehow.

His mother looked up at him, waited.

"Did you . . . hear anything last night? Like, anything strange?"

Julia blanched. "No," she said, a little too quickly,
almost before he had finished asking the question. A
splash of coffee slopped over the side of her cup. Had
Peter heard them? What must they have sounded like?
But, wait, that wasn't last night, was it?

Julia tried to recall when it had happened. Had it

happened again? Now, when she tried to remember it, what had been so present—had she sat there on the side of the bed yesterday, feeling it all over again? or was that this morning?—seemed many times removed, as if it were not only a dream, but a dream from a long time ago, only just now remembered.

"You're going on about ghosts again, are you?" Phil said as he entered the room to refill his coffee cup.

"No," Peter said sullenly, embarrassed.

"I told you, son, towns have memories, and you have to expect that sort of superstitious reaction in a place like this. People here can't tell the difference between spirituality and spirits. I expect you to know better."

"Yeah, I know," Peter said. He felt foolish, and grabbed at something to change the subject. "Listen, Dad, I can't get the wireless to work up in my room. Do you think you can mess with the router or something so it works?"

"Of course it's not working, Peter. I haven't set one up yet. If you need to go online you can come downstairs and use my computer. Or I'll give you money to buy a router and you can set it up. You're much better at these things than I am, anyway."

"Yeah, sure, Dad, I'll do that," Peter said, and thought about Virginia, up in her room all the time, IMing with her friends, she'd said . . . but did she actually ever say that, or had he just assumed?

"I wanted a chance to talk to you before I left, Peter," Julia said.

He knew that he'd been intentionally cruel last night, lashed out with those things he knew she'd feel bad about. He didn't want to meet her eyes.

"Maybe we could take a walk down by the lake? We haven't spent any time together all weekend."

"Yeah, sure, that'd be okay," he said. She was absolving him, he could tell by her tone. There was only the formality of the apology to get out of the way. "Lemme go get some shoes on. I'll be right back," he said, and dashed up the stairs.

He didn't come straight down, though, after he'd pulled his flip-flops out from under his bed. He first went and stood by Virginia's door.

In the light of day and the face of his father's insistence, he was starting to doubt what he'd heard last night. It did seem pretty unlikely. Maybe something he'd smoked, snorted, or swallowed the night before had been spiked with something else, something trippy.

"Gin," he said, as he rapped on the door with his knuckles.

"What?"

"Can I talk to you for a minute?"

No answer but the squeak of bedsprings, and then he heard her walking toward the door. The sound brought him back to last night, and he felt a quick chill, but the door opened a crack, and it was just Virginia looking out at him. She was leaning over to look through the opening, keeping her body behind the door, like somebody not dressed for company.

"Is Mom gone yet?" she asked.

"She's leaving soon, I think."

"Good," she said. "I hate her." She started to close the door.

"Wait. Listen, last night . . . did you hear—"

"Did I hear what, Peter? Did I hear you sneaking around listening to me? Did I hear you trying to come in the door? Yeah, I heard that. But, surprise, Peter. I lock it."

"What? I heard something, I was worried, I was just trying to . . . "

"I know what you were trying to do, Peter. Now that you've got a girlfriend, you think everybody thinks you're so hot—"

"What?"

She pulled the door partly open again, a focused anger on her face. "You know what, Peter? Stay out of my room, and you can stay *away* from my room, too. I know you're spying on me."

"Virginia, I don't know what you're talking about."

"You're spying on me. You were spying on me last night, weren't you? You've been spying on me since we got here. Don't even try to lie. I've seen you at the window."

"But I'm not—"

"Yeah, right. Just, here, look . . . " And she came out of the room. She had a bathrobe on, nothing to hide from him.

She outlined a semicircle around her doorway with her foot. She dragged her toe over his feet, bared in his flip-flops, to make part of it.

"Just stay out of there, okay?"

Peter looked from the imaginary line on the floor up to his sister. "Are you fucking kidding me?"

"Like, *now*?" she said, and pushed him in the chest so that he stumbled back a step.

"Thank you," she said, and went back in her room and closed the door behind her, leaving Peter standing there, bewildered.

When she'd closed the door, Virginia walked to her bed and sat down. With the curtains drawn and the lights out, the room was filled with a twilight gloom.

"Okay," she said. "You can come back now."

She turned and looked at the handsome, long-haired man sitting beside her on the bed.

"You know, darlin'," he said, "you really cannot trust that boy at all."

"Yeah, I know," Virginia said. "He's always been sort of sneaky."

"You know what else? I don't know about you, but I just don't see how he manages to be so popular, when you're the one who should really be popular."

Virginia said nothing. She sighed and fell back onto the bed, her arms up over her head, her robe falling open as she moved, exposing the fresh cuts across her breasts.

"You see that, don't you?" he asked her. "How unfair it all is to you?"

Virginia nodded, silent.

"Personally, Virginia, I wouldn't let him get away with it. I wouldn't let any of them get away with it. If it were up to me, they'd all regret the way they've been treating you."

Virginia's eyes were filling with tears as she thought about how unfair it all was, how she really couldn't depend on anybody else, because they were all so busy having friends, and having girlfriends and boyfriends, and how she was never going to. She sat up and looked at her new friend, who was always so nice to her.

"Thanks. Will you help me get even with everybody?"

"You bet, darlin'," he said. "Soon."

"Okay," Virginia said, and shook her head and wiped her eyes. She stood up in front of him, and her robe fell off. "What do you want to do to me today?"

Outside, the sky hung heavy and gray, a luminous shade paler where the sun tried to shine through the dense cloud cover. Peter carried his mother's bag to her secondhand Beetle and put it in the backseat, and then they walked around the side of the house to the pier, started walking south on a path that ran along beside the shore of the lake. His mother commented on the old rowboat pulled up from the water next to the pier. It wasn't visible from the house, and she hadn't noticed it before.

"Yeah, I found it. It was in the grass way up under the pier. I had to get all the way under to even see it. It barely leaks. I'm gonna paint it maybe, and try going out fishing in it," Peter said.

"My little outdoorsman. . . . It's good for you guys up here, isn't it?" she asked, hoping to address her own misgivings about leaving her kids behind.

"Listen," he went on, focused on his own guilt, "what I said last night—"

"I forgive you," Julia said and smiled, and she reached out and put an arm around his shoulder and pulled him to her for a second.

"Mom," he said, and shrugged her arm off. "Really, I didn't mean it. I know you have to be in the city for work."

The path they followed was little more than a dirt rut worn through the grass by countless passages over countless years. To their right, a dozen feet away, the ground dropped off to the water. Today, the lake was a dull greenish gray, a leaden reflection of the sky above, a small chop lapping everywhere across its surface.

"You know that's not what it really is, don't you, Peter? You're old enough to understand that things haven't exactly worked out between me and your father, right?"

Peter glanced at her, didn't say anything. Last night, is that what it sounds like when it doesn't work out? he thought. He shook his head.

"Don't be that way, Peter. We need the time apart. Really," she said, more to herself than to Peter, thinking about it logistically, "I could work up here, most of the time"—she came back to the emotional reality of the situation—"but your father and I just can't live in the same place anymore."

Peter sighed. It was true, it wasn't news to him, even if he had chosen not to think about it. "Yeah, I know. It's not like having your parents divorce makes me a freak."

"I'm going to try to get up here more," she said.

"That'd be great. I think Virginia would really like that . . . I mean, I'd like it too, but—"

"I know. You're pretty much grown up and don't need me anymore, right?"

She smiled at him, and however much it was patronizing, it was balanced by affection.

"Well, yeah. But Ginny, she's getting pretty strange, and . . . "

"I know. I'm worried about her, too. Your dad thinks I'm being an alarmist, and I know he wouldn't let anything happen to her, but, well, you know your father. Some things, he doesn't exactly notice."

Peter blew a puff of air through his lips, a sound that succinctly conveyed the idea that they were barely scratching the surface of the set of things that his father didn't notice, and they both knew it, it was just a fact of life, so why bother getting into it?

"Ginny's not doing too well at school, is she? I mean, socially."

Another understatement.

"Nah, she's . . . well, really, she's pretty much a leper. She said something to some girl, one of the really popular girls, and I guess word got around not to hang out with her."

They walked a bit while Julia absorbed this. The Heather had been dethroned. There had been a time when she thought Virginia could stand to be shaken up a bit, taken down a notch, see what it's like not to be at the top of the social scene; maybe, she had thought, Virginia would develop a little more empathy for kids who weren't as successful with their peers as she was. As it turned out, though, Julia didn't like seeing it at all.

They had come by now to the woods, which started at the end of their property line, about fifty yards beyond the pier. From there south, along the shore, was nothing but trees and whatever lived in them, until you came out the other side, a couple of miles away, into the old cemetery that Peter and his friends frequented.

A cool wind, heavy and wet, blew off the lake, suggesting the rain about to follow.

"I hear you have a girlfriend now," Julia said, as they walked in among the beeches and oaks.

"Yeah, I guess," Peter said, looking at the ground as they walked.

"Is she nice?"

"She's great, Mom," Peter said, in a burst of enthusiasm that managed to escape him unmediated. "Her name is Patricia Willits, but everyone calls her Trish, and she used to go out with this other guy, who is really cool, so I thought . . . " His voice trailed off, as be became self-conscious about sharing his feelings about a girl with his mother.

"I don't suppose you and your girlfriend could be Ginny's friends at school. . . . "

Peter shot her a look, which she correctly interpreted as "You're not serious, are you?"

"I suppose not," she said.

"It just doesn't work that way, Mom."

They had walked another quarter mile or so into the woods, the dirt path still roughly following the shoreline, the trees on either side of them growing more closely together the farther they walked. To their right, the trees grew all the way down to the water, some of the last ones leaning over the lake with roots exposed, time having whittled away the stable ground beneath them.

The path turned up away from the lake here, and as they continued deeper into the woods, the trees seemed to trap darkness beneath their tangled branches.

Julia stopped a pace ahead of Peter and turned to face him, compelling him to stop, too.

"It would make me feel a lot better if I knew you would look out for her, Peter."

"I don't know what you expect me to do. It's her own fault."

"She's just a little girl, Peter. She's your sister. You could spend some time with her, you know. At least make sure she's not alone so much."

Just then, over his mother's shoulder, deeper in the woods, Peter saw somebody. No, two people, a guy and a girl. They passed through his line of vision in a second, and then vanished back into the cover of the trees. The guy looked sort of like Weaver. At this distance, he couldn't be sure. The girl, though, it definitely wasn't Karen; she had too much hair. Could that have been Trish? No, of course it wasn't.

Was it?

What would Trish be doing with Weaver?

"Peter, are you listening to me?"

"Huh . . . oh, yeah. What?"

"Are you going to start spending more time with your sister?"

"Oh. Okay, sure. I'll, I don't know, I'll help her out."

"Thank you, Peter." Julia put her hands on his shoulders and kissed him on the forehead. She had to get up on her toes to do it. "You know, you turned out to be a pretty decent kid."

"C'mon, Mom. You sound like a Lifetime movie," Peter said.

Julia shook her head and laughed. "I don't know if you're aware of this, but people had relationships and feelings long before they made movies about them."

"So you claim," Peter said.

"Very funny. C'mon. Let's head back before we get rained on."

"Yeah, okay," Peter said, but he let her start back and then announced, "You go ahead, I'll catch up in a second."

"It's starting to rain, Peter. You'll get soaked," she said, but overcame the impulse to order him to turn around and return to the house with her.

"Don't worry. I just want to walk a little more. Have a good trip, okay?"

Peter turned and headed deeper into the woods, leaving his mother to return on her own.

The sound of rain falling on the leaves above started gradually, a staccato patter at first, and the canopy of the treetops had held the worst of it off for a moment, but within minutes the sound turned into a steady curtain of noise. By the time he turned and looked back the way he'd come and could no longer see his mother, Peter's hair and clothes were soaked, and water dripped steadily down his face. Cold, wet leaves, yellow and brown, were getting into his flip-flops, pasting themselves to the soles of his feet.

Peter never would have found them if he hadn't become aware of the smell of pot, a smell that made him more certain it was Weaver he had seen, and just a touch more concerned that it was Trish with him. He had to leave the path to follow them, and one way would have seemed as likely as another but for the tangy sweet scent, strong even through the rain.

He saw the fire before he saw them, flickering orange flame, nearly invisible, through the trees in a clearing up ahead.

"Hey! Weaver, that you?" he called ahead of him as he hurried forward and stepped out from the trees into the clearing.

There was nobody there. He had been mistaken. There was no fire, he saw as he approached the center of the clearing—how could there be in this much rain?—just the charred remnants of wrist-thick branches resting atop a heap of cinders, being beaten by raindrops into thick black mud.

"Hey, man," somebody said right behind him, and Peter whirled around to look.

Okay, this was fucked up. He was hearing things. He scanned all around him, saw a flicker of movement on the ground by his foot: a snake, poised to strike.

"Shit!" he yanked his foot back and lost his balance.

"Ow!" He'd stepped right in the fire with his nearly bare foot. He pulled his foot out, spun, and lost his balance. He fell on his back and looked quickly to his side, afraid he'd landed in biting range, but all he saw was a crooked branch on the ground. The smell of burning rubber flip-flop reached him. He lay there for a moment, looking up at the circle of gray sky framed by the surrounding woods,

the drops of rain falling in steady lines right at him. He blinked as rain splattered his face.

"Okay, this is *really* fucked up," he said, out loud this time.

"Sorry, man, but I've seen fucked up and this does *not* come close."

Peter sat up fast. On the other side of the blazing fire—what the fuck? how could he have made that mistake? and why wasn't the rain putting the fire out?—sat a guy with dark brown shoulder-length hair parted in the middle. Definitely not Weaver. This guy was a lot older, almost old, at least twenty-five. His face looked hard and amused.

"See, if you're gonna do the back-to-nature thing, son, you're going to have to do a better job following some of the basic rules. Now, it might not be written down anywhere, but when you went and stuck your foot in the fire—"

"Who are you?" Peter asked him.

"—you broke one of the basic rules."

"Are you from the college?"

"Sort of," the guy said. "Does it matter?"

"Where's that girl you were with?" Peter looked around the clearing.

"Don't get ahead of yourself, man. You'll get yours."

"I'll get my what?" Peter saw a movement to his side and jerked his head around to look. A pretty young woman with long, curly blond hair was standing right beside him. She smiled, and dropped down to her knees.

"See, man? For everything bad there's something good. Your yin? It always comes with a side of yang. You don't want to fight it. You can't fight it. You gotta work with the universe. 'Universe,' you gotta say, 'what have you got up your sleeve for me?' Then maybe you get a pleasant surprise. You got burned, something nice is gonna happen for you, too."

Peter was listening to the guy, but he was looking at the girl.

"Uh, hi," he said to her, a bit unnerved.

"She don't talk, man. Pretty cool, huh? She does other stuff, though. Good stuff." He looked at the girl, raised his eyebrows expectantly. "Well?" he said.

She leaned in toward Peter, put her hands on his shoulders, and pushed him down onto the ground. Peter was too surprised to do anything at first, and once he was flat on his back and she had crawled on top of him, that part of the male brain that kept the species alive kicked in before actual thought, as it will, and he stayed there in the wet grass. She held his shoulders down straight-armed, and where their bodies made contact below the waist she began to rub herself against him as he grew hard. Her breasts hung inches from his face, her cotton peasant blouse rain-soaked and transparent, as though she wore nothing at all.

The thought of Trish flashed through his mind—that's why he'd come here, wasn't it? Because he'd been afraid that his girlfriend might be in the woods with Weaver?— but it was pushed aside as the girl brought her face closer to his, pressed her lips to his, and . . .

Memories surged forward in his mind, memories of dreams of memories, all filled with bodies, wet, hot, thrashing against each other. Images and sensation rushed toward him like a wave, completely enveloped him, picked him up and tumbled him over. He could feel the girl at the same time, reaching down, into his pants, and he did not want her to stop, and the greater his desire grew the more out of control he felt, the more not-real, not-in-the-world he felt, until he couldn't tell which way was up, whether he was in a dream or in the world, which way to go to find the surface, the air, waking life. He felt the weight of the girl on top of him, felt himself responding to her, his lust growing bigger than he was, he couldn't contain it . . . was he dreaming now?

And then he couldn't breathe, her lips were pressed to his so tightly, he drew in air, constricted, through his nose, tried to fill his lungs, but his nostrils filled with water, he breathed in the rain that ran down their faces, and he felt like he was drowning, falling deeper away from the sky, and if he drowned he'd fall into the dream forever. . . .

"No!" he shouted, but it came out a grunt, and while a part of him wanted to cling to her, enter her, drown in her if that's what was waiting at the end of it, he pushed her violently up and away and rolled out from under her. He got up on his knees, and stayed there, panting like a dog, looking back and forth, from her to the guy, from the guy to her.

The guy smiled. "You're sure now, little buddy?"

Peter got to his feet and then he knew, in his conscious mind, what he'd been hiding from himself. He remembered, suddenly, the visits at night, how he'd been looking forward to them, falling off into sleep every night, waiting, hoping, to slip again into that dreamworld where everything was about the pleasure of his body, where fucking and death were right next to each other and he didn't care. That's where he had just been. This girl had taken him there; it was her he waited for every night.

But this, this isn't what he wanted.

It was too much for him, and as much as his body cried out for it, it was too big for him, too intense. With

Trish . . . there was nothing frightening about it, it was thrilling, not scary, and they shared it. That was real. This other thing, this thing that picked him up and shook him, it scared him. He'd disappear inside it and get lost forever.

"Yeah, I'm sure." He started to back away from them. It was an admission of defeat, in a way; he felt he was giving up something important, passing by a challenge that would make him strong, an adult, but it was also the right thing to do.

The guy shook his head in mock wonder. "You're thinking about that cute little girlfriend of yours, aren't you? That's really sweet. But do you understand I'm offering you something here? Something big. This"— he gestured toward the girl—"she's just the handshake that signs the deal. I have big plans, son, and you can be a part of them, and what you get out of it . . . well, she's just the start." He grinned. "All you can eat, a buffet of the good stuff. You don't have to give up the jailbait. You can have them both. You want, I can make her like this one, too."

"No," Peter said to the guy, then he looked toward the girl, who just stared up at him with unblinking emerald green eyes. He didn't want to think about what that meant. "No, uh, thank you." He started backing away. "I don't know what you're talking about, and I'm just gonna go now, okay?"

"No, it's not okay," the guy said, and grabbed his shoulders to stop him.

"C'mere," he said to the girl, and the girl stepped over and dropped to her knees in front of Peter, between them, began to stroke him through his jeans. Peter tried to pull away, but the guy was too strong. He couldn't even turn.

The woman put a hand on one of his hips and pulled him closer, unzipped his fly, took him in her mouth. The guy was looking him in the eyes, a big smile on his face. Peter shuddered and closed his eyes, started getting lost in the feel of her mouth on him. He didn't notice when the grip on his shoulders disappeared.

"So? How's she doing?" The guy was standing next to him now, spoke right in his ear. It made Peter jump, enough to disengage himself. He put his hands on her shoulders and pushed her away. He must have pushed harder than he meant to, because she snapped back onto the ground as if she were thrown. He heard her head hit something, a rock in the ground. Just the sound of it was painful.

The guy laughed. "Yeah, you can hurt them some, too, if that's what you like. I got a knife you can borrow."

The girl on the ground wasn't moving. He dropped to his knees, turned her face toward him, shook her.

Peter stood up and started to back away. "I didn't mean to do that," he said.

"Sure you did. You wanted to."

"No, that's not true. You wanted to hurt her, not me. You're sick. You're crazy."

The guy just laughed, and came toward him again.

Peter turned and ran out of the clearing toward home, the mud and wet leaves sucking at his flip-flops. He went down, fell right on his face, and when he stood up, the guy was standing over him again.

"You're absolutely sure, now? One-time offer. You can fuck them when they're dead, too, if you want."

Peter got up again, kicked off his flip-flops and left them there in the woods, and then ran as fast as he could through the trees toward home.

10

Molly Dellinger took her seat in Probst Hall, the lecture hall where Phil Coulter taught his class in the history of Western religion. She sat only a few rows back from the stage in the raked semicircle of seats, at eye level with the lectern. Windows in the wall to her left reached almost all the way to the high ceiling, heavy curtains pulled back to flood the hall with light.

Fewer than fifty students were scattered among more than three hundred seats, some forming clumps and groups consistent with the laws of random dispersion. Those in groups ceased talking when Professor Coulter, entering from the back of the hall, turned up the lights, then threw the switch that caused the high, heavy curtains to draw shut over the windows, as if invisible assistants had been cued to pull them closed.

He walked down through an aisle, looking neither right nor left, up the short flight of stairs onto the stage, and arranged his papers on the lectern. Molly sat ready to take notes. He began where he had left off the week before.

"To understand the Second Great Awakening, the bout of evangelical revivalism that swept the United States in the nineteenth century—or for that matter, to understand the First Great Awakening of the eighteenth century, or what some are calling the Third Great Awakening, which we are living through now—it's necessary to look back to the first centuries of Christianity.

"The American tendency to rise up in fits of righteousness and condemn the worldly ways of modernity, to insist on withdrawal and purification, has its roots in Christianity's most persistent heresy, a dualist belief system that has cropped up again and again under various names: the Cathars, the Albigensians, the Manicheans, and so on. All of these are both specific and general terms for various instances of Gnosticism, from the Greek *gnosis*, a secret knowledge. Followers of these faiths believed that there was a hidden truth, both symbolically, within the teachings of the Church, and literally, an underlying truth about the world hidden by the world as we experienced it . . . ."

At Seneca High School, Ms. Bourne paced in front of her nineteenth-century American history class.

"In the middle of the nineteenth century, there were so many revivals here in western New York State that the whole area was called the Burned-Over District; everybody who could be saved had been saved, some of them many more times than once. Nowadays, we think of the religious as being very straitlaced and rigid, but the people we're talking about were really the hippies of their era. These revivals were more like the Woodstocks of the nineteenth century than what we think of as church services."

"The first Woodstock or the second?" Peter asked.

Ms. Bourne laughed. "Depends who you believe. Lots of people went for entertainment, and some thought the circuit preachers were as commercial and cynical as the worst of our televangelists. But many of the people who were turning to new religions and new religious leaders were very much like the young people of the sixties who 'dropped out and turned on.' They were unhappy with the values of contemporary society and they were looking for a better way to live. Both in the early nineteenth and the mid-twentieth century, young people left mainstream society to live on communes. The Oneida Community—"

"My brother goes there," said a guy in the back.

"That's very unlikely," Ms. Bourne answered. "You're thinking of Oneida Community College. The Oneida Community only lasted until around 1880. It was pretty successful, though, and it might actually still be there if it weren't for their unconventional ideas about sex and marriage. Even if we associate it with Woodstock and San Francisco and hippies, it was John Humphrey Noyes, the founder of the Oneida Community, who coined the term 'free love'. . . ."

As she knew she would, she suddenly had the rapt attention of every teenager in the classroom.

Molly had grown up in a conservative churchgoing Methodist family in the very small town of Putney, Vermont, where things hadn't changed all that much since John Humphrey Noyes had been run out of town in 1847 for his libertine beliefs. Tourism supported the town instead of paper mills now, but the people of Putney believed the same things their great-grandparents had. For Molly, who had both attended and taught Sunday school until the week she left home for Harcourt College, freshman year had been a revelation.

Molly was not stupid, nor was she ungenerous of

spirit, so when she found herself rooming freshman year with Laura Fox, a graduate of New York City's private school scene, she could not overlook Laura's essential decency, despite what appeared to Molly her depraved indulgence in alcohol and boys. Within weeks Molly found herself forced to reevaluate what she had been taught about such things. Laura was neither afflicted with venereal disease nor smote from above, and by the end of midterms it had also become apparent that she was maintaining a better grade point average than Molly. As hard as she tried to peer into their futures, Molly could not discern that Laura's was made by her indiscretions any less promising than Molly's own.

By the time Molly went home for Thanksgiving break, she brought with her a small bag of marijuana and a number of new tricks she shared with her high school beau, leaving him too grateful and dazed to even realize that she had broken off their secret pre-engagement until she was already back at school.

Still, despite having embraced the idea that the boundaries of what a good girl could do without going over to the other side were rather more elastic than she had originally supposed, Molly had neither let go of nor examined too thoroughly the idea that there *were* sides and that Jesus was the captain of hers.

Which was why she got such a rush from Professor Coulter's class, and was the only student in it who had actually read his book. Molly conceived of herself as cosmopolitan and sophisticated after two years of college, but the unquestioned assumption that people's religious behavior had political and economic causes, the implication that there was no God, and therefore, no absolute right and wrong, this still seemed to Molly on some essential level daring, even wicked. It was thrilling.

Professor Coulter looked up and caught her eye. She smiled at him.

Molly found herself thinking that there was something very appealing about him, a sort of bearish authority that made her feel both safe and vulnerable at the same time. She'd never been with anyone that much older than her, no one even close, and the thought of doing it with a man who held views that her father would have thought blasphemy, a man old enough to *be* her father . . . she realized that she was growing a little warm. She squeezed her legs together and concentrated on taking notes.

" . . . Gnostics also believed that the literary character referred to in the Old Testament as God, the great rumbling voice in the sky who breathed life into Adam and fashioned Eve from his rib, and then evicted the two of them from Eden like a cranky landlord, was not actually God. They believed that the creator of our world, whom we referred to as God, was a being they called the demiurge. A powerful but still lesser being within the larger universe ruled over by the one true God. The demiurge is not all-powerful, and nowhere near all-knowing: the demiurge did not even know that he was not God.

"The creation of the demiurge, our world, our bodies, all things material, were by the very nature of their creation corrupt. We now use the term 'Manichean' to describe a black-and-white vision of the world for very good reason. To the original Manicheans the nature of things *was* black and white. What was spiritual was good, what was physical was evil."

*   *   *

". . . but what he was describing wasn't the free love of the sixties," Ms. Bourne said. "He preferred the term 'Complex Marriage,' and what it meant was that everyone in the community was married to everybody else in the community." She paused a moment to let that sink in.

"Why would they do that?" Annabelle, a pretty, pale-skinned girl wearing even paler makeup and dressed all in black, asked. "I mean, what's the point?"

"Well, the Oneida Community came out of a movement called Perfectionism. They believed they could live perfect lives, the same lives they would live when they were in Heaven. So, there was no private property, and in the same way, they believed that there should be no 'ownership' of one person by another. The way Noyes described it, life was like a big banquet, and it would be selfish to claim one dish for yourself and not share it with your neighbor. It was the same if you kept one person to yourself."

Sitting next to Peter, Crisp caught his eye. He looked toward Annabelle, who used to be his girlfriend, when her name was still Anne. He was still unhappy about being dumped, and he was still pretending the breakup had been his idea, although everyone in school knew better. "She gets passed around a lot," he said, making no effort to keep her from hearing.

Annabelle pointedly ignored him. She spoke up again. "But who says that's what it's like in Heaven? I mean, what did he know? And wasn't it against the law?"

Last year, when she'd gone out with Crisp, Anne had been a semi-stoner, but in the course of rehearsing *Our Town*—her involvement in the school play being one of the things that kept her from being a full-fledged stoner—she had decided that she was in love with Jordan, the boy who played George to her Emily. When he revealed to her at the cast party, both of them pretending to be more drunk than they actually were, that he was pretty sure he was gay, she decided that she was not just in love with him, she was *tragically* in love with him. That was when she broke up with Crisp, became the school's sole Goth, and changed her name to Annabelle. She began writing poetry and spent much of her free time visiting various websites, where she learned about Wicca and Magick.

"Good questions, Annabelle, and they're very much related. The Perfectionists, and specifically the Oneida Community, were"—and she stopped to write the word on the board—"*antinomian*. This means . . . well, you know those old television commercials for Hebrew National hot dogs? They talk about the federal standards that Oscar Meyer and everyone else follows, and then they say, 'But we answer to a higher authority,' and the thunder lets you know they mean God?

"That's what antinomian means. It's a religious group that believes it gets its instructions directly from God. That means they can ignore the morals of society, or even the laws of the government. Groups like this, and there were a lot of them, still are, believe that their leaders are in direct communication with God, and they feel justified, even obliged, to ignore the standards of the society they came from and follow a revealed higher morality."

"Do what thou wilt shall be the whole of the law," Annabelle said. "Aleister Crowley said that. A messenger from the gods dictated a whole book to him, but that was the main thing."

There were comments and laughter throughout the

classroom, something Annabelle had grown used to. Ms. Bourne smiled at the girl, helping her ignore the derision. She liked the girl, and sympathized with her attempts to defy convention in a small community, even if her attempts were straight out of *My First Book of Teen Rebellion.*

Despite her best efforts, Molly's mind kept wandering back to this newest possibility for transgression. To someone of her background and bent, crossing those boundaries was almost an irresistible temptation. And, really, what would the big deal be? It would just be an experiment, and that's what college was for, wasn't it? Maybe she'd even get an A out of it.

". . . From the Gnostic perspective," the professor continued, "much of Christian mythology had a very different meaning. To the Gnostics, if we believed the account of Genesis, then we had been tricked. The knowledge that was forbidden to us in the Garden of Eden was a knowledge that was larger than the world, the revelation that there was a greater reality behind this world. This was the secret knowledge of the Gnostics, and it meant that whomever would bring us that information was our friend and ally, and not the enemy.

"The snake in the garden, then, instead of being a liar and deceiver, instead of tempting us to sin, is the source of truth and wisdom. The god that curses the snake is our enemy, a frustrated petty tyrant, who does not want what is best for us. He wants us to remain unconscious of the truth."

"But," Peter said, "doesn't that mean that, like, anybody can say anything and then they can do whatever they want? Because they said God told them to? What if the guy who says what to do is lying?" Peter said.

"Good question, Peter. Because Noyes's critics at the time pointed out that he came up with his theory of Complex Marriage not long after a woman he had proposed to married someone else in the community. And from a feminist perspective," Ms. Bourne said, and a few groans arose in the classroom, as they did whenever Ms. Bourne mentioned a "feminist perspective," a term that sounded to her students as yellowed and musty as "Earth Day" or "Sputnik," "it's hard not to notice that the way it was practiced tended to give the most powerful men in the community, most specifically Noyes, sexual access to many if not all of the young women."

". . . but Gnosticism was not considered the most dangerous heresy within Christianity just because of the blasphemy inherent in this characterization of the god of the Old Testament—in some cases actually identifying him with Satan—but because the Gnostics questioned the bodily resurrection of Christ.

"In the early days of Christianity many believed that Christ's resurrection was meant by the apostles to be interpreted metaphorically, or, alternately, that what the apostles saw on the third day after Christ's death was his spirit. A ghost, we'd call it.

"The political hierarchy of the established Church was based as much as anything else on the belief that a resurrected Christ appointed his apostles to carry on his work, and that they in turn had the power to appoint their successors. This is the basis for an institutional structure that has persisted for almost two thousand years.

"The Gnostics, though, believed that Christ was a manifestation of the true God, the god from beyond the corrupt material world. Christ was God's way of piercing the deception of the demiurge and bringing us the Word, the secret knowledge, in much the same way that snake entered Eden to lead Eve to the apple.

"Now, if flesh was corrupt, and Christ was pure, then Christ could not have been flesh. And if Christ was not flesh, not truly an inhabitant of the human form, then he would not have been bodily resurrected. If Christ had not been resurrected, his apostles did not have an experience unique in history; that is, they did not encounter the bodily resurrected Christ. And if that were true, then anybody's direct experience of Christ was no less valid or authoritative than that of the apostles. . . . "

"It's not like they were the only ones who did that," Peter said.

"Yes?" Ms. Bourne said.

"I mean Joseph Smith. He had, like, forty wives, and some of them were really young. The Mormons had polygamy until, I don't know, whenever Utah became a state. In 1890, I think."

Ms. Bourne looked surprised.

"Okay. Very good, that's true. Let's put that on the table, too. I'm sure you've all heard of the Mormons, the Church of Latter-day Saints. Joseph Smith founded the Church not far from here, in Palmyra in 1830. Around the same time that John Noyes was establishing the Oneida Community, Joseph Smith was leading his followers west, looking for somewhere to live their lives according to their own beliefs. And one of those beliefs was the practice of polygamy"—she paused to write the word on the board—"which is one man marrying many women. Joseph Smith said that God told him that this was the right thing to do, despite society's rules. In order for a saint to enter Heaven, he had to participate in 'celestial marriage,' which is the term Smith used for taking multiple wives."

"Did women get to have more than one husband, too?" Annabelle asked.

"A good question, and it occurred to Joseph Smith's first wife when he announced his new instructions from God. She wasn't happy about it, and after burning the document he'd shown her proclaiming his latest revelation, she announced that if her husband was going to take more wives, then she was going to take another husband."

"So, did she?"

"No, because Smith had another communication from God right after that, specifying that only men can do that."

"That's not fair," Annabelle said.

"Well, first you might want to consider why anyone would want more than one husband"—the girls in the room laughed—"but, no, I suppose it isn't," Ms. Bourne said.

"Well, how come, then?"

"I suppose it's because polygamy occurs in cultures where women are considered the property of men—first their father's property, and then their husband's. But, keep in mind that this isn't something Joseph Smith invented. Women have been treated that way in most cultures through most of history. In Joseph Smith's time, an American woman's property was controlled by her husband and he was responsible for her behavior, the way your parents are ultimately responsible for yours. It would still be a while before women even got the vote. Women have been property in many different cultures throughout history, and polygamy is just one of the results. Even now, though, right here in America, there's a radical offshoot of Mormonism in Arizona where they've exiled hundreds of young men, no older than you; made them leave their families behind, so that the young women in the town can become the third or seventh or twelfth wife of one of the community's elders."

". . . By the eleventh century, Christianity, specifically the Roman Catholic Church, had the religion franchise for Western Europe sewn up, but despite their best efforts, there were still pockets of Gnosticism. It was in response to the largest of these that the Inquisition was formed.

"In southern France the Gnostic Cathars were thought to be as numerous as Catholics. Their leaders, the elders of their communities, were called Perfecti, and they devoted themselves to living lives as close to perfect as humanly possible, if not more so. They ate no meat, accumulated no wealth, and engaged in no sexual activities. . . ."

Annabelle looked down at her desk, agitated, and fiddled with a pen, quickly, almost aggressively, then started talking in a rush of words.

"Okay, I don't want to say anything that it's wrong to say, but those people, they're just crazy. What they believe in, they're like a cult. They're not normal. People from around here would never do that. Everybody knows it's wrong."

"Okay," Ms. Bourne said, after looking up at the clock on the wall. "Let's do this. For your homework"—a mild boo arose from the students—"*for your homework*, I want you to pick one law or belief that we've discussed this semester that has changed since the nineteenth century. I'd like to see three pages on why it changed, if you think it should have changed, and what you would have done if you disagreed with it at the time—"

The bell rang, interrupting her and setting off a cacophony of slamming books and squealing chairs and desks, and a flurry of bodies heading toward the door. "*. . . And why,*" she finished, raising her voice.

"Peter," she added, as he reached the front of the room, "could you stay a moment, please?"

Peter looked at Trish, with whom he was walking, and shrugged his shoulders. "See you outside," he said.

Ms. Bourne seated herself behind her desk, and when the last kids had left the room, she looked up at Peter.

"If you're a member of the Mormon church, I hope you weren't offended."

Peter drew his head back and squinted his eyes, an outsized expression of bewilderment. "What? I'm not a Mormon. I don't even go to regular church. I don't believe in any of that stuff."

It was Ms. Bourne's turn to be puzzled.

"I'm sorry, I thought you must be. Not many teenagers who aren't in the LDS know as much about them as you do."

"Oh, that," Peter said. "It's my dad. His last book was about Joseph Smith and the Mormons, so he's been talking about them for years, at dinner and stuff. I didn't even know I knew that until I said it. I never paid much attention."

"Really? Would I have read any of his books? What's your father's name?"

"Philip—"

"Philip Coulter. Of course," Ms. Bourne said, interrupting. "*Taking the Measure of Heaven.* A remarkable book."

"Well, he sure thinks so."

"And you just moved here? He's teaching at Harcourt, I assume?"

"Yeah."

"I'd love to meet him sometime. Where are you living?"

"Out on the lake, on Route Nine. That old house that used to belong to the college, before you get to the cemetery."

Ms. Bourne's smiling, animated face was suddenly still.

"You're living in Oneida House?" she asked quietly.

At that moment, just from the sound of her voice, the way it changed, became tightly held instead of open to whomever might hear, Peter felt relief from the tension he'd been living with equal to the tension that he now sensed in her. She knew something about the house. He could talk to her.

"Yeah, I think my dad said they used to call it that. Listen," he said, almost pouncing on her, "do you know anything weird about that house?"

"What do you mean?" She didn't allow any emotion to show in her voice at all now.

"Well, some of the guys said, you know, said that there were . . . ghosts."

"Ghosts!" she said, and laughed, relieved. "No, I'm sorry, Peter. I'm not aware of any ghosts there or anywhere else." She'd heard those stories, and knew how they got started, and didn't take them seriously at all.

The disappointment Peter felt was plain in his face. "Oh. That's great that you know the house, though. So, thanks anyway. " He turned to leave the room.

"Peter."

He stopped, turned back and waited. "What?"

What was she going to do, tell him the whole story? It was the past, and it wouldn't do anybody any good to bring it up again.

"Nothing, Peter. Except I'm sorry I can't help you."

Peter left the room, not bothering to reply.

Ellen Bourne hadn't thought about Oneida House in a long time, had in fact put a lot of effort into forgetting it, maybe more than she'd ever put into anything else. She hadn't been there in over thirty years. She didn't want to think about it, and she certainly never wanted to see the place again. Anyone who had lived through what she had would feel the same way. Except there was no one else, was there?

1971

"Oh, hey, Ellen," Seth said when he opened the door. "Smile." He held up a Polaroid camera, a new toy with which he had been annoying everybody. Ellen smiled and waited impatiently until Seth had taken the picture. She could hear music, Grateful Dead, sounded like "Dark Star," floating out of the house from behind him. Seth wore his frizzy red hair in an Afro twice the size of his head, which, coupled with the oversized bands of sideburn wrapping around his face into a mustache, made him look like a Fabulous Furry Freak Brother. "Come on in," he said, looking at the picture he was shaking in his hand as he turned and headed back into the house.

Ellen stepped in off the porch and closed the heavy wooden door behind her. She followed him into the living room. Paul was in there with Keith and Amy, the house couple, all sitting on a heavy-looking couch, low to the ground, tattered and torn, its ancient-looking textured fabric gone from some shade of white to somewhere in the yellow-gray family. Paul sat at one end; Keith and Amy were entangled at the other. There was room next to Paul for Ellen to wedge herself in if she wanted to, but instead she took a seat on the arm of the old leather armchair Seth returned to. It had been recently patched up with fresh duct tape.

Centered between the couch and the armchair, and another chair on the other side, was a big wooden spool, salvaged from a construction site, serving as a table. A candle was burning there, planted in the rippled melt of previous candles. They had been passing around a small wooden pipe in which a chunk of hash glowed red with each toke.

"No, really. That's where the word 'assassin' comes from, from hashish," said Paul, a quick-witted poli sci major with scruffy blond hair and a tuft growing out from under his lower lip. He took a hit off the pipe and then held it out to Ellen. He lifted his eyebrows, querying. She leaned forward, took the pipe and drew on it, then passed it back to Keith, directly to her right, who held it out for Amy to get a hit, and then took one himself.

"Bullshit," Seth said, rejoining the conversation. "How could that be? Hashish mellows you out. Nobody's going to go out and kill somebody from smoking hashish. More like you'd go out and give somebody a back massage."

"Mashish," Keith said. "Mashashin." Amy giggled.

"I'm telling you, there was this eleventh-century sheik, and he used it to brainwash soldiers. He'd get them all fucked up on hash until they passed out, and then he'd take them to this place he had in the mountains, and they'd wake up there, in this paradise he built. Fountains and fruit trees and women. And they'd wake up and have all these women, you know, fucking them and stuff, and feeding them delicious food, and later, when they were back in the desert, this sheik would tell them he'd sent them to paradise. That he could do that, and if they did whatever he said, he'd make sure they got in when they died. So he had the most dangerous followers, assassins, who'd kill anybody he said because they didn't care if they died. I'm telling you, it's true."

"Huh," Seth said and stared at the hash pipe he was now holding. He took a hit, held it in, then blew it out. "They must have had better hash back then."

"So, where's Alex?" Ellen asked. She'd expected to find her in here with everybody else.

"In the kitchen with Mike," answered Paul.

"I don't get why he can't hang out with the rest of us. He's spending all his time with Alex," Seth said, almost petulantly.

"Well, she's the one that made the contact, Seth," Amy said. "He wouldn't be here if it weren't for her."

"I dunno, man. I don't think it's such a good idea, him being here," Keith said. "We're perfectly capable of planning an action ourselves. This guy, who knows what he's gonna want us to do?"

"If it were up to you, Keith, there would never be any action," Paul said.

"That's not true," Keith said, shaking his head in mock weariness, as if he'd been over this point many times. He *had* been over this point many times before. Keith was a big athletic guy, a reformed jock who'd quit football in the middle of senior year of high school, after his first acid trip, to the great consternation of his coach, his teammates, his parents, and his soon-to-be ex-girlfriend the cheerleader. He'd continued to drop acid, announced himself a Buddhist and began throwing the I Ching every day, after his morning joint.

"But if we're going to do something, it should be the right thing, not just some big, showy gesture so everybody knows what revolutionaries we are. It should actually do something, not just destroy something."

"So no violence, right?" Seth said, sarcastically.

"That's right," Amy said, jumping in, defending him. Although her slight frame and freckles made her look younger than the rest of them, she'd done as much reading as anyone in the house. Of the two of them, she was even more aggressively nonviolent than Keith. "And don't act like you're more serious about the Movement than he is just because you like to talk about blowing things up."

"Revolutionary consciousness without revolutionary action is just talk, man," Seth responded, looking very satisfied with his answer.

"So, what are you saying, Seth?" Paul said. He sucked on the pipe when it was passed to him, studied the ash for a second, and then tapped it against the side of a dinner-plate-sized ashtray on the table, emptying it. "You want to lead the workers in the overthrow of your father?" Seth's father owned a very successful shoe factory in his hometown of Lowell, Massachusetts.

Seth, called on his rhetoric in front of his friends, had no choice, and had to follow through. "Whatever's necessary, man. Whatever's necessary."

Paul took a matchbox from a pocket on the front of his overalls, slid it open to extract a gram-sized chunk of hash, then shaved some pieces off of it into the bowl of the pipe with a Boy Scout knife. He offered the pipe back to Ellen.

"What do you think, Ellen? Ready to join the revolution?"

Like the rest of her generation, Ellen had grown up with the Vietnam War in the background: nightly body counts on TV; the increasingly violent protests in the streets; the growing clear-cut division in the country between the young, antiwar, overthrow-the-Establishment Us and the old, America-right-or-wrong, stop-the-Commies Them.

In every way, Ellen was an Us, a child of her time; she grew up knowing that it was her generation's job to stop the war, but there was another division, the one that split the young Left. How far were you willing to go? That was the question. Did you really want to see everything torn down? Right now, on campuses and in communes and in downtowns all over the country, everybody knew that they had to choose, but whichever side you chose, the greatest respect was reserved for those who went the furthest. The real revolutionaries among them, the ones that threw bombs, went underground, carried guns and were prepared to use them, they were the heaviest characters around.

Ellen knew that Alex was poised to become one of them, if she wasn't already, and Ellen could go with her.

Ellen shrugged. "No, thanks," she said, ambiguous about whether she was turning down the Revolution or the pipe. To be honest, after her conversation with Alex yesterday, she was afraid she was already in over her head, but she wasn't going to let anyone know, if she could help it.

Alex was sitting at the kitchen table, sipping at a water glass full of red wine. Nearby, a half-smoked joint sat cold in an ashtray, surrounded by crushed cigarette butts, Marlboros and Camel straights. On the stove behind her, a big pot of vegetarian chili bubbled, and on the counter was a big bowl of salad.

Alex looked up at Ellen, standing in the doorway. "Hey, El. Want a glass of wine?"

"Sure. That'd be great," Ellen said.

Alex had been talking to the tall, thin, good-looking guy leaning back against the counter. He looked sort of like Jesus, but so did every third guy on campus, really. Ellen was immediately certain that she'd seen him somewhere before, although she had no idea where. She was pretty sure he wasn't a student; he was too old, at least twenty-five and maybe as old as thirty. Besides, while at first glance he looked like another long-haired Harcourt student, the impression didn't hold up. Just the way he held himself, he was too comfortable, too confident, to be a student, as if he already knew where he stood in the world, and was satisfied with it; there wasn't any posturing there. There was something else about him, too, something in his face. . . .

The guy watched Ellen looking at him, taking him

in, and his amused smile was almost enough to make you overlook the assessing, almost predatory, nature of his stare, like a big cat lazing near a watering hole, in no hurry, not yet hungry, looking over one of the ungulates that had come to drink. Ellen felt naked when he looked at her.

He blinked, slowly, then sort of unfurled himself in her direction, and took the few steps toward her across the kitchen.

"Ellen," Alex said, standing up and stepping over to his side, putting a hand on his shoulder for a moment, "this is Graham Walker, the guy I told you about."

Ellen felt a wash of jealousy flow through her, and she was disconcerted to realize that she was not certain which of them she was jealous of.

He stood there, his hand held out, head cocked slightly to the side. Ellen took his hand, and he immediately pulled her into a hug. "Welcome to the Revolution, Ellen. You can call me Mike," he said, quietly, intimately, next to her ear, and it sent a shiver through her.

"I hope we get to spend some time together," he said when he stepped back, still holding her hand. His voice was smooth and thick, a bit of a country drawl to it. "From what Alex tells me, you have a whole lot to offer." Ellen was glad that Alex had turned to the counter to pour her a glass of wine, because she didn't want her to see the flush she could feel warming her cheeks.

Dinner was over, and they all still sat around the long wooden table in the dining room, off the kitchen. A couple of gallon jugs of cheap red wine had been emptied, and joints were working their way around the table. The chili had been unexceptional, but they were mostly all used to it, having committed as a house to both vegetarianism and the rejection of mass-produced food.

The only light in the room came from the thick round candles lined up down the center of the table. There were seven people at the table, all told: the five residents of the house, Ellen, and Mike. Their faces were dancing patterns of shadow and the orange glow of candlelight, as the flames flickered, diminished, grew and guttered in the shifting breezes passing into the room.

Although winter was not far enough behind them that the day's warmth lasted into the night, the doors at the end of the room were open to the back porch. Ellen sat next to Alex at the end of the table closest to the doors, and between the darkness and the cold night air, Ellen's senses were telling her that they were actually outdoors. It felt as if the table they sat at jutted out of the house like a finger into the night, suspending them between the incredibly pure white light of stars shining down from trillions of miles away, traveling millions of years from the past, and the still black mirror of the lake, reflecting the glimmering lights back up at the sky. Ellen could feel the lights of the stars almost as solid things, which they were in a sense, long needles of phase-shifted matter, anchored to their own reflections, but still streaming back into the history of the galaxy, and she realized that if you could somehow climb back up those shafts, you would actually be . . .

Ellen realized that the acid had kicked in and opened her eyes.

The dinner table conversation had been the usual Oneida House mix of politics and campus gossip, side conversations breaking out here and there, Keith and Amy whispering and laughing together, the sound of them by now as much a part of life in the house as mediocre chili. Mike, sitting next to Alex, joined in the various conversations from time to time, but mostly he just listened; Ellen noticed that everyone kept glancing over at him as they spoke, checking his reactions, no matter whom they were actually addressing.

When they'd first sat down, Mike had fished a small yellow envelope out of the breast pocket of his denim work shirt and passed it around the table. Ellen had hesitated for just a second, but everyone was looking at her, so just like the rest of them, Ellen dropped a hit of windowpane.

Now, almost an hour later, the conversation had died out, as all around the table people were getting off on the acid, turning their attention inward, to the sensations in their own bodies, their own expanding, blossoming, sinuous thoughts, getting distracted by the flickering of the candles and phantom patterns in the shadows in the corners of the room.

"You were saying," Mike spoke suddenly, his words bursting into the group's awareness with the clarity of a rifle shot.

Everybody looked his way.

"You. Red," he said, focusing on Seth, sitting across the table from him. His camera had finally been forgotten on the floor by his feet, after everyone had started complaining about the flash as the acid made it seem more and more like a physical assault. "You were saying something before. It sounded pretty smart. You remember what it was you were saying?"

Seth looked down at his hands, then back at Mike. It was true. He'd been saying something, and he'd trailed off, lost in his own thoughts, not aware that he'd stopped speaking out loud. Everybody was looking at him now. He reached back, tried to retrace his thoughts to where they'd started.

"Oh, yeah. Yeah. I was talking about this paper I wrote, for a seminar . . . on the labor movement in America. And how violent it got when the workers first unionized. And if they fought back enough, things could have really changed. But they backed down when confronted with overwhelming force, and let the owners and the government sort of have a monopoly on real violence, and that's why it didn't grow into a genuine revolutionary movement. This paper I wrote," he said, "proves that violence is an inevitable part of any genuine revolutionary movement." The cadences of his own rhetoric pleased him, made him more comfortable, the sentence itself familiar, something he'd heard himself say so many times it was almost like a single unit of speech.

"Good, Seth. That was it. Now," Mike said, rising up out of his chair, leaning forward on his hands, looking Seth right in the eyes, "what I've been wanting to ask you is, *What the fuck do you know about violence?*"

Ellen could hear breaths drawn in around the table, and Seth's eyes grew wide. The discomfort level in the room notched way up.

As she looked from Mike to Seth and then back again, Ellen realized what it was about Mike, about his face, that made him seem so different from the rest of them, different from every student she knew. His handsome, angular face was finished in a way theirs weren't, hardened into its final shape, everything soft and malleable gone. He looked, more than anything else, like one of those chiseled-looking cowboys in a cigarette ad. Compared to Mike, Seth's face was rounded, childlike.

Mike looked around the table. Ellen's eyes followed his, and she saw that same softness, that same malleability in everyone but him.

What it was was he was the only grown-up there.

"Any of you kids, what do you know about being revolutionaries? You're just playing at it, just talkin', while you're running a tab on daddy's money, the bunch of you."

And if he was the only adult . . . that was it! she realized, and it illuminated her mind like sudden dawn: he was right! They *were* children! They weren't done yet. College, it was like a big playground, where you were safe to play grown-up, play sex, play scholar. Anything they did now was what *children* did, and what they talked about at Oneida House was playing soldiers. And that meant they could stop any time they wanted to. She could call a time-out.

She turned to Alex, to tell her what she'd realized, but seriousness was coming off Alex in waves, as she concentrated on what Mike said, her pretty brow furrowed, and Ellen let go of what she'd figured out, let it get washed away, forgotten. This was important to Alex, so it would be important to Ellen, too.

"Well," Mike said, "I'm here to teach you a thing or two about revolution. That is, if any of you are serious. If any of you can forget your middle-class conditioning long enough to stop acting like goddamn *citizens*," and he spat the word out like an insult.

"Then, maybe, we can do something about stopping the war." He stood there, looking at them, arms folded, waiting.

A murmur went around the table, which resolved itself into a group protestation of seriousness.

"I'm as committed to stopping this war as you are," Alex said.

"Is that right?" he said, cocking his head a bit to one side and looking her in the eyes.

Ellen leaned toward Alex fractionally, an idea of protectiveness externalized.

"So am I," said Keith from the other end of the table. He put his arm over Amy's shoulder. "We all are," he said.

"Well, that's good. I'm very glad to hear that," Mike said, and he started pacing the length of the table. In the dark, he was a voice moving behind them, his steps silent, his form unseen. It occurred to Ellen that he hadn't done a hit of acid when the rest of them had. "Because without commitment, without a conscious ongoing effort to transform yourselves into revolutionaries, what's going to happen is that you'll revert to the values the Establishment has built deep down inside you, the rules they've been forcing on you to keep you in line since you were crawling around in diapers.

"A conscious and ongoing effort," he repeated. "Because you cannot trust your impulses. You cannot trust what you believe you know about right and wrong, because that's how the Man controls you. The fucking Man decided what was right and wrong, and then he got inside your brain and wrote it there.

"Now, what I have to ask you, what you have to ask yourselves, is how far are you willing to go to overthrow the fascists running this country? Are you willing to go deep inside and rip that conditioning out of you? Our government has declared war on the innocent people of Vietnam, and they will not stop until they have killed every last one of them. Every father, every mother, and every fucking child.

"They are shipping our brothers over there to die with them, shipping us over like we were their property, the way peasants and slaves and sharecroppers are property. They won't stop this war because the war is about profits, and all it costs them is . . . you know what it costs them?

"Here's a hint, boys and girls: Fall in love! Get married! Get a job to support your family, and raise up strong little kids! You know why they want that? You know why the American Way of Life has been drummed into your heads since the first day you sat down in front of a television? Because all it costs them to run a war is us. As long as we keep on turning out more little soldiers for them, everything's going just the way they want it."

Despite her initial resistance, despite whatever fears she had about where this would lead them and what might happen to Alex when they got there, Ellen couldn't help herself. All of what Mike was saying was as obviously true to her as gravity, as evolution. That *is* what society wanted, it wanted you to keep doing what had always been done, because otherwise, society couldn't survive.

She was starting to get excited, starting to feel herself pulled along by Mike's words. His vehemence, his certainty, it all seemed to be sweeping her up, pulling her along like her little Beetle getting caught in the slipstream of a big semi on the interstate.

"Now, *right now*, you have to ask yourselves what it's worth to stop that. Are you willing to fight the Man any way you can? Are you willing to put your life on the line to stop the war? You think maybe that's worth a little violence?" He leaned in among them now, hands on the table, and everybody could tell this was no rhetorical question. It was time to speak up.

Ellen had to pull herself from the glint of the candlelight reflected in his intense dark eyes; when she did, she saw glances flying around the table, Seth and Paul looking at each other, Alex looking down the table at Amy, all of them, the whole house, bucking each other up to take the step and do what they'd been talking about all this time.

Ellen closed her eyes, tried to get straight in her head, tried to find her way back to where she was before she got on this train. She remembered: We don't have to do this! She thought it at Alex as loud as she could. We can stop right now! But Alex couldn't hear her and then Seth stood up, brought his fist down on the table, making plates and glasses jump and clatter all around him. "By any means necessary!" he said. Around him, others echoed Malcolm's call to arms.

"Alex," Ellen whispered, and tugged on her arm. Alex looked at her, but Ellen didn't know what to say. "Don't." Alex shrugged her off and turned back to Mike.

"We have some pacifists here, don't we?" Mike asked. He looked at everyone but Keith and Amy, and Alex looked down at the table in front of her.

Alex told him, Ellen realized. "Briefed" him.

"Well, yeah," Keith said, from the end of the table. "I'm a pacifist."

Amy, sitting next to him, said, "Me too." Amy put her hand on the table, and Keith covered it with his. They both looked up at Mike.

"So, what you're saying to me is," Mike said, and walked toward the two of them, "that you don't believe in violence." He stopped behind them, a hand resting on each of their shoulders. He leaned over between them.

"Yeah," Keith said, defiant. "That's what I'm saying."

"Stand up, son."

Keith did. He stood up and took a step back from the table, but he didn't look happy about it. He suspected what was coming—they all did—and he braced himself.

"So you're saying if I do this, you're just gonna take it?" Mike was as tall as Keith, but Keith had some serious shoulders, looked like he had twenty or thirty pounds on him. Still, when Mike drew back his fist and slammed it into Keith's jaw, hard, it sent him sprawling back into the wall. Keith didn't go down, but he had to lean back against the wall to stay up.

Hand on his jaw, Keith said, "Yeah, that's right, man. Last thing we fuckin' need is more violence."

"Great," Mike said, "just checking." He reached around and grabbed a handful of Amy's thick brown hair, and yanked hard. Her chair went over and Amy screamed in surprise and pain as he dragged her along the floor, and then threw her up against the wall next to Keith.

Everyone at the table saw what happened, but it was so far out of their experience, so unexpected, that filtered through the veil of the acid, it was like watching a movie you weren't supposed to take seriously. One guy hitting another guy, that made sense, they could reference it, but this? Things like that don't happen. Nobody moved—nobody but Keith, who started toward Mike.

Mike turned on him, body tensed, hands out to his sides, and the way he stood, it was as if he'd suddenly revealed himself to be armed.

"Believe in violence now, son?" he said, smiling.

"I'm okay," Amy said. "It's okay."

The potential motion in Keith's body drained away.

"No, I don't. What I believe is that you're an asshole, and blowing up some lab or the ROTC isn't
going to make any difference. That doesn't change
anything."

"Whatever you say," Mike replied, and turned back
to Amy. He ripped open her shirt, exposing her small
round breasts, pale, almost glowing in the candlelight,
against last summer's tan.

"Very nice," Mike said. "Don't you think?" he asked
Keith. Keith said nothing.

Mike reached out and grabbed one of her nipples
and twisted, hard. Amy screamed and went to her
knees, and Keith launched himself at Mike. Mike side-
stepped him, casually, and pushed a fist into his stomach, sending him doubled over to the floor. Keith lay
there, his face squeezed tight in pain, Amy beside him
on her knees, crying now.

"I guess you've rethought your position on violence
then?" Mike asked him, and then turned to everybody
else.

"You don't get to choose nonviolence," he said,
calmly, slowly. "Violence exists. What you choose
doesn't mean shit. These folks here, they chose nonviolence, but did that make violence go away?

"Willingness to do violence is everything. You're
going to have to be like holy warriors, turn yourselves
into holy warriors. If you want to change anything,
you gotta be committed to violence, because the
American empire will not be overthrown without an
armed struggle. The American empire is built on violence. It is *made* of violence. They will fuckin' laugh
at you, you come at them with anything else. They'll

fuckin' brush you aside like bugs. This is a government that uses napalm on children. That means fuckin' nothing to them.

"You think your little march on Washington made any difference to them? You think they're going to give up because you take a walk in the sun with your friends? If they thought you could make a difference they would have machine-gunned the whole crowd right there."

Mike reached down to Keith, to give him a hand up. Keith ignored him and got to his feet on his own, while Mike squatted down beside Amy. "I'm sorry, darlin', but this is an important lesson you kids have to learn if you're ever going to make any difference in this old world. Now, you understand that I'm doing this for a reason? So that you can take the next step? So that we can all move forward together?" Amy looked up through teary eyes at Keith.

"Don't look at him, damn it. You gonna let him make your decisions for you? Is your loyalty to him or to this revolution? What if you had to hurt him to stop the war? What if your old man had to die before the war could end? What if that one man there, you had to kill him to save every goddamn kid in Vietnam? You ready to do that?"

Amy looked down. "I don't know," she said quietly.

"Well, okay, okay. That's honest." Mike stood up, held his hand out to her. She hesitated for a moment, then took it, and he pulled her to her feet.

Standing there, holding Amy's hand in his, Mike said to the room at large, "Lesson over, people. We will continue tomorrow. Right now I need to do some special work with our pacifist friends. Anybody else need to join us?" He looked right at Ellen; her eyes dropped to the table and she didn't look up until she heard him start to walk out of the room, pulling Amy with him.

At the doorway, he stopped, looked back at Keith. "I can give all of my attention to Amy, but I don't know, man, I think you'd want to be there."

Mike walked to the stairs and headed up to the bedrooms, Amy right behind him, Keith now hurrying after.

Nobody else went upstairs that night. They all stayed downstairs until they'd come down from their trip, and nobody said a word about the noises they heard coming down through the ceiling, from Keith and Amy's bedroom, even sort of got used to them, so that by the time they could see the first sign of the sun lightening the sky in the east, they weren't even flinching anymore.

11

At five fifteen, the setting sun was exactly low enough in the sky to shine directly in Phil's office window and straight on into his eyes. He might have gotten up and lowered the blinds, but he was caught up in an article in *Speculum*, one of the journals he regularly skimmed. The article was by a brash young historian with some very interesting ideas about the varying standards for miracles used in the canonization of saints in the twelfth and thirteenth centuries. Phil recrossed his legs, settled an elbow on his desk, and rested the journal in his lap.

The religious were like children, he thought. Miracles . . . and they still believed in such things. God was so much a projection, the great daddy in the sky, so obviously what people wanted to be true, he was sometimes actually embarrassed for them, for so clearly and unconsciously revealing themselves. Miracles were like Daddy doing tricks with quarters when he came home. *What's that behind your ear? Why, it's a statue of the Virgin, crying real tears!*

They were no better than "abductees," or conspiracy theorists . . . in fact, hmm, there wasn't that much difference between religion and conspiracy theory, was there? Somebody was watching you all the time, secret meanings and patterns everywhere, only the truly enlightened saw beyond the pretense. Yes, religion as conspiracy theory. There was an essay in that.

How could so many people accept such things? In fact, if there was one question left for him, it was why so many smart people had been taken in over the years. He shook his head and returned to reading just as he heard a knock on his open door.

"Professor?"

Phil had thought he was safely past his office hours; by five, not only were the hallways clear of students, but on most days his colleagues had all left, too. "Yes," he said without looking up, doing his best to express his displeasure at being interrupted with the one word.

"I was wondering if you had a few minutes?" Rising inflection at the end of the sentence, sound of submission.

He recognized the voice in the second before he looked up and saw that it was Molly.

"Oh," he said. "Come in," but she had not only already come in, she had closed the door behind her.

"What can I do for you, Molly?"

"Well . . ."

"If you're here to talk about your term paper, it's really too early in the semester to—"

"No, no, it's not about that," she said and took the three steps from the door to the desk.

"Well, what is it then? Is there a problem at the house?" He sounded a little impatient.

"No," she said. "No problem, it's, um . . . " This wasn't going as she'd planned. Or hadn't planned. In her mind, the scenario had gone from showing up directly to having sex with her professor. It hadn't occurred to her that she'd have to initiate it. The way she'd imagined it, he'd know why she was there, and he'd know what to do, and he'd take care of all that.

"I'm sorry, Molly, you're going to have to—"

Damn. Well, in for a penny, in for a pound . . . she reached down and lifted her shirt off over her head; she wasn't wearing a bra. When she had it off, the look she found waiting on Phil's face was so cartoonishly shocked that she laughed out loud.

"Oh," Phil said. He stood up and the journal in his lap fell to the ground; reaching for it, he banged his elbow into the keyboard on his desk. "Ow."

They stood there, the moment growing increasingly awkward, and Molly suddenly wondered about the wisdom of what she was doing. To stop thinking about it, she stepped over behind the desk and leaned into him. Phil threw his arms around her, lowered his head, and they kissed. He ran his hands up and down the bare skin of her back; reached down, ran his hand over her ass.

Phil was growing more aroused with each passing second; for Molly, however, the experience was quite the reverse. She found reality moving her further and further from the fantasy that had brought her here. He was growing more and more frantic in his movements, his tongue thrust into her mouth, his hands grabbing for the waist of her jeans, trying to pull them open and off. He was twitchy, and too rough, and while he didn't smell bad, exactly, his scent was very much present, and it was not the presence of somebody she could imagine having sex with. He smelled to her like a stale room or an old leather chair, not particularly unpleasant, but not something that inspired her to passion of any kind.

God, she'd made a huge mistake. She pushed herself away from him.

He looked at her, not comprehending, all his internal mechanisms, for the next few seconds, still moving forward, responding to a stimulus that key parts of his brain had yet to understand were no longer there.

"Oh, God, Professor! I'm sorry! I don't know what I was thinking."

His confused look turned to anger as quickly as he realized he wasn't getting any.

"I'm really, really sorry," Molly said, picking her shirt up off the desk where she'd dropped it and putting it back on. She could see where he was pressing out against his pants. Pants that he wore up around his waist, pants that were, what? suit pants? old man pants? Not pants that anyone her age, anyone she wanted to see take *off* their pants, would ever wear. "I have to go." She turned and scrambled out the door before he had a chance to say anything.

Phil's anger was as involuntary and physically based as his excitement, and it ebbed quickly. Later, he'd think about this and get angry in another way, an anger produced by thought and not frustration, but for now he just sank back into his chair, and picked his journal up from the floor. In a few minutes, he started reading again.

Trish Willits lived with her mother and two younger sisters in a small one-story house on a side road off High Street, about a quarter mile south of the school, well past where the paved sidewalks ended. From the outside, it looked like a place that somebody had given up on. There were shingles missing from the roof, and the rust-colored paint was coming off in fist-size flakes. The house had a front lawn, but if the lawn were a carpet, you'd call it threadbare; what rough and hardy grasses remained were challenged everywhere by the dry, hard-packed dirt.

Inside, there was nothing—not the furniture in the living room, not the pots and pans in the kitchen, not the eight-year-old thirty-two-inch TV with built-in VCR, no DVD player in sight—that could not stand to be replaced. In the kitchen, where the yellow linoleum floor was dulled and fading, worn through in spots to a previous layer of linoleum, there were fourteen souvenir spoons hanging on the wall, one from each of the thirteen original colonies, plus Texas. Trish's mother, Marjorie Willits, had abandoned her honeymoon notion of collecting all fifty states when Trish's dad disappeared. He'd gone looking for work on the oil rigs of the Gulf, but instead of sending back money so they could join him, the last thing he'd sent was a package postmarked Port Arthur, containing the Texas spoon and three plastic bracelets that lit up and flashed. Their batteries had long since worn out.

In the kitchen a door led out to the backyard, and another opened up to the basement, half converted by Trish's dad into a rec room before he had left. Amid the faint smell of mildew, Trish and Peter had been down there making out on the slightly oily fabric of a burnt umber couch for hours. They had been making out for so long and with such intensity that Peter could no longer have told you where he was, if he would have even heard you ask: they might have been in a suite at the Plaza, as far as he was concerned.

Peter and Trish had been making out for so long that their tongues hurt from encountering the sharp edges of teeth; they'd been making out for so long that their lips were chapping and numb; they'd been making out since they got home from school, but Peter had only just now fumbled Trish's bra open, and as his palm moved over the hard nipple on her inconceivably soft breast, he came in his pants for a second time, a slow blossoming that did little to lessen the thrumming intensity of his hard-on, and he was kissing Trish with redoubled passion when he felt her pull away from him.

"What are you looking at?" she said sharply as she disentangled herself and sat up, crossing her arms to cover her chest, although nothing untoward was visible under her long-sleeve T-shirt.

Peter looked up to the top of the stairs, where Trish's eight-year-old sister, Sarah, stood watching them, wide-eyed, through the partly opened door.

"Amanda!" Trish shouted.

"You said you'd keep her out of here!" she said, when her other sister poked her head into the doorway above Sarah's.

"I don't need anybody to watch me," Sarah said, opening the door the rest of the way, and starting down the stairs. "I wasn't even looking at you. . . ."

"You've been down there since we got home," Amanda said. "You and your boyfriend can hang out with her now. I have homework to do."

"And besides," Sarah said, now down in the basement and standing right in front of them, hands on the hips of her hand-me-down jeans, "I just came down here to get"—she looked around the room—"this!" she said triumphantly, spotting the water-stained cardboard box of playground balls and Frisbees against the wall. She grabbed one of the balls and held it up over her head. "Who wants to see you sticking your tongue down his throat anyway?"

Trish leapt up from the couch and snatched up one of her sneakers from the floor all in one motion, then threw it at her little sister, missing by inches as Sarah let out a full-throated scream and ran up the stairs, Trish right behind.

Amanda stepped back out of the way as Sarah flashed past her in the doorway, and Trish stopped there to plead.

"C'mon, Mandy. I'd do it for you," she said.

Amanda looked down past her at Peter, who had stood up and was straightening his clothes. "As if. I mean, *ick.*" She held out her hand. "Five dollars."

"Three," Trish said and reached into her pocket.

"Okay, plus you make dinner."

Trish pulled her hand out of her pocket empty. "Forget it." She turned to walk back down the stairs.

"No, wait. Three dollars and I still make dinner."

Trish smiled down the stairs at Peter, then turned and paid her sister off.

"One more hour," Amanda said, and headed toward the sound of the TV in the living room.

Trish returned to the couch, reached under her shirt and refastened her bra, then plunked herself down next to Peter. "She's such a pain," she said, and rolled her eyes.

"Yeah, you don't have to tell me. I've got one, too," he said, putting his arm around her shoulder and leaning in to reengage.

"You know, I had an idea," Trish said, pulling away.

"Me too," Peter said, and reached down to slip his hand up under her shirt again.

"Stop," she said, and pushed his hand away. "Seriously. About your sister."

Peter, with just a hint of pique, withdrew.

"Okay. What about my sister? She's hopeless.

What's your idea? Sell her to the Mormons so we don't have to go to the same school anymore?"

"No, really. I've been thinking. It's not fair. She got fucked over from the first day. Melanie and them are such jerks. I hate how everyone does what they want."

"Okay, so what's your idea?"

"Amanda's in your sister's class. Maybe we could get her to hang out with Virginia some, so at least she had one friend. Then maybe other people will stop thinking she's the school loser."

"Why would Amanda do that?"

"You ask her. I think she's got a bit of a crush on you."

"On me?" Peter was not used to girls having a crush on him, even if they were his little sister's age.

"Yeah," Trish said, and leaned in to kiss him. "You're pretty cute. Why shouldn't she?"

Peter blushed. "I don't know."

"Good, then. Ask her," she said, and called Amanda downstairs.

"What?" Amanda said, when she got to the top of the stairs.

"Could you come here for a minute? Peter has something to ask you."

Amanda walked hesitantly down the stairs and gave Peter a quizzical look.

"What do you want?"

"Well, uh, you know my sister?"

"Everybody knows your sister."

"Well, here's the thing. You know how nobody will talk to her?"

Amanda raised her eyebrows, crossed her arms, and assumed a posture of impatience.

"Peter wants to know if you'll hang out with her," Trish cut in.

"Why would I do that?" Haughty.

"Because you know it's not fair what happened to her, and you hate Melanie as much as I do."

"So, how is it my problem?"

"It's not," Peter said. "We just thought maybe . . ."

"Come on, Mandy. Do it. Because Peter and me asked you to."

At the top of the stairs, Sarah peered down from behind the door. "What are you doing down there?"

"Come on, Mandy," Trish said, ignoring Sarah.

"Is it a secret?" Sarah asked.

Amanda held out her hand. "Five dollars."

Trish shook her head. "Forget it."

"No," Peter said. He'd said he'd help. This would cover it. "Five dollars."

"Can I have five dollars, too?" Sarah asked, coming down the stairs with her hand held out.

"Okaaay," Amanda said to Peter, drawing out the word, ignoring Sarah along with the others. "How much do I have to hang out with her?"

"Just give her a break, okay? She's really an okay kid. Maybe eat lunch with her?" Peter said.

"I don't know. I don't want everybody to see."

"You figure something out then. After school, maybe. Just talk to her."

"Who are you guys talking about?" Sarah asked, after looking at them, from one to the other, waiting to be included. They continued to ignore her.

"Okay," Amanda said, "but now you have to make dinner," she told Trish. "And I'm done watching Sarah."

"Nobody has to watch me!" Sarah shouted and kicked the couch.

"Fine," Trish said and got up. "I'll make dinner."

Peter rose with her. "Come on, I'll walk you out to your bike." She took his hand and led him up the stairs. Amanda followed, leaving Sarah alone in the basement, where she crossed her arms, stuck out her lower lip, and sat herself forcefully down on the couch. "I hate those guys," she said. "I hope they die."

12

Phil had been staring at the girl on the pier for some time before he actually became aware that he was looking at somebody. His mind was elsewhere . . . or rather elsewhen, because his thoughts so often drifted back to this place: this house, this land, this particular part of the world. What was it? So many men had been inspired here—in*spired*, touched by, filled with, a spirit. The Iroquois believed that the Finger Lakes were created when God reached down and laid his hands upon the land, to bless this place among all places. They believed that this was the place where God made physical contact with earth.

The Old World had its holy places—Jerusalem, of course, and Lourdes, and Medjugorje, in Bosnia-Herzegovina, where the Virgin was apparently still putting in curtain calls two millennia after the last act was over—where men experienced miracles, contact with the divine, but two thousand years of Christian history in Europe seemed to have worn off the rough edges, turned down the thermostat. Here things had stayed raw. New religions arose in Europe out of politics, like the Anglican Church, or differing interpretations of scripture, like the Lutherans or the Wesleyans or the Anabaptists.

Even the violence of Islamic terrorism came not from any new revelatory experience but out of opposing readings of the Koran, and political conflict over territory, physical and cultural.

Here, though, in America, particularly right here, in western New York, religious movements still sprang from visionaries, men who had seen something that transcended the small and incremental changes that a society could tolerate, and were left with a revolutionary, almost violent, determination that didn't always stop short of apocalypse. It was nonrational.

Phil had been thinking about religion for a long time, and could have told you the political, social, and economic causes of just about every significant religious movement in Western history, but the more he looked into the history of this area, the more details the framework of his understanding was having trouble accommodating.

The story of Moses receiving the Ten Commandments, that was a myth of the ancients, and if contemporaries had believed it, well, they were primitives, and knew nothing of the world except for the tiny, frightened, blinkered moment of their own existence. They were trying to understand a whole movie from a single frame. They had no inkling of what was happening over the horizon, or in anything but the immediate past; no insight into the physical laws that made the sun rise and set. If somebody came along and said that Yahweh, his tribal god, had given him these stone tablets, and he wanted them to follow these rules, well, it was no less likely than anything else. You have a soul that survives your body! The poor shall inherit the earth! I died and came back! God loves you!

But people were born in Joseph Smith's lifetime

who lived to see the atomic bomb. This wasn't in some uncivilized and barbaric backwater. It wasn't before science had explained enough of the world that we still needed supernatural explanations. He had witnesses, and untold followers, all of whom believed he found golden tablets, a third testament for Christians, buried in the ground not fifty miles from this spot.

Phil had seen the actual signed testimonies, the primary documents, had looked into the backgrounds of the signers. It made no sense.

Phil had come into the kitchen from his study looking to get himself some coffee, and the scenery out the window—the leaden gray weight of the lake that drew your eyes, as if it exerted its own localized gravity; the buildings of the college directly across on the opposite shore, rendered by distance into scale models; the patchwork quilt of farmland that blanketed the rise beyond them; the dull, muted browns and reds and yellows that had these last few weeks slowly crept over the trees that covered the hills as far down the lake as he could see—had cast him back into these questions once more. Now, though, he was pulled from his thoughts, and though it took a while to sink in, he was a little alarmed to discover there was someone in his backyard, out on the old pier.

The girl had long, curly blond hair, and despite being nicely rounded, there was something adolescent about her body. She wore low-waisted jeans and a loose white shirt, a hooded sweatshirt over it. It wasn't anyone he recognized. It could have been one of Peter's friends, but that didn't lessen his concern about the possibility of legal action should someone get hurt on the shaky pier, any more than if it were a trespassing stranger. He should have had the contractor pull it down before they even moved in here; he had to remember to call and take care of that.

"You!" he shouted through the open window. "What are you doing? Get off of there!" And though the figure looked his way for a moment, she gave no indication of going anywhere. More shouting produced no more satisfactory a response, so he set his coffee cup down in the sink and headed toward the back of the house.

By the time he got to the backyard, the girl was gone, the pier looking as undisturbed and desolate as if nobody had stood upon it for years. The wind coming off the lake blew against it, shifting it however slightly, and carried with it the creak of wood against wood, the sound of incremental collapse.

There she was.

He was looking to his left, toward the south, and he saw the girl moving along through the high grass toward where the trees began. She had already almost reached them.

"You!" he called again. "Wait!" If it wasn't a friend of Peter's—and what would one of his friends be doing here without him?—it was, he was sure, a student from the college. He knew from other faculty that students wandered down this way, along the shore of the lake, and that the old cemetery on the other side of the stand of woods was a popular destination. This was the first time he'd actually seen anyone, though, and he wasn't about to allow a precedent to be set; let word get out that this stretch of shore was a great shortcut. Not only was the pier a dangerous place, particularly for no-doubt pot-smoking students, but his home was not a playground.

He hurried along behind her, but she moved faster

than he could manage; with the grass almost waist high, he couldn't see her legs, and she appeared to be floating through it, but that same grass only slowed him down and tripped him up. The grass was still wet from that morning's rain, and the legs of his pants soon grew soaked, and by the time he reached the edge of the woods, where he'd lost sight of her, his breath was coming in gasps. He briefly considered turning back, but in a moment, he plunged on, into the woods.

The trail he followed soon petered out. Even with some of the trees already bare, it was hard to see too far ahead. The ground was soft beneath his feet, a layer of wet leaves everywhere he looked, and each step released a rich, almost fetid smell that made him think of rotting wood and worms wriggling in dark moist earth just below.

He heard something ahead of him, an indistinct crash, and wanted to call out, but he didn't even know the girl's name. He continued on in the direction of the sound. When he stopped to shake off the wet leaves that clung to his shoes, he leaned his hand against the light gray bark of a tree, and almost fell over when the bark slid right off, and his hand slipped onto the pale green viscous flesh of the tree beneath it. He wiped his hand on his pants leg, and turned around. Had he come from that direction? Looking back, he could no longer see his house through the trees, or the water of the lake where he thought it should be. He was lost. He felt the slightest hint of fear. Ridiculous, he thought. He was minutes from home. Walking in any direction a few miles, at the most, would bring him out of the woods.

But what if he kept getting turned around? He had never had a feel for the outdoors; until now, he'd spent his entire life in cities. How long was it until dark? He tried to pick the most likely direction, the girl completely forgotten.

Which is when he felt as if there was someone standing behind him. He turned around, and there she was. She smiled. She was really very fetching, this girl.

"Excuse me," he said. Excuse me, what? He was no longer so concerned with reprimanding her as he was with getting her help in walking in the right direction to get back to his house. "I feel a little foolish, but I seem to have gotten turned around. Could you show me the direction out of here? Back toward the pier?"

The girl was silent, continued smiling. Inclined her head slightly. She reached out and took his hand. Phil was taken aback, but didn't pull his hand away. Her hand felt good in his, cool and dry, so small it was practically weightless. She tugged at him and they began to walk.

He was glad to be headed back, but her silence made him a little self-conscious, and he felt the need to fill it, explain himself.

"I was actually looking for you. That was my house, you know, where you were. I appreciate very much the help right now, but I need to tell you that doesn't change the fact that I feel I should say something. I don't mean to sound harsh, and when I use the word 'trespassing,' I don't want you to think that I would necessarily ever call the police, particularly now that I've met you, but if you can imagine things from my perspective for just a moment—"

The girl stopped, turned, put a finger to his lips. She shook her head, then turned and continued on, Phil in tow.

Silenced, Phil paid more attention to where she was

leading him, and realized that the trees around them were growing denser; they looked older, the bark thicker and more gnarled, and they grew closer together. Phil vaguely suspected that the underbrush they were trampling through as she pulled him on was at least partly made up of poison something or other. It seemed to him very unlikely that this was the way back to the house.

"Just a minute," he said, and stopped. The girl didn't even look at him, just tightened her grip on his hand and pulled; he stumbled forward into a walk and then tried to pull his hand back.

She squeezed his hand even harder. A sound of pain escaped him. He wouldn't have believed she had that much strength in her whole body. "I'm not going any farther with you," he said and grasped her wrist with his other hand, pulling as hard as he could to peel her hand away, unsuccessfully. She gave a final tug, and he stepped with her into a clearing, a large circle of soft-looking grass.

There was a fire blazing in the middle, branches piled chaotically a foot high, sending up flames three or four feet.

Sitting at the fire, looking up at him, was a long-haired young man, a definite Harcourt student type, if a less collegiate-looking example. He was thin, wiry, dressed in jeans and a hooded sweatshirt, like the girl's; neither he nor his clothes appeared to have been washed for some time. The planes of his face were striking, his eyes remarkable, intense, almost black; he was good-looking in a way that Phil associated with lead singers with rock bands, even though his face was dirty, with sharp, dark lines of grime on his cheeks and forehead.

"Hey, man. Welcome," he said to Phil. "Take a load off," and he gestured to the ground on the other side of the fire.

The girl released Phil's hand and walked over to join the guy, sat down into a cross-legged position next to him. The young man threw his arm over her shoulder; she leaned into him and smiled up at Phil. He ignored the invitation to join them.

Phil had been disarmed at the appearance of the young woman; though she was young enough to be his daughter, he was not immune to the fact that she was quite attractive, and she was obviously harmless, and by the time he had caught up to her, he was glad to see anyone at all. His immediate response to her friend was very different. There was something about him that made Phil very uneasy.

"If you could just point the way out of the woods, and in the future, if you and the young lady could avoid crossing my property—I live in the house over there . . ." But he didn't know which way to point.

"I know where you live, Professor."

"Fine, then, if you could just show me the way."

The guy laughed. "That is exactly why I'm here—to show you the way." He stood up and walked over toward Phil. As he drew close, Phil could see that the lines on his face were cuts, a pattern of horizontal and vertical lines that had been carved into his forehead and down his cheeks. Closer, and Phil could see the dark crust of blood in some, dark red blood welling minutely from others, almost pulsing. He looked over at the girl. Her sweatshirt was gone; she wore only her light white top. Phil's eyes were immediately, involuntarily, drawn to her full breasts, distinctly visible where they pressed against the thin fabric, and it was like an afterthought that he comprehended that she was also cut and bleeding. Her arms, from the insides of her wrists up to her elbows, all across her biceps up to where they disappeared into the sleeves of her shirt, were scored with dozens of cuts and scars. She stood up, walked toward him, too.

Phil took a step back, toward the edge of the clearing.

"I wouldn't go that way, man," the guy said, and pointed to the ground by Phil's feet. Coiled not a foot away, head up, mouth open, fangs bared, was what even Phil could recognize as a rattlesnake, three or four feet long. Another second and he would have stepped right on it. Phil jumped back toward the fire.

"Good. We need to have a talk anyway. There are things you need to know."

"What are you talking about? Who are you?" His eyes anxiously swept the ground around him, then he looked back up at the couple by the fire.

"Doesn't matter who I am, man. What matters is I've been waiting for you, Philip Coulter. I've been waiting for you a long time, right here. Great things once happened here, because this is a special place. The land around here? It's not like other places. You're starting to realize that, aren't you? And you, you didn't come here by chance. You were called."

"Ridiculous," Phil said, but he spoke almost inaudibly, and with no conviction at all. He took a step away from them in another direction and found himself backed up against a tree. It would be hard to say if he was more alarmed by what he was hearing or the fact that this stranger, this very odd and somewhat scary man, knew his name. The two were on him then, one taking each arm and pulling him back to the fire. He looked from one to the other as they walked, and their faces were now smooth, unmarked, as clear as youth.

They reached the fire. They were scarred again. Their faces were changing as he looked, alternately scarred then unmarked then bloody then clear, flickering like an old movie.

"Who *are* you? *What* are you?" Phil pressed the heels of his hands to his eyes, rubbed hard, looked at them again. They looked perfectly normal.

"I'm a messenger, man, a vessel. An emissary from the great beyond. I'm the message that's been sent to you. And this"—— he waved his hand to take in the entire area; the woods, the lake, the land they sat on—— "this is where I hang out. Call me Walker."

Phil didn't know what to make of any of this, but he no longer felt in control of his own body. He had no will to move, would have been surprised, really, to realize that his legs were still holding him up. All of his effort was at that moment going toward processing what he was seeing, what he was hearing, making some sense of it so that he could respond.

The guy smiled at him. "Not convinced, are you?"

Phil opened his mouth to speak, but nothing came out.

"Wait! What's that, behind your ear?" He reached out toward Phil's head. Phil flinched, pulled away, but the guy was fast; Phil felt his touch by his ear and in a blink he was holding up a quarter in his hand, a look of mock surprise on his face.

Hadn't he just been . . . He pushed everything else back, all that he'd just seen, concentrated, pulled himself together. Finally, something he could comprehend and address.

"You're doing party tricks? Do you think I'm some credulous bumpkin—"

The guy had reached out again, and this time his hand came back holding a quarter the size of a small hubcap. The face on it was Phil's.

"What were you saying?"

Walker tossed it aside, then reached down and picked up a stick by Phil's feet.

"Look out," he said.

"What?" Phil asked, unnerved, glancing around.

"Snake." He tossed the stick down to the ground, and there was a snake there again, writhing at Phil's feet. Phil gasped, jumped back.

"An old favorite. Doesn't always do the trick, though." He snapped his fingers and the snake froze, a stick again.

"Sometimes I have to pull out the big guns. Do I have to pull out the big guns, Phil?"

Phil held on, feebly. "Stop. Just stop. Please."

"Come here, darlin'," Walker said, and held his arm out. The girl, whom Phil had forgotten in his confusion, seemed to materialize out of nowhere, and stepped toward Walker. He pulled her to him, facing Phil, wrapped his left arm across her belly, his hand resting on her waist. The glare of the sun glinting off the blade was what made Phil aware of the frighteningly large bowie knife now in Walker's other hand.

Phil looked back at the girl, who smiled and blinked her green eyes at him, just as Walker slashed her throat with the knife, the cut deep, all the way through the tracheal cartilage, leaving her neck gaping open like a mouth. Blood splashed out in a gout, reaching all the way to Phil, three feet away.

"*No!*" he screamed, his first impulse driving him forward, his arms reaching out toward the girl, but as Walker released her and she fell forward, dead, he caught himself and, finally, he did what he'd been wanting to do all along; he turned and ran . . . right into Walker, who grabbed him and led him back to where the girl lay on the ground, her head tilted at a stomach-turning angle.

"Hey, man, it's okay, really," Walker said, and reached down, and the girl grabbed his hand, and he pulled her to her feet, her neck unmarked.

"How did you do that?"

Walker shrugged. "It's a miracle, man. Now, listen, I have some things I want to tell you."

The perverse thing, what some might call the ironic thing, was that if Phil had known less, he would have been better equipped to deal with miracles. Somebody else, somebody who had not yet worked out a system for understanding the world, who was still dealing with each new bit of previously unencountered information on the fly, might have assimilated these events without sacrificing too much of himself, without having to start from scratch. For Phil, though, who had long ago worked it all out, the clear failure of his understanding created an extreme and unsustainable stress, and it could only be resolved when it all collapsed into something new.

The human brain is a pattern-discerning machine, which is why we have astronomy and agriculture, and why we like to solve puzzles, but it's also the reason we see animals in the shapes of clouds and a face in the asteroid rubble of the moon, and burn women for witches when the crops fail. The brain wants to find patterns, needs to find them, and will not rest until it does, even when there is no pattern to be found. If necessary, the brain will invent one.

Phil's pattern, the one that had sustained him, made sense of the world for him through all his adult years, explained to him who he was and where he fit, was shattered. His mind remained awash with information, but without a system to process that information, to put it in order, it meant no more to Phil than the shiny mobile dangling over a crib meant to a baby; it was a constant babbling in a foreign tongue. And now, like somebody subjected to brainwashing, he would cling to whatever would make sense of the world for him, whatever pattern he could live with, whatever explanation allowed him to again inhabit a world where things didn't just happen for no reason.

"Okay," Walker told Phil, collapsed to the ground beside him, his face sunk into his hands. "First of all, God made the world. Got it? Are you paying attention? God also made man, and not in some metaphorical, evolutionary way, using natural law as his tools. Made him out of dirt. First there wasn't man, then there was. And then he made woman to serve him. And he made her pleasing to man's senses, because that was her purpose."

Phil took it in as fact, no longer had any reason or method to doubt it. It made as much sense as anything else right now. These were the starting points, not the conclusion. It was a relief to know that some things were true and unchanging, the most welcome thing he could imagine, in fact, and as soon as he heard these things spoken, he began to feel better, calmer. He knew where he stood.

"You still with me?" Walker asked. "Because here's the part where you're really going to have to apply yourself. You ready?

"Because the world was made by a Creator, all of his Creation was made by His choice. Nothing exists without a reason, and His intent is present in everything. If you can learn to read the world, his Creation, you shall know his mind. . . ."

Phil did not know which way was home, wasn't even aware of which way he was walking, but he headed the right way nonetheless. His mind was too busy with the changes in the world around him to pay attention to things like direction; he let that take care of itself.

Everything looked different now. There was nothing that manifested itself in the world without a purpose, and all of it was meant to speak to him. Things were clearer, sharper, more distinct, each leaf almost vibrating with meaning, every stone beneath his feet humming with purpose. He too was filled up with purpose now, and not the vain, petty purposes that had driven him before. But, wait, that couldn't be. Hadn't he been directed all along, just unaware of the larger plan?

Phil understood now that faith wasn't a failure of intellect; it was a triumph. To take as fact the existence of a supernatural creator when all logic told you otherwise, and then *force* into being an intellectually rigorous system that accommodated both God's existence and the evidence of the world that denied it, that took a very special mind. All Phil's years of study had been leading to this, preparing him for this, even if he had not been aware of it, even if he thought he had been making choices himself.

He laughed out loud at the idea that the world around him was all random. How could he have ever thought that?

There were very few men who could do what he was about to attempt, perhaps no more than one in a generation. Philip Coulter would know the mind of God.

Molly had been avoiding Phil for a week now; she hadn't gone to his classes, and she hadn't been out to the house to clean or cook. Finally, though, she talked herself into facing up to what she'd done and getting the entire sorry incident behind her. She knew that Phil would be home that day, and she drove out from campus early, to get the confrontation out of the way before Peter and Ginny got home. They were good kids, she liked them, even though Ginny was sort of strange, and it was when she thought about them that she grew most ashamed of herself. They didn't need to know about any of this.

When she arrived, Phil wasn't home. His car was there, though, so he couldn't be far. While she was waiting, she started cleaning up the kitchen; it had gotten ugly in there pretty quickly. There were dishes stacked in the sink and boxes and wrappers all along the counter.

She hadn't been at it long, had really barely made a dent, when she glanced up from the sink. It had begun to get dark already, but not too dark to see Phil walking across the backyard from the woods. While cleaning, she'd managed to forget what it was she'd come here to do. She immediately became nervous about the encounter.

Phil came to his house and went inside, and things here, too, seemed to have taken on new meanings, seemed to speak to him differently. For instance, he thought, as he walked into the kitchen, that girl, Molly.

"Hello, Professor," she said, looking down. She couldn't meet his eyes, and no wonder.

"Hello, Molly." One of the rules, true since the beginning, was that woman existed to serve man. God had made it so.

As he remembered what had happened between them, he grew both angry and excited; excited at the thought of her body, angry that it had been dangled in front of him and yanked away. That was wrong.

"I wanted to apologize for what I did," she said. "Can you forgive me?" She looked up at him shyly.

"Yes, of course." He smiled back. "After we've worked out your penance." He stepped toward her.

13

That night, Peter left Trish's house well after dark, after another damp and heated session down in the basement. The ride from there, the two miles south on High Street into town, and almost five miles along the lakeside road to his house, was almost all downhill, so he'd made good time on his bicycle. Twice, though, he'd been startled into a wobbling near spill by a car suddenly appearing in the lane beside him, moving up fast at fifty or sixty miles an hour. It wasn't until the car was right there that he noticed it, which sent him veering away to catch himself at the last minute.

For a teenager, Peter was normally a careful enough bike rider, but tonight the sound of a car coming up behind him out of the dark, the crisp whine of the tires in the chilly October air, the wash of headlights, throwing his shadow ahead of him, kept going unnoticed until the very last moment. Peter's thoughts just weren't on the road. He was riding along what was becoming a very familiar route on autopilot. His mind kept being drawn back to the feel of Trish's body against his, the soft warm weight of her breasts in his hands, the moment when she had run her finger along the length of his erection through his jeans, setting off an exquisite shudder through his entire body that had not stopped echoing even now.

It was all some kind of ongoing miracle to him, that Trish would let him touch her; that, having it in her power to make him feel this way, she chose to. The promise of even more amazing things seemed to hang in the air between them, when they weren't pressed so tightly together that there was no room for even a promise to slip in.

It was better even than pot, he'd decided a while ago. When he was with Trish, his concerns about what was going on at home—his sister might be a little jerk, but it's not like he didn't care about what was going on with her, and you'd have to be an idiot not to notice that neither his mother nor his father was complaining about the fact that they barely saw each other—went away, the unease he carried with him so much of the time fading in the face of the way she made him feel. They were still there, somewhere, waiting for him, but it was like pouring a glass of salt water into the lake; they became so diluted by the larger force that it was like they weren't there at all.

Even if he didn't eagerly dive into the heady whirl of sex and emotion that they stirred up between them every chance they got, he probably wouldn't have told her about the things that were bothering him at home, anyway. Trish's mom was a loser, and none of his friends back home in Brooklyn had been as poor as they were, but the Willitses seemed to Peter somehow normal in a way that his family just wasn't. What went on in his house, it seemed to him, was uniquely shameful, and it wasn't something he was eager to share with his first girlfriend, or anybody else, for that matter. If he did, he was afraid Trish wouldn't think of him the same way.

She'd see him the way all the cool girls in Brooklyn had
seen him, and that was not the image that led to what
they were doing tonight, and what he was hoping they'd
be doing soon. There was a flash in his head of her lips,
full and wet, her tongue darting out to lick them, as she
pulled down his zipper and lowered her head—

It was fortunate that Molly's car swung wide as she
raced out of the driveway, because he came up to his
house without being more than a quarter aware of his
surroundings at that moment, and she surely would
have hit him otherwise. On the side of the road, he
stopped his bike and put his feet down, looked back
the way he had come after Molly's car. She was speeding away and—there, her headlights had just now
come on; she'd been driving without them—she
hadn't even stopped before she turned out onto the
road. He hoped she was okay; that wasn't like her.

"Sorry I missed dinner, Dad," Peter said after he'd
put his bike away and come inside to find his father
sitting by himself at the dining room table, three books
open in front of him. Two of them were Bibles, and the
third was the Book of Mormon. There were some papers spread out around them.

"Mmmph," his father said, without looking up.

"I meant to call," Peter explained on his way into the
kitchen, although he hadn't thought of it once the entire
evening. An excuse was apparently unnecessary. His father said nothing. "I'll just get myself a sandwich."

"What did you guys have?" Peter called out to his
father in the next room.

"We didn't have anything. Dad just got home a little
while ago. Molly was here. She said she was going to
make dinner, but then Dad got home and she just left,

and I guess she didn't," said Virginia as she came down the stairs.

"Yeah? So why didn't you make something?"

Virginia stood in the kitchen doorway and shrugged. She wore his gray sweater again, the cuffs of the too-long sleeves grasped in her hands. Peter thought she was looking worse. Her skin, her weight, even the way she walked now. It was like she was another person.

"You want pizza?" he asked her.

"Sure." She walked to where Peter was standing and looked at him.

"What?" Peter said.

"I wanna tell you something."

"Okay. Let me call for a pizza first. Dad," he said as he walked into the other room, "I'm getting us a pizza. You gotta give me money." He stopped still. "What happened to your face? Are you okay?"

"What?" Phil said, looking up at his son. He raised his hand to his cheek, brought it away with blood on the fingers. There were four furrows down the left side of his face, gouges filled with blood, and his right eye was blackening.

"That must have happened when I fell. In the woods. I took a walk, and I fell." He got up and went to the kitchen, where he got a paper towel, wet it, and started to wipe his face. He turned and saw his daughter watching him. She looked different now, too. She could hardly be called a child anymore, could she? He stepped toward her, leaned in. His nostrils flared. He stepped back and looked her over again.

"What?" Virginia said, stepping back from her father and drawing into herself, hunching her shoulders a bit and crossing her arms. Did he just smell her? "What are you doing?"

"Hmm. Nothing." Interesting.

Virginia and Peter, who'd come back into the kitchen to witness the interaction, looked at each other.

Peter shook his head, then picked up the phone and called the local Domino's. Phil went back to his Bibles.

"Okay, what did you want?" Peter asked Virginia when he got off the phone.

"I don't want anything," she said. "I want to know how you like being friends with the biggest asshole losers in town."

"Fuck off."

"I just thought you'd want to know that Karen's been pregnant twice. And Crisp's got three DWIs. And perfect Trish, you want to know something about her mother and, like, the whole volunteer fire department?"

"Please. What do you care who I hang out with anyway?"

"I don't. It just sucks living here, and I'm gonna move back."

"Right."

"Or something. Okay, forget it. Have fun with your gang of losers. I know you're all doing drugs."

"You don't know shit."

"Dad!"

"What are you doing?"

"I'm telling Dad that you're doing drugs."

"Are you fucking crazy? What's wrong with you?"

She walked to the doorway, and Peter made a grab for her arm, but she was already in the dining room, where their father could see.

"Dad?" she said, Peter standing right behind her, ready to call her a liar.

"Dad?" she asked again, and they both waited.

He was reading from a Bible on the desk, his finger
following the words on the page, his lips moving rapidly.

They were used to their father being distracted. It
was something they just understood to be part of the
deal. Phil's mind was seldom where his body was, and
even if he might have seemed to a stranger to be par-
ticipating in a dinner-table conversation, he was generally just reflexively presenting rote responses with
some superfluous portion of his mind assigned to dealing with family—the parental lobe, maybe. Now,
though, he wasn't just preoccupied. When he finally
looked up, he looked at them like they were strangers,
didn't even speak. He didn't bother to hide his annoy-
ance at finding them standing there.

"Dad, Peter's doing drugs. And not just marijuana,"
Virginia said, but feebly, without the assertion that had
been in her voice before. Peter waited for him to respond, prepared to protest, deny it, accuse her of something in turn. Phil stared at them for a moment, while
a drop of blood ran down his cheek and dripped from
his chin onto the Bible open in front of him. "Tell your
mother," he said, and turned back to his reading.

1971

It was late afternoon when Ellen woke up, the sky
out the bedroom window already getting dark. Alex
was gone when she opened her eyes. After pulling on
her jeans, she found Alex in the kitchen with Paul and
Seth, the three of them working on their first cup of
coffee, smoking cigarettes and passing around a joint,
everybody still in yesterday's clothes. There was a cup
already poured for Ellen—Alex had heard her coming
down the stairs—and she took the last seat at the table,

opposite Alex, and got the joint the next time around. They were all still a little strung out from the acid and all the pot they had smoked coming down from it, and having gone to bed that morning before the sun was really up, it felt like she'd missed the day completely, like they'd all entered a tunnel that led from one night to the next, cut off from the world that lived in the daytime.

Not much was said over the next ten minutes, but what wasn't said the loudest was what was on all their minds. Without being aware of it, each of them kept throwing glances up toward the ceiling, as if they unconsciously believed that *this* time they'd be able to see right through it, up into Keith and Amy's bedroom. They were still sitting there when Mike appeared in the doorway. Nobody had heard him coming down the stairs, so they didn't notice him standing there until Seth, who was facing that way, jerked his head a little, eyes wide, and then looked away.

They all turned to look, and of the three of them— Ellen, Alex, and Paul—only Alex did not avert her eyes when they saw that he was standing there naked, tan all over, dick flopping down out of a dense black thatch of pubic hair. Alex kept her eyes on his, looking neither away nor down.

"Good morning, comrades," he said, although there was now little sun left in the sky, and even less coming in through the window. He reached over to the wall and threw the light switch, and the overhead came on, leaving them all blinking in the sudden brightness. "Any coffee left?"

"Not much," Seth said, and got up to fetch him what was left from the percolator on the stove. "I can make some more if you want," he said over his shoulder as he poured the cooling coffee into a cup for Mike, all without looking in his direction.

"No, that right there will be just fine," Seth heard from directly behind him, and he almost dropped the cup. Mike had walked over to stand next to him. He took the cup and turned to face the others.

He stood there smiling and shaking his head, sipping his coffee. "Look at you," he said, indicating Ellen and Paul, studiedly not looking at him, and Alex, less willing to be intimidated, but obviously uncomfortable. "You want to be revolutionaries, and you're freaking out because I'm not wearing any clothes? You want to change the world, and you're worried about some bourgeois social convention?" He shook his head. "When did you say graduation was?" he asked Alex.

"Next week. Friday."

"We're going to have to make a lot of progress before you people are ready for this. We're still in kindergarten."

"I was wondering," Paul said, "when you were going to tell us what *this* is, exactly? Do you have a plan yet? Have you decided on a building? Since Alex told us you were coming, I've been going around the campus at night and checking which buildings are empty on which nights."

"That's good, Paul, but right now you should be more focused on what you need to do to transform yourselves into a genuine revolutionary cadre. A weapon's gotta be forged before you can use it. Look at how you get just because I don't have any clothes on." He held his arms out, took a few steps to the table. "This is the simple stuff. . . . " He stopped while he drew in a breath and sneezed into his hand.

"God bless you," they all murmured.

"See!" he said, shaking his head. "You're all still hung up on the ridiculous conventions you were raised with. How can you expect to overthrow the structure that created these behaviors when the smallest ones still control you? You," he said, and pointed to Alex, "take off your clothes."

Everyone turned to her to see what she would do.

She reached up and began to unbutton the flannel shirt she wore over bare skin.

"Stop, I'm just kiddin' you, darlin'," Mike said, but not before she had exposed a significant portion of her breasts to the room, which Seth and Paul made no effort to look away from. "That was very good, but we all have a lot of work ahead of us."

He turned to head back upstairs.

"Mike?" Alex called after his naked ass. "What's up with Keith and Amy? Are they coming downstairs?"

Big smile. "They'll be joining you later. They're making a lot of progress."

It wasn't long after that that Mike had come back downstairs and fed them each a hit of acid, put it on their tongues like a priest delivering a sacrament. Masses of fog had formed over the lake with the night, drifted up over the shoreline, creeping up the lawn behind the house and in among the trees. Mike led them into the woods just as the acid began to overtake them, and as they plunged deeper into the mist that hung in the air around them, it was as if they were the same thing, the trip and the mist, each an expression of the other. The physical world they knew was being blotted out by the fog just as the acid lifted them to another plane, a place where higher truths and Platonic forms resided.

The fog seemed to gather up the moonlight into

itself, hold it there so that it was almost luminescent. At times they each found themselves alone in the glowing mist, unable to see anybody or anything else, only avoiding becoming completely lost, without direction, by following the sound of Mike's voice.

He'd brought them to a clearing where a fire had already been blazing, burning off the fog around it, so that it seemed like an island of clarity, a bit of solid land that had materialized out of nothingness. Once they were all seated around the fire, Mike had begun speaking, picking them up where he'd led them the night before.

"So, we are all agreed then?" Mike said. "There's nobody here who still believes we're going to end this war without violence?"

Ellen had misgivings, mostly concerned with Alex's safety, and the safety of the others. She could see that the things Mike said were true—literally; as he spoke, they were communicated through the medium of the acid into things that visibly resonated with truth—and even earlier that day, when she was almost completely straight, she couldn't disagree in principle with breaking the law to achieve an important goal, but still, when she considered the actuality of it she balked. What if something went wrong? What if Mike sent them to plant explosives in some building and they went off too soon?

She couldn't help imagining Alex caught in the blast, being torn apart by the force of it, dismembered, burned, dying.

Mike wasn't new to this, though. He was some kind of leader, an expert, somebody who tapped into truths she hadn't seen before, and if Alex could trust him, so could she.

Mike looked across the fire to where Keith and Amy sat; they both wore hooded sweatshirts, with the hoods pulled up. Keith nodded his head, almost so slightly that you had to be looking right at him to catch it. They all were, though.

"Very good," Mike said. "Now . . ."

"The administration building," Paul said. He'd explained to Alex and Ellen earlier, back at the house, while they were waiting for Mike to come back down. He'd figured it out. The one place they could be sure there wouldn't be anyone around at night was Garrick Hall.

Mike looked his way.

"The administration building is a sure thing," Paul said. "There's never anyone in it at night. All the other buildings, I've checked them out, you can't count on it. People have study groups sometimes, the professors work late in their offices. But Garrick, it's all bureaucracy, all of them go home at five o'clock when they close up. They're, like, drones. Like Bartleby." He stopped and thought for a minute, staring off. "They might even be robots. But that gives us time to go in there, set up a bomb, and get out. We can set it to go off anytime before six in the morning, and nobody gets hurt."

"Is that what you think we've been talking about, Paul?" Mike asked.

Paul was brought up short. The extent of his imagining at that moment made it hard to reorient.

"You think this is what it means to be committed to a cause? Blowing up a building?" Mike asked.

"Well, yeah. Isn't that what we've been talking about? I mean, isn't that what you do?" He didn't sound so sure of himself anymore. Mike didn't say anything. "We aren't going to blow anything up?"

Mike stood up, started pacing around behind them again, wisps of fog streaming around him, trailing in his wake as he walked.

"You know why I split from the Weather Underground? They think they're committed to ending the war and overthrowing the government. They believe that because they've gone underground, given up their old lives, their bourgeois lives, they've demonstrated their commitment. They think that because they've blown up a statue in San Francisco, a couple of buildings here and there, they're a serious threat to the stability of this nation."

"They're not?" Seth asked, but Mike rolled on over him.

"Let me tell you what they are—they're a joke. They're no threat to anything. They blew up some things, man. Things. They even called in warnings whenever they planned something, so nobody would get hurt. Even the pigs, they warned them. They finally kill one or two people, and it's a goddamn *accident*!

"I talked to them and I talked to them, and I was very patient in allowing them the time to see that unless they got serious, nothing was ever going to change. We are responsible for a revolution, people, there is a war going on and we have to stop it, and they couldn't take that last step, so I took it for them. I sent them a message in Greenwich Village, where they were playing at revolution like rich kids at a debutante ball."

Ellen remembered the three Weathermen who had died in an explosion on West Eleventh Street in New York City just last year. Mike had done that? Did everyone else know this?

"And then they turn on me. As if we were going to

get through this without sacrifice. A revolutionary," Mike told them, "has to be ready to do two things, or else he's no revolutionary. He has to be ready to kill, and he has to be ready to die. Anything short of that and he's just taking up space." Mike stopped behind Paul. He rested his hand on Paul's head and leaned over and said, quietly, "Are you ready to hurt someone? Because until you are, until you all are"—he stood up, looked them all over—"we're not going to get anywhere and nothing's going to change."

Mike went back to his spot in the circle and sat back down. He pulled out a couple of joints, big fat ones, and lit them both up from a wooden match he pulled out of a pocket. He passed one in each direction around the circle.

"Mike's right," Keith said. He'd been sitting there, staring down the whole time they'd been there, but now, as he spoke, he looked up and around the circle. They could see now the gash in his right cheek, a clean, straight line, black in the light of the fire, but surely red in the daylight, running from just next to his eye almost all the way down to his chin. "Violence against things is hardly violence at all. It's like punching a wall. You can do it over and over and everything just goes on. But if you hurt people . . ."

Mike was looking into the fire, a satisfied expression on his face, but everyone else was staring at Keith.

". . . well, then, change is going to occur. People notice when they start getting hurt and dying."

"Very good, Keith, thank you," Mike said. "It's not what we're going to blow up, Paul. It's who."

Ellen saw Alex stiffen at this, and Paul started to object, and Ellen was relieved to see she was not alone in feeling that there was something wrong about all this. She thought maybe she should just get up and walk away, and then maybe Alex and the others would follow her, but . . . she looked around at that glowing mist that surrounded them, and she felt as if there was no solid place out there anymore, just this one clearing by the fire, that everything else was gone.

"I'm not going to ask you to do anything until you're ready, so just relax, okay? You want to change things, though, you have to expand yourselves, accommodate new ways of thinking, find out what your real limits are. Isn't that right, Amy?"

Amy nodded her head, her hood still mostly covering her face.

"I wouldn't ask you to do what I wouldn't do, and you won't have to ask anyone to sacrifice what you wouldn't sacrifice yourself. You understand? Change in this world doesn't come for free. People will get hurt, but that's the nature of the task we've taken on. It's the price. But I'm going to help you get ready for it; I'm going to prepare you to be the kind of person who can do that. When we're done, you'll be real revolutionaries.

"The way you do that, the way you get ready to hurt somebody else, is to make sure you know what real pain feels like, to go through pain, to come out the other side and realize that this is something you are willing to do to achieve your goals. Amy, you got that knife?"

Mike pushed up his sleeves before he reached over to take the big bowie knife Amy had under her sweatshirt, and the light of the fire clearly illuminated the striations covering his forearms, running from wrist to elbow, scars and cuts, some of the scars so new they were almost shiny, some badly healed, rising up in ridges and lumps.

"Now, Amy, show them some of the work you and Keith did last night."

Amy pushed her sleeves up, too, and they could now see that her arms looked like Mike's, except the cuts were fresh, still oozing blood. To Ellen they seemed to pulse with her own heartbeat.

Ellen gasped. "How could you do that to yourself?" she asked.

Mike answered for her. "She didn't do all of it, darlin'."

"I did," Keith said quietly, not looking up at any of them.

"They surprised me, these two," Mike said.

"It wasn't so bad," Amy told Ellen, but everyone could tell she was saying it for Keith.

"That's right," Mike said. "It wasn't so bad. They both made it through, and they've been transformed by the experience into the kind of people who can make a difference in the world."

"Here," he said, to Seth, and held the knife out to him. "You're next."

Seth took the knife and pushed up his sleeve, looked around at the rest of them.

"You can't hesitate," Mike said. "You do it or you don't." He leaned over the fire and snatched the knife away from him. "You, next," he said and handed the blade to Paul.

"Fine," Paul said, and, wincing, drew the tip of the knife slowly down his arm, leaving a thickening line of blood there.

Mike lit up. "Very good! See," he said to the others, "that wasn't hard. Now, who's next?"

The knife went around the group, and in the end, they all did it, each for their own reasons; the boys a bit out of face, Alex because she would not back down, all of them because they believed Mike, that this was the way to change, but Ellen did it mostly because she didn't want Alex to leave her behind.

After an hour of it, everyone's arms were bloody and raw, and it had stopped being pain; it had become something else, the slashes more like a lover's remembered caress, but sharp and burning. Mike had reached out—somehow it was him, no matter whose hand held the knife—and branded them each with his mark.

"Okay, dig it. That was good," he told them. "I'm very proud of you. You put aside the boundaries and went somewhere you could not previously go, somewhere you'd been taught was wrong and perverse."

Despite everything, they all, every one of them, felt a little glow inside at his approval; they'd have been embarrassed if they'd realized how much their response just then resembled a child's to an approving father, but they were leagues away from any sort of self-analysis. They had shut off their internal governors to travel to where they were; it wasn't a place that they were equipped to go as their own captains. They had turned it all over to him. And at that moment, they were as opaque to themselves as they were transparent to Mike.

"Now, though, we have to go further. Further, man. We have to take every internalized aspect of the bourgeoisie and smash it. Smash private property. Smash authority. Smash monogamy. Fuck it, smash heterosexuality, too!" He winked at Ellen.

"I think," Mike said, "that you're all ready to move on."

14

It seemed to Virginia that she had been walking for hours. She was cold, and hungry, and her backpack was heavy, and she was starting to be afraid that she had missed the driveway to her house in the dark, walking home along Route 9. She'd never walked all the way home before, and she could have missed the house behind all the trees, and maybe she hadn't been paying attention when she passed the driveway.

The *shhhh* of tires on asphalt and the growing white glow of headlights lighting up the fog that had crept up and surrounded her warned her that another car was about to speed by, and Virginia moved farther away from the road again, but here the ground fell off in a slope, and she kept stumbling as her feet landed on different levels. As soon as the car passed, she moved back toward the road, onto the dirt and gravel shoulder, where it was flat, at least.

There had still been a little light in the sky when Virginia had started out from Amanda's house, and by the time it was dark, she'd made it all the way down High Street to Main Street, where the town's few streetlights illuminated her way. But that was far behind her now, and the road curved so that she wouldn't see the lights anymore when she turned and looked behind her, even if it hadn't gotten so foggy. She slogged forward, her ankle hurting from where she'd twisted it some, jumping away from a car that had come up too suddenly for her to notice until it felt like it was right behind her, sure to run her down.

She had to be coming up to the house soon. Unless she'd already passed it. She thought she recognized the really bent-over tree on the right; she thought maybe the house came a little bit after here, but she wasn't sure. She started counting as she walked, one, and, two, and, three, and, to see how far she went after that, but when she got into the hundred and twenties, she lost track and didn't bother to start over, because how could she measure anything if she didn't know where she was starting from? She felt like crying. All she had to do was think one sad thought and she knew she'd start, or if she just once pictured herself walking alone down the road, head down, feet dragging, all alone, she would break right down, but she knew that wouldn't help, so she kept on walking, not even bothering to look ahead anymore, because even the ground was hard to make out a few feet away.

The first time she'd been to Amanda's house, Peter and Trish had been there, too, and when Buddy came by to pick them up to go out, to go drinking and doing drugs, of course, Peter got Buddy to give her a ride home in the backseat. She huddled in the corner there, Peter and Trish next to her; they'd been quiet the whole ride, except for Trish asking a couple of polite questions, but Buddy had talked really loudly, about fucking and stuff. Virginia knew he was doing it to freak her out, but she didn't care how gross he was.

She'd been so happy that day, maybe the first time she'd really been happy since school started.

Amanda had startled her at lunchtime by passing her a note when they were in line to pay. Sitting alone at one end of a long cafeteria table—two pimply guys eating sandwiches from home, ignoring her and talking about Halo II at the other end—she'd opened up the note and read it.

Virginia had barely stopped to think why Trish's sister would invite her to walk home with her after school; in her mind it made some vague sort of sense, since Peter went out with Trish, so maybe Amanda wouldn't hate her like everyone else did, and it didn't even bother her that the note said not to tell anyone. She'd been waiting in the French classroom after school, as instructed, when Amanda showed up, and after Amanda was sure that both buses were gone— she kept looking out the window to check—they'd left together.

Amanda had been quiet at first, and Virginia didn't really know what to say either, but she hadn't had anyone to talk to, not really, not in a long time, and she had just started talking. About how much she missed her friends, and how she didn't mean to do what she did when she first got to school, although really, she knew it was her own fault, she wasn't saying it wasn't. About *Buffy* and *Angel* and *American Idol*, and when she mentioned the *Gossip Girl* novels, Amanda had jumped in. She'd read them all, too. By the time they turned off High Street onto Amanda's block, they were chattering away, and they'd even laughed together a couple of times.

At the Willitses' house, she'd met Amanda's mom, and then they'd gone to Amanda's room, where they'd listened to some music, made fun of Amanda's old Barbies, and presented an outraged and united front against Sarah, Amanda's little sister, and her attempts to join them, rebuffing her again and again, until Peter had told her that she better come now if she wanted a ride.

Today, they'd gotten along even better, like they really were friends, like maybe Amanda would talk to her in school, in front of the other kids, someday. It had transformed Virginia's experience of everything: the street they walked on to Amanda's house, the air she breathed on the way, her understanding of herself, of the future. They'd hung out in Amanda's room again, and this time she showed Amanda her cuts—just the ones on her arms, though; she'd only pushed her sleeves up to her elbows—and Amanda had promised to teach her how to throw up next time she came over, because her mother was home tonight.

Amanda didn't have a cell phone, none of the Willitses did, except their mom, so Virginia let her mess with hers, and they called a boy Amanda liked and pressed the speakerphone button, and listened to him say "Hello? Hello? Is this Debbie?" which was the name of the girl Amanda knew that he liked, so she shouted, "Why don't you have *sex* with her!" and they'd snapped the phone shut and fell back on the bed, unable to stop giggling even when they tried to stop by shouting out horrible things to each other, like war and AIDS and dying without ever getting a boyfriend, but each horrible thing they said seemed even funnier than the last.

When Amanda's mom invited her to stay for dinner, Virginia really wanted to, but she said no, because, one, obviously, she was fat and gross and she knew what they'd be thinking if they saw her eating, duh, and, two, their kitchen smelled kind of funny, and she didn't think she'd want to eat something that Mrs. Willits cooked.

Mrs. Willits offered to drive her home, but Virginia could tell she didn't want to, so she said no to that, too, and when the Willitses were ready to have dinner, she'd set out walking.

It always seemed like such a short ride in the car; it was a short ride even in the bus, with stops, and she just didn't think it would take that long to walk. By the time she realized she'd made a mistake and thought to call home to see if her dad could come and drive along Route 9 until he saw her, and discovered that she'd left her cell phone in Amanda's room, she had already walked too far to go back and get it, because she was sure she'd be getting to the house any minute.

Well, just think about Amanda's room, Virginia told herself, think about Amanda, your new friend, your new *best* friend, think about something good, and then you'll be home. It was so dark, and hard to see, though; clouds filled the sky above her, no moon, no stars, fog all around. There were trees on both sides of the road, and most of the time the fog was so thick she couldn't see the trees on the other side, sometimes so thick she couldn't see the trees on *this* side of the road.

There were sounds from the woods sometimes; after a long stretch of silence, she'd hear something heavy go crashing through brittle branches. Sometimes it would feel like it was right next to her, just a few feet away, and she'd stop still, hold her breath, just in case it was coming for her; maybe it wouldn't find her if she was completely quiet. After it was silent a few seconds, she'd start walking again, but since the first time it happened, she couldn't get rid of the feeling that something was right there, watching her, following her. A big wolf, maybe, but not the regular kind, the smart ones with the pretty eyes you see on the Discovery Channel sometimes; the big ugly kind, with the big hump on its back and coarse, scraggly fur. The were-wolf kind.

Well, that was smart, Virginia. Now she'd scared herself. She could feel her heart beating fast. She listened to her feet as they crunched through the gravel. Maybe she should hitchhike when another car came?

She'd never hitchhiked before. She didn't even know a single person who had ever hitchhiked; nobody hitchhiked in the city. In fact, the only thing she knew about hitchhiking was from TV, and even though some old movies made hitchhiking look like fun, like you were going to meet somebody great and have an adventure and fall in love, mostly it ended up with somebody having a big knife.

She didn't even know that she'd started to cry until she had to blow her nose, and then she lifted her arm to her face and wiped the tears from her cheeks with the arm of her sweater. It was so dark and cold and her backpack had gotten so heavy, and she just wanted to give up. Why wasn't anybody even looking for her?

She'd start counting again, was what she'd do, and if she didn't see the house by five hundred, she'd turn around and walk back, try the other way, and she'd just started counting out loud, her voice sounding small and pathetic in the dark night even to her, when she heard somebody in the woods call her name.

Virginia froze. She didn't really hear that, did she? She listened as hard as she could, moving her head just slightly to her right, straining to make out something in the hushed night. She listened so hard, her breath held in, that she could hear the gravel beneath her feet as her weight shifted.

"Hello?" she said, weakly, the sound barely making it out of her throat. "Is somebody there? Because . . ." She couldn't think of a because.

In the gray opacity of fog between two trees, a portion grew darker, took the shape of a person.

"Get yourself lost, did you?"

Virginia relaxed, let out her breath, when she saw it was Walker.

"Oh. It's you."

"That's right, darlin'. I'm here to rescue you . . . I'd think you'd be a little happier to see me."

"No, I am," she said. She'd always been glad to see Walker before, looked forward to it all day, sometimes; there were days when it felt like he was the only one in the world who didn't hate her. And he did lots of stuff with her that made school easier to get through. But she realized that it had been a couple of days since she'd seen him, or even thought of him.

"C'mon, it's shorter if we go this way," he said, and he turned and headed back into the woods, Virginia following.

Relieved to be headed home, Virginia started telling Walker about her visit at Amanda's house. Virginia could feel the moisture of the fog on her face as they walked deeper into the woods; it was growing thicker, and she could see less and less around her.

"That sounds like fun," Walker said, when she was finished telling him how they were laughing about AIDS. "But . . ."

Virginia was a little thirsty. She tried opening her mouth wide as they passed through the fog, to see if she'd get any water in her mouth. It tasted bitter and oily on her tongue. She spit loudly.

"But what?"

"But I don't know if you can trust her, Virginia. I think she's probably like everyone else, all those other girls."

Virginia walked into a branch, got slapped by it as it sprang back after Walker's passing.

"She's my friend. . . ."

"You have to be really careful about who you trust."

"I know that. Are you sure this is even the right way home?"

"Well, first we have to see some friends of mine."

"You said you were taking me home."

"I just want you to meet some people first. Then we'll take you right home. If you still want to."

Up ahead, there was an orange glow in the fog: a fire. As they got closer, Virginia could see the darker outlines of people forming around it.

"You'll like them way better than Amanda. She's not like you, Virginia. She's not as smart as you, and her mom's really poor. And did you notice that smell in their house?"

Virginia didn't say anything. They were almost to the fire now. The people there were becoming more distinct, a bunch of hippies from the college, looked like, and one of them looked like . . . Walker. Virginia stopped, did a double-take.

"I don't think I want to meet your friends."

"They'll be your friends, too."

"I have a friend now. A real friend."

"I'm your real friend, Virginia. Amanda's probably calling up somebody from school right now and making fun of you."

Virginia stared at him for a minute.

"Probably telling everybody about how you cut yourself. You can't trust her, Virginia. Probably she's on the phone with Melanie right now, telling her how fat you are."

"She is not!" Virginia shouted, and turned and started running, away from Walker, away from those people by the fire.

1971

They had been waiting, sitting there around the fire, waiting for what seemed like a long time, twenty, thirty minutes, while Mike sat there with his eyes closed, like he was in a trance.

"Damn," he said, and opened his eyes. "Hold on. Just a bit longer." He closed his eyes again. "She'll be back."

Virginia ran and ran, into trees, through bushes, scraping her legs, falling down, getting up again, but the fog started thinning as soon as she got away from Walker, and soon she could see the lake through the trees and she just knew her house had to be the other way, away from them. She was too mad now to be scared, too determined to get away from Walker and whatever weird thing he wanted her to do to stop running. Her pack was bouncing against her back as she ran; it would probably leave bruises, she thought, and she'd show them to Amanda, tell her how this guy had said Amanda wasn't her real friend, and Amanda would get all resentful at him, too.

That cheered her as she ran, and then she was sure she could see the lights of her house, she was getting closer, and she slowed down to a walk, breathing heavily. She would call Amanda and tell her all about it as soon as she got home.

But who's Walker? Amanda would ask. How do you know this guy?

Okay, maybe she wouldn't tell Amanda, Virginia thought, as she walked across her backyard to her house. Because, well, how did she know this guy? What was he, anyway? How did he get into her room? She'd always known there was something weird about that, but she'd made herself not think about it. She was so lonely, and felt so bad, that she didn't think about it on purpose.

The wood-framed door to the back porch banged shut behind her, but the back door was locked. She pounded on it with her fist.

The sleeve of her sweater, stretched and loose, fell back as she banged on the door. She looked at the cuts on her arm, thought of the hundreds of cuts all over her body, and the other things Walker made her do. Okay, not made her, but still. Maybe . . . no, not maybe. She didn't want to visit with Walker anymore at all.

A light came on and Peter opened the door for her.

"Where the hell've you been? I called Trish's house looking for you, and they said you left hours ago."

"You're not in charge, Peter. I can stay out as late as I want."

"No. You can't. It's almost eleven."

She'd had no idea it was that late. "It is?"

"Yeah, what, you forget how to tell time?" He grabbed for her wrist to show her her own watch, but she responded more violently than he might have reasonably expected, yanking her arm back and swinging with her other fist at him as soon as he touched her. He let go immediately, and they both stood there looking sheepish.

"You were worried?" she asked.

"Well, yeah."

"Was Dad worried?"

His father had done little more than grunt when he'd knocked on the door of his study the first time to tell him that Virginia was late, and then as he got more worried, he'd knocked again, to ask if they should go looking for her, and his father hadn't even answered. When he tried the door, it was locked.

"Yeah," Peter said. "You hungry?" he asked, quickly changing the subject. "I saved you some spaghetti."

Virginia was; she hadn't realized in all this time how hungry she'd become.

"Yeah. Did Molly make it?"

"No, I did. Molly didn't come today."

She made a face. "I guess I can eat it anyway," she said, joking.

"Right, come on."

They headed toward the kitchen.

"Peter, can I ask you something?" Virginia said, as they went into the kitchen.

"Yeah, sure, what?" Peter said as he opened the refrigerator door.

"You haven't, like, seen anybody weird in the woods . . ."

Peter stopped still.

". . . or in your room?"

Peter could almost cry with the relief he felt. He turned to look at her.

"That guy?"

"Walker," Virginia said. "His name's Walker."

"Yeah, him," Peter said, slowly nodding his head.

"He's, like, a ghost, right?"

"I guess. I don't know what he is."

"I let him—" Virginia started to say. Peter thought of the things he'd remembered from his dreams, or not-dreams, and didn't want to hear.

"Yeah, I know," he said, cutting her off.

"You think Dad knows?"

"I don't know," Peter said. "Sit down. I'll get you some dinner."

Virginia dropped her pack on the floor, and sat down at the kitchen table, while Peter dished up a plate of the spaghetti and put it in the microwave. It took him a minute to find the plate, though, because so many of them were in the sink, dirty.

He brought the hot food over for Virginia and sat and watched as she started eating. She must have been starved, because she really dug in. She saw Peter watching her, and smiled at him self-consciously. He realized he hadn't seen her this animated since they'd moved here, really. Despite whatever physical changes she'd gone through, there was something about her that was like she used to be. Her eyes were clearer, her face open, unguarded, in a way he realized now had been gone for a long time.

She caught his eyes and looked down at where a drink would sit. "Well?" Demanded it, as if he were there to serve her.

Peter got up and went to the fridge to get her the last can of Diet Coke. He smiled to himself. His obnoxious, insufferable, infuriating little sister was back.

15

Peter woke up panicked. Somebody was in his room, by his bed, leaning over him. He felt a hand on his shoulder, a girl's hand he was sure, and he knew what was coming next. *"No!"* he shouted.

Since his encounter in the woods with that girl, since he'd realized where he'd been going, what he'd been doing, every night, and consciously rejected it, the succubus—he'd looked it up; he'd known there was a word for it—had stayed away. He'd been sleeping well and steadily, undisturbed, for over a week now. Not that his dreams were sex-free; he was, after all, a sixteen-year-old boy. But now, waking up out of them, or waking in the morning many dream cycles later, he could tell it was a normal dream he'd had; there wasn't anything ambiguous about it. He could recall them in daylight, how it felt, in what wisps of memory still circled his head, less and less as the day progressed until they'd dissipated completely. They weren't pushed away and repressed, so intense they terrified him in his sleep and he had to claw his way out of them, back to the surface, to lay there gasping afterward, as if he'd just escaped drowning.

But now he woke to the sure knowledge that the

girl, the thing, was back, and he sat up and pushed her away.

"Peter, stop!"

Peter shook his head to clear it and wake up a little more. It was his sister. He could see her standing there now in the moonlight coming in the window. She looked pale and ghostly in that light, but also solid and undeniably real in her sweatpants and baggy T-shirt.

"What, why'd you wake me up?"

"Can I sleep in here with you?"

"God. Grow up."

"C'mon, Peter, I'm scared. I don't want Walker to come to my room. He'll make me . . . do things."

Peter hesitated for just a second after that.

"Fine, get your blanket and pillow and you can sleep on the floor."

"I don't want to sleep on the floor." She just about stamped her foot, but then her voice mellowed. "Let me just get into the bed with you, okay?" She grabbed a corner of the blanket and slipped under. He slid over to the very edge, so they weren't touching.

"You're not getting my pillow," he said.

"Thanks, Peter. Brought my own." She rolled over to face away from him, shifted a little to find her spot, and let out an unconscious sigh.

She sounded relieved, unconcerned.

Peter fell asleep a little annoyed at having to share his bed, but glad he could do that for her.

The only light visible downstairs was leaking out under the locked door of Phil's study. It had been days since he had slept. There were multiple Web pages open on his computer, open books stacked on his desk, open books surrounding him on the floor. At first he had been parsing only religious texts—various translations of the Old and New Testaments; the Koran, the Book of Mormon, Dianetics; Anton LeVay, Aleister Crowley, Sri Chinmoy—but now he'd moved on to histories and biographies and law books. He was getting very very close to figuring it out. He could feel it, like an electricity coursing through his body.

He ignored the first knock on the door, snapped "Go away" at the next disturbance, and had forgotten completely that someone had knocked when Walker dispensed with knocking a few minutes later and walked through the door.

"What?" Phil said, glancing up. "What is it? Can't you see I'm busy?" Phil turned back to the book he'd been reading.

"Have you forgotten who led you to all this?"

Phil turned to Walker again, impatient. "Yes, I appreciate it, but I don't think you fully understand how far I've come. I believe I'm about to put my finger on what everyone else got wrong. I believe I am about to get to the bottom of things.

"You were a messenger, and set me to my task, so thank you very much, but now if you could just leave me alone to my work." He waited. Walker smiled.

"You can just let yourself—" Phil gasped, or tried to. He couldn't breathe. It was as if his throat had been plugged closed. He stood, pounded himself on the chest. After a minute he began to see flickers of colors at the periphery of his vision, like floaters, and then a blackness moving in from all sides as he began to lose consciousness. Walker stepped behind him, wrapped his arms around his chest, and performed the Heimlich maneuver, one squeeze.

Phil gagged and retched, and from his mouth shot a silvery fish, six inches long, that landed, flopping, on the open book he'd been reading. It created a dark wet patch on the white pages, where it writhed for a moment before dying.

Phil glared at Walker, angry. He wiped his wrist across his mouth.

"Come with me," Walker said and walked back out through the door.

By the time Phil had unlocked the door and followed him out, Walker was halfway up the stairs. He caught up with him at the door to Peter's room, which swung open as they stood there.

"Yes, what is it?" Phil snapped, but keeping his voice low, a parent's instinct that had not yet deserted him. His eyes still hadn't adjusted to the darkness, and Walker waited until he saw his children in bed.

Peter and Virginia had in their sleep rolled over and come together in the middle of the bed. They would both be quite uncomfortable about whatever inadvertent contact had come about when they woke up.

"Do you see what almost happened here?"

Phil considered.

"Yes. Yes I do. What of it?"

"She's to remain a virgin—"

"How is this my problem? And how am I supposed to manage that? Perhaps you should speak with her mother—" Phil felt a tightness in his throat. "All right, fine. The girl will remain a virgin. Although why you care, I don't know."

"She is to remain a virgin, because you will be called on to sacrifice her, and if she's not a virgin, God will be displeased."

Phil shook his head, said in a put-upon tone, "Fine.

Virgin. Sacrifice. I kill the girl. Do you want me to kill the boy, too?"

Walker smiled at that. "That's more the spirit I'm looking for, Phil. But no, he just wants the girl."

"Right. I'll just get it out of the way now, all right? And then I can get back to work." Phil started into the room, looking around for something heavy to use to crush his daughter's skull. He stopped when he felt Walker's hand on his shoulder.

"No, not yet. I still have uses for her. But I really do appreciate your enthusiasm."

16

Saturday, already getting dark, not quite six. Virginia sat in her bedroom at the vanity, experimenting with makeup. A little lipstick, that was easy. Bright blue eye shadow—she kept on stroking it onto her upper eyelid with a finger and then wiping it off. She liked the color, but she knew people would notice it, and she couldn't decide if that was what she wanted or not.

These last few months, she'd gotten used to dressing and holding herself in a way that deflected attention, so people wouldn't notice her. She was just creeping up to the idea that she wasn't so gross that people would laugh or be disgusted with her if they really looked. Or else why would Amanda have invited her to go bowling in Canandaigua with her and her friends?

The last week, Virginia had sat at Amanda's table at lunch, and the two other girls she always hung out with, Jeannie and Kathy, had been pretty friendly. They didn't say anything on Monday when Melanie had pretended to be smelling something gross when she walked by and all her friends laughed, but when the boys at the next table had thrown some food at her on Wednesday, they'd glared at them until they stopped. All three of them.

Virginia looked at herself in the mirror and smiled. Maybe she wasn't as ugly as she thought. Her skin was clearing up a little, she'd noticed, it was just her forehead right now. She moved her hair over her forehead in sort of an emo-sweep, and you could barely tell she was broken out at all.

Her mom had taken her shopping for some new clothes the last time she was up—a really tense weekend, even Virginia had noticed, everyone pretending things were normal. Her dad had spent the whole weekend on campus, sleeping in his office. Honestly, Virginia didn't mind having him gone at all. When he was here he was always locked in his study, or you'd find him skulking around the house looking at you weird.

As unpleasant as it had been trying on things— she'd almost cried at the Gap, trying on jeans; okay, no, she did cry—but she had stuff that fit for the first time since last spring. She wasn't squeezed into something too tight, reminding her all the time how fat she was, or wearing something of Peter's that anybody could tell was for hiding in. She stood up and turned around. Maybe it was the clothes, but she didn't even look that fat, really.

She went to the bed and changed from her cute blue Nikes into her high-top Cons—New York sneakers, Amanda called them—and back again, then returned to the mirror to play with makeup some more until Amanda and her mom got there to pick her up. Amanda said there were these boys who were always at the bowling alley on Saturday night, tenth-graders from Canandaigua High, who were sort of jerks, but kinda cute. She wiped off her lipstick and started over.

*   *   *

Phil had not been leaving his study except to use the bathroom and fill the water bottle he kept with him. He'd been driven, pulled on by the promise of a new sort of enlightenment. He'd always wondered about smart people and faith, and at the thousands and thousands of intellectual man-hours that had been wasted by the Church throughout its history pursuing the fine points of sin and virtue and God's intent.

Now he understood: it was the most rewarding thing he could imagine, the most important thing in the world. To know God's mind, to know his will for us, what could be a higher calling? The churchmen, he could see what drew them now. He understood why brilliant men like Augustine and Aquinas could devote their lives to this.

But, of course, history had not yet in their time unfolded; the face of God's Creation had not yet been fully exposed. They could only see their own small pieces of the world. It was as if they were trying to understand a book by reading a handful of pages; comprehend a symphony for which only the overture had been composed.

Phil leaned back in his desk chair, a feeling of satisfaction such as he'd never known, never even imagined possible, washing through him. He put the book he'd been reading onto the head-high pile at the edge of the desk; it collapsed, books falling over onto more books, a haphazard pile on the floor, exposing on his desktop folders of materials he'd been working with weeks ago, documents he once would have handled carefully, filed properly.

He paid no attention; none of that mattered now. His new book would share with the world what he had uncovered. He was a prize-winning author before, re-

spected among his peers, but now what he wrote
would change everything.

Really, it couldn't have been more obvious, once
he'd realized. He wasn't even the first one to suspect.
The Gnostics had been on to something, but they'd
only been half right.

People had always grappled with the problem of
pain, the existence of evil, wondered why the world
was full of disease and insanity, famine and death.
Why was man's nature such that there was no end to
murder and rape and poverty? Why were innocent
children born with fatal, disfiguring diseases that beg-
gared human imagination? Why was suffering so
much the substance of the world?

Centuries had been spent wrestling with these questions. Entire libraries had been filled with contorted
scholastic logic and Panglossian theodicies, an endless
supply of mysterious ways and holy paradoxes sum-
moned up in the attempt to explain it away, and he suspected that nobody had ever, deep down, really bought
any of it. It was all so forced, all so clearly a case of
protesting too much. Now Phil had puzzled out the
answer.

The secret, the hidden truth about the nature of God
written in his Creation, was that there was no hidden
truth. There was no secret meaning. It was right there,
out in the open. God *wanted* man to suffer. That's the
way he had created the world. He *liked* it.

It was so obvious, now that he'd figured it out. In
retrospect, it was a wonder that it had taken a man of
his intellect and learning to piece it together.

Did people have to be tortured with an awareness
of their own mortality and the steady degeneration of
their bodies, until every motion was painful and death

was a welcome relief—unless it struck you down out of nowhere, cutting your life short—before they understood? Oh, wait, God had done that.

Did people have to be battered with tidal waves that wiped out innumerable villages for no apparent reason? Yes, he'd done that, too.

Earthquakes and hurricanes that left cities in rubble, their populations cut in half? Check. Horrifying parasites that ate you from within? Covered. Diseases that brought slow, creeping misery? Lots of them, a catalogue full. Plagues that destroyed entire ways of life in a heartbeat? You bet.

It was an inextricable thread in the fabric of Creation, perhaps the dominant one. It was the one constant drone beneath all the various grace notes people blithely made of their lives. The world was made in such a way that pain and suffering could not be avoided. That was the nature of Creation and that was the nature of God. God was a sadist, and our suffering meant nothing to him . . . or, no, not nothing. Our suffering was the point of it all. He had made the world so that we would suffer in it.

It was as plain as day, but it had still taken him, Philip Coulter, to decipher it.

"Very good, Phil."

"Thank you." Phil wasn't surprised that he had company now. Really, he wouldn't have been surprised at trumpets and fireworks. This was a great moment in human history. He turned in his chair to face Walker.

"You understand now," Walker said.

"Yes. Yes, I do."

"And you know what you have to do?"

"Of course. I must make this known. I'll begin work on my book—"

"No, before you begin something like that, you're going to have to demonstrate that you can live these principles. That you're truly the man to present these things to the world."

"A sacrifice, you mean? Yes, that makes sense. Fine." Phil stood up. "Is Virginia here? And I can get to work on my book when I've taken care of that?"

"No, not your daughter. Not yet. She has things to do before you take her."

"Then who? You can't really expect me to go out and start snatching girls off the street, can you? People are very wary with their children these days."

"Relax," Walker said. "I sent out. You can play with them some, too, if you want. But only after. They have to be virgins when you kill them."

When it came down to it, Marjorie Willits just wasn't doing that good a job of being a mother. She tried, she did her best, but somebody had to work, and so she was always leaving the girls alone, and *still* money was always as short, which made her temper shorter.

Here it was, one of her rare nights off, and she was going out. On a date. What would a good mother do? Insist on Amanda staying home, probably, and the four Willits girls having an evening together. But Trish hadn't objected to keeping an eye on Sarah with that new boyfriend, and Marjorie was pretty sure nobody was getting anybody pregnant with Sarah around, so that was two birds right there, and if she didn't let Amanda go out with her friends, she'd be bitchy all night anyway, so she might as well drop the bunch of them off and take up that cute customer on his offer to buy her a drink. Not just cute—a good tipper, and as best she could tell, single. Not that a wedding ring would necessarily stop her. She was thirty-six and showing it, and the field of eligible bachelors around here didn't exactly include, well, the Bachelor. Really, any one of those three—cute, a good tipper, or single—qualified him for at least a friendly drink.

"Turn on the radio, okay, Mom?" Amanda asked from where she sat in the backseat with her friends.

"It's not working," her mother replied, and the least of my concerns, she didn't bother to say out loud.

There were so many bills that had gone unpaid, so many things that needed repairs, that Marjorie Willits had put off taking her car in for months now. It ran well enough to take her to work, and shuttle the girls, and pick up the groceries, which was all she really asked. Besides the radio, the AC and heater were out, but the summer hadn't been too bad, and it hadn't even really gotten cold yet. And the horn didn't work, but honestly, how often do you use a horn for a real emergency? If somebody cut you off, you honked after, to let him know you were annoyed, but Marjorie'd never even heard of an accident that hadn't happened because somebody blew their horn.

"Is this it, Mandy?" Marjorie asked, raising her voice to be heard over the girls' chatter. They were coming up to a driveway that turned off of Route 9.

"My name isn't Mandy, it's Amanda," Amanda said, from the backseat, where her two friends now shut up in case she was going to get into it with her mother.

"I think I know your name, *Mandy*, I named you. And if you want me to pick up whatshername, your new little friend, then you better tell me if this is where she lives, and stop making every conversation into a fight."

"It isn't," Amanda said, and crossed her arms.

"And you can drop the attitude, missy," Marjorie added, looking at her daughter in the rearview mirror, "unless you want to get somebody else's mother to drive you to Canandaigua. I have plans, too, you know, and I don't have all night."

Amanda glared back at her, said "God" under her breath, and held her middle finger up to the back of her mother's seat, out of sight of the mirror. Kathy and Jeannie covered their mouths in mock shock, then started laughing again.

"It must be here, then," Marjorie said a minute later, and pulled into the driveway and drove slowly down to the house. It was dark, only the one light by the front door on. She looked in the rearview mirror again. The backseat was empty; or rather, the girls had slid down in the seat so that she couldn't see them. "Amanda, I hope you're not expecting me to get out of the car and get your friend."

"Yes, slave," she whispered so just her friends could hear, and then sat up and opened the door. "Come on," she said to them, "come with me." Together they walked to the front door to fetch Virginia.

Looking forward to her evening out, Virginia had gotten to thinking about what a good time she used to have back home, when she was popular, when she did things with her friends all the time. She used to have so much fun! She hoped so much that everything went well tonight. She was remembering a particular birthday party, two summers ago, when she and her friends had danced all afternoon. Two of the boys at that party had even danced, and guess who they danced with? Virginia, of course.

What was the song they all loved that year? Oh, yeah! "Hey Ya," by OutKast. What a great song that was.

Virginia had gotten up to go to the bathroom, and when she came back, her iPod was sitting right out on her bed. She didn't remember leaving it there; it must have been under the blanket or something. Maybe she'd bring it with her tonight, so her new friends could hear all her favorite music? No, that would be rude. Maybe the other girls didn't have one. She knew Amanda didn't.

You know what she wanted, though? She wanted to hear "Hey Ya." That would really put her in the mood for going out. Virginia put the earphones on, and clicked through to "Hey Ya," the long version, and then, well, she couldn't help getting up and dancing a little.

The door swung open before Amanda could knock, and the three girls took a step backward when they saw Phil standing there, his hair sticking up in back, dressed only in his blue bathrobe.

"Yes, come in," he said. "I was waiting for you."

"No, thanks," Amanda said. Virginia's dad was a college professor. Her mom had always said all those people from the college were freaks. "Is Virginia ready?"

"Come in. I'll see," Phil said.

Jeannie pushed Amanda from behind, and the three of them walked in the door.

To their right were the stairs up to the bedrooms. "Come in here," Phil said, walking into the living room, switching on the light. Clumped together, the girls followed him.

"Are you going to get Virginia?" Amanda asked.

"I need to ask you a question first," Phil said.

The girls looked at each other. "What?" Amanda said.

"Are you all virgins?"

As recently as five years ago, had an adult male stranger asked a group of thirteen- and fourteen-year-old girls if they were virgins, they would have thought it was vastly inappropriate, plainly wrong. Having been subjected for the last two years to federally sponsored abstinence education, however, and having attended more than one mandatory virginity pledge rally, this was not the first time the girls had been subjected to middle-aged men openly poking at their virginity. They could understand how a father might ask, to see what kind of kids his daughter was hanging out with. Still, it made them all uncomfortable.

"Yes," they said together, two of them looking down. Kathy, who never looked away from Phil, was the only one lying.

"Good," Phil said, gruffly, and stared at them for a moment. He hadn't considered the logistics of the situation. If he grabbed one, the others would no doubt flee. He could grab two, they were small, but, same problem with the third, and he wouldn't even have a hand free to do anything to them . . . there was some twine under the sink in the kitchen. That would hold them.

"Good," he repeated, nodding his head. "Wait here for me, please." He left the room. The girls stood there, uneasy.

"Do you think he went to get her?" Jeannie asked.

"Well, yeah, I guess," said Amanda.

"Maybe she's not even here," Kathy said.

"Maybe she's upstairs," Amanda said.

"Yeah," Jeannie said. "Probably. Right?"

"Yeah," Amanda said. "I'll go see, okay?"

"Let's just go, okay?" Kathy said. "He's really creepy."

"Don't be a baby," Amanda said, asserting her leadership. She walked out of the room and over to the stairs, leaned her head up, and said, "Ginny?"

In her room, Virginia, watching herself in the mirror, shook it like a Polaroid picture. She didn't notice that the music had just gotten fractionally louder.

Amanda put her foot on the first step, called out again. She turned to rejoin her friends in the living room, and saw Phil coming down the hallway from the kitchen.

Bent over, rooting around below the sink for the twine, holding the large knife he'd already taken from a drawer, his robe had fallen open. When he'd stood up, twine in one hand, knife in the other, he hadn't bothered to tie it closed again. What difference did it make? Now, his erect penis was plainly visible from all the way down the hall.

For the first time since entering adolescence, Amanda was speechless.

In the living room, Kathy and Jeannie saw the look on their friend's face, hurried out to join her by the stairs to see what was wrong. They turned and saw Phil coming at them, and as one, the three girls now screamed, then turned and ran out the door, shrieking all the way to the car. Amanda pulled open the door and they all piled into the backseat.

If Marjorie never heard the shriek of a teenage girl again, it would be too soon. She turned in her seat to face the girls, who had just tumbled into the car.

"Shut *up*!" she barked at them.

"Mom, Mom, her dad, her dad was—"

"What?"

"We saw his—" Amanda didn't know what word she could use in front of both her friends and her mother.

Jeannie knew why she stopped and giggled nervously, waiting to hear what she'd say.

"You saw what?" her mother asked.

Now Kathy laughed, too.

"Stop it!" Amanda said, turning to glare at them.

Marjorie, annoyed, turned back around and started the car.

"Is your friend coming or not?" Marjorie asked over the sound of the engine.

"No, but I think her dad is, though," Jeannie said, and now Amanda couldn't help it, she started laughing, too. The three of them couldn't get two words out after that, all of it released as laughter.

Marjorie shook her head wearily, backed the car up to turn it around, then drove away.

Virginia thought she heard something from downstairs as the song ended. She took off her headphones, but when she walked out on the landing, and said, "Hello?" nobody answered. Around seven, she went downstairs to wait, and then she called Amanda's house at seven thirty. Sarah answered the phone, and called Trish up from downstairs, leaving Peter to cool down a bit. Trish told Virginia that they'd left a long time ago. Virginia sat in the living room, waiting until just before ten for Amanda to pick her up, and then finally went upstairs to bed.

*   *   *

Walker was waiting for Phil when he opened the door to his study.

"That could have gone better," Walker said.

"It couldn't be helped. They got away. I don't know how you thought I was supposed to control all three of them," Phil said, annoyed, wanting to get started on the book it was his destiny to write. He brushed past Walker, pulled out his chair, and sat down . . .

. . . and fell to the ground, sprawled on his back, rocks pushing up sharp into his back and thighs. He turned his head. He was on a small patch of grass, right beside the lake. Wind, fast and strong, blew through the trees that surrounded him on three sides, branches swaying; clouds raced across the sky, across the face of the moon hanging low over the choppy lake. Walker stood looking down at him.

"You're going to have to take a little more personal responsibility than that," he said.

Phil tried to get up, found himself pinned to the ground. He grunted, attempted to move, but something was holding him down, and his struggles pressed the shards of rock more painfully into his back.

"Let me up!"

"No," Walker said. "I don't think you should get up until you've got a better grip on your place in the workings of things."

Phil's head whipped from side to side, the only way he was free to move. Shapes, human shapes, were forming out of nothing by his arms and legs.

"I understand!" Phil said. "I understand more than you know!"

They were kids, kids who looked just like students, holding him there. Now someone grabbed his head and held it still.

"No, Phil," Walker said, kneeling down beside him. "You understand in your head, not in your heart. Not in your soul, Phil." He pulled open Phil's robe, so that he was completely exposed to the night; the mound of his belly, the gray hairs scattered across his chest, his balls, hanging loose between his legs, his cock above them, shrunken now, like a boy's.

For a moment, the full moon was clear of clouds, and like a spotlight it shined down and glinted off the bowie knife in Walker's hand. To Phil, it looked as long as a sword.

Walker lowered the knife to Phil's chest.

"No! Stop! What are you going to do? *Stop! Ow!*"

Walker had sliced into his skin, made a cut in the center of his chest, just below his neck, a half inch long, a little less than that deep.

"We reach the heart through the gut, Phil, not the mind. All that thinking, that's after the fact. That's just making stuff up. The Truth, Phil," and he reached down and slid a nail into the cut, started pulling at the skin, started peeling it down, using the knife to help it along, so that one long strip of skin tore away from Phil's chest, and now he had to raise his voice to be heard over Phil's screams, "that's something we feel," and now he ripped at the strip of skin so that it came off completely, leaving a raw, oozing, red slash, like a stroke of paint down Phil's chest, "not something we think."

Walker tossed the skin aside into the water beside him, where small dark shapes darted up from the mud to taste it. He stood up, then wiped away the blood that had gotten on his hands.

"Here," he said, and held out the knife. "Your turn."

The figure holding Phil's head, a big guy with long

hair, stood and stepped over to Walker and took the knife from him. He knelt down and began another cut, in another place.

Phil's screams weakened after the first hour, until they barely carried out over the lake, no louder than the wind.

Monday morning, Virginia woke up with a stomachache, or she got one as soon as she remembered what had happened on Saturday night, anyway. She'd been afraid to call Amanda on Sunday, and now she was afraid to go to school, but staying home and wondering why Amanda had stood her up, that was worse.

So, tense, muted, Virginia rode the bus to school and went through her first few classes of the day. Whenever she thought nobody would notice, she'd look around at the kids in the room, to see if any of them were looking at her, to see if they knew she'd been left waiting, to see if they were laughing. She sort of wished she'd never had a friend; that would have been better than this. Once, rounding the corner into the second-floor hallway, she saw Amanda and her friends at Amanda's locker between classes. She could have just walked up to them, but she turned around and took the other way to get to her class.

It wasn't until lunchtime that she got up the nerve to talk to Amanda, and she probably would have turned around and run again if so many people—she could tell—hadn't been watching her.

Tray in hand, she walked up to Amanda where she was sitting with Jeannie and Kathy and started to put her tray down to take her place among them.

Kathy, who had never been that happy about adding Virginia to their group, reached out her hand and stopped her. "That seat's taken," she said, without turning to face her. Virginia stood there.

"Amanda?" Virginia said.

Amanda said nothing.

"Please, Amanda?"

"She doesn't want to talk to you. None of us want to talk to you, so you can go sit by yourself or something because we don't care where you sit, except you're not sitting with us," Kathy said.

Kathy had been the one who had talked the other two into this. Amanda and Jeannie, best friends for years, didn't think it was Virginia's fault, but Kathy, who had known from the beginning that the natural size of their little gang was three, felt her standing threatened by the addition of another girl, and had seized the opportunity to ditch her when it arose.

"But I don't understand why you're doing this to me."

"Like you don't know," Kathy said, suddenly turning toward her. She looked really angry.

Immediately, though, Virginia did know. It had taken a couple of weeks, but they all finally saw what a fat, disgusting loser she really was. Why did she think they wouldn't notice? She began to back away. "I'm sorry," she said, barely audible.

Amanda was feeling awful, really feeling bad for Virginia, and was about to say something, was changing her mind, but Jeannie kicked her under the table, and she kept her mouth shut.

"You're sorry? Who cares if you're sorry? That was just the grossest thing that ever happened to us," Kathy said.

Virginia wanted to cry. She *was* gross. How could Amanda have stood to hang out with her as much as she did, anyway? She looked around and saw people all over the room looking at her. From somewhere a fish stick came flying out of the air and hit her on the side of the forehead. All the noise in the room sounded like laughter to Virginia, and she dropped her tray and ran, the laughter following behind her until she found a spot beneath the stairs, where she curled up in the dust of a corner with her hands over her ears.

She stayed there under the stairs until after the bell rang, until everybody had gone to their next classes and the last slapping footsteps had faded and the halls were empty. She would go find Peter. Maybe he would help her get home, let her take his bike or something, so she wouldn't have to wait for the bus after school and she wouldn't have to see anybody else. Shoulders slumped, she walked up the stairs to the second floor, where most of the eleventh-grade classes were, and peered in the little window in each classroom door. There were four in all, and she couldn't see Peter in any of them.

At the landing by the stairs, she looked out the window for a while, over the baseball diamond and the football field and then the other way, out over the empty fields that were supposed to be farmland but were just sitting there empty now. There, by the annex, she saw someone. Maybe Peter was hanging out there with some of his burn-out friends. She scooted down the stairs and out the door by the gym, across the bare stretch of asphalt to where she could see around the corner of the little building. She hesitated, didn't really want to interact with anybody back there except Peter.

Virginia stepped around the corner. Peter wasn't there. The only one there was Buddy, sitting on the poured-cement steps up to the building. He had a note-book open in his lap, and in his hand a pen he was alternately chewing on and writing with. When he wrote, his left hand curled over the top of the page and then down, and he got a look of concentration on his face, like someone walking a tightrope. It was a few seconds before he noticed her.

"Whatta you want?" he asked.

"You seen my brother?"

Buddy scanned the landscape around them, sarcastically. "You see him anywhere?"

"No," she said, looking down at the ground.

"Whattaya want him for anyway?" Buddy asked. He turned back to his notebook, but now gave up on the essay he'd been struggling to produce, word by recalcitrant, grueling word, and started drawing the logo from the cover of an AC/DC album. He'd have to start over again, and copy out what he'd written, but it was only a few lines. He concentrated just as much, maybe more, on the picture, and the tip of his tongue poked out of his lips as he brought his mind to bear on the page.

"None of your business," she said, but she didn't make any motion toward leaving. Buddy was being mean to her, but she knew he wasn't being any meaner to her than he would be to anybody else. It made her feel comfortable. "Do you know where he is?"

"Nah," Buddy said. "You want a beer?" He reached into the rumpled paper grocery sack sitting in the dirt, held out a Rolling Rock.

"No, thanks," Virginia said.

"Hey," she heard from behind her, and Weaver walked past her, looking her over curiously as he passed, then reaching out to grab the beer that Buddy was holding out. He opened it and turned toward her. "You're Peter's little sis, right?"

"Um-hm."

"How's that deal with Trish's sister working out for you?"

"It's not," Virginia said and thought of the horror she'd have to face the next time she had to walk through the halls to a class. But how did he know . . . it didn't make sense. "What do you mean?"

"You know, Peter paying her to hang out with you and all."

Virginia's eyes widened as her heart fell, and the one was a fairly accurate physical gauge of the other. Everything she saw just then—Buddy sitting, scribbling something in his notebook; Weaver standing next to him, beer bottle now upturned as he drained it; the rusty gray bulk of the annex, the fields that surrounded them, everything bleached out in the midday sun—was frozen in her mind like a snapshot, as if her brain had chosen to take a picture at just that instant, before moving on, a souvenir of that moment of her life.

Anybody could have told from the surprise on her face that she hadn't known, that this was news to her. Even Weaver and Buddy could see that.

"Yeah, and everybody says I'm the asshole," Buddy said, shaking his head over his picture.

"Fuck you," Weaver replied.

"Three bucks for the beer," Buddy said.

"Again, fuck you. The six-pack only cost you eight."

"Don't matter what I paid. It was my beer, you drank it, and the price is three bucks. Pay up," Buddy said.

"I'll owe you a beer," Weaver said.

"Don't need a beer," Buddy said, looking over at him. "Want my money for the one you drank."

Weaver finished his beer, then took the bottle by the neck, turned, and threw it high into the sky, to fall to the ground with a distant *thunk* in the field behind them. He turned back to Buddy.

"What beer?" he said, and held his hands out like a magician demonstrating they were empty. And then, "Hey, where you going?" he called when he noticed Virginia walking away, a vague feeling of guilt prompted by the dejected slump of her shoulders. "You want me to tell your brother anything?"

Virginia didn't answer, and Weaver and Buddy promptly lost interest, and returned to squabbling about who owed whom what, not stopping until Weaver pulled out some reefer for them to smoke before sixth-period math.

In the woods, Phil woke up midafternoon, and the first thing he knew was pain. Searing hot pain, radiating from his chest, but so much of it that it felt like it filled up every part of his body. He opened his eyes, and squinted away from the sun shining down on him, making his skin hot and clammy.

He lifted his head, looked around. The lake was still now, and there was nothing to show that anybody else had been here with him. He sat up, and the additional pain made him scream out, and he bit his tongue trying to silence himself.

When he looked down, he saw that his chest was a patchwork of red and white, blood and flesh. Dozens of strips of his skin had been torn from him, and while he lay there unconscious, bits of leaves, little twigs, struggling insects that had yet to die had been blown onto his raw flesh by the wind, and were now stuck in his coagulating blood.

Phil swiped at himself once, but the pain of contact was worse than the awful feeling of having bugs and bits of compost clinging to him. Tentatively, the pain flaring when he was forced to bend his torso, he got to his feet. Stopping to lean against trees on the way, over the course of the afternoon he slowly made his way back to his house and let himself in.

Upstairs, he locked himself in his bedroom and collapsed onto his bed. He knew what he had to do. He had to sacrifice his daughter and do it slowly, subject her to worse than he had himself experienced, to show God that he understood his Creation not just intellectually, not just in theory, but in his actions. Then he would be permitted to write his book.

But first, he had to sleep and heal.

That was his plan, anyway, which had not accounted for the infection that spread from his open flesh into his blood, and the fever that seized him later that night.

Phil lay in his bed, sometimes thrashing, sweat drenching the sheets bunched around him. Pus and blood oozed from his wounds, but not enough to clear the many tiny eggs of the flies that his sores had attracted while he lay unconscious in the hot sun beside the muck at the edge of the lake.

When he finally came out of his fever, he would find that the pain had lessened considerably, but on the whole he might have preferred it to the feel of maggots squirming in his flesh.

17

Who else knew? Did everyone know? It was bad enough that Amanda and them didn't want to be her friends anymore, it broke her heart, really, but she hadn't even suspected that it could turn out that she was even more pathetic than that. Her brother, who'd been nice to her the last few days, who wasn't acting like he thought he was so cool, like he had been lately, or like a hopeless geek, like he'd always been before: he did this.

Had he been off laughing at her with his friends all along?

She was already a mile down High Street from the school, shaking her head slightly back and forth, an unconscious little moaning sound periodically escaping her, before she even realized that she had set off walking home. She'd left all her books and stuff in her locker, but there was no way she was turning around and going back to school. Maybe she was never going back to that school. She could run away, hitchhike back to New York, maybe sneak into her old house. There was a basement there, and it was only used for storage. She could live there, and then get a job at one of those cool stores on St. Mark's Place in the East

Village. The kids in Seneca thought they were so much cooler than her, but they didn't even know what cool really was. Maybe they'd come to visit New York and see her, and then . . . she didn't know what.

But maybe when her mother heard she was missing, if she waited a while and stayed down in the basement, she'd be so glad to find her that she'd let her stay. She wouldn't have to even take care of her anymore; Virginia could take care of herself, with her job. And she wouldn't go back to school at all, just work and have a boyfriend, somebody cooler than anyone at Seneca High School. There were so many boys in bands in New York, she could have a boyfriend in a band, and then they'd come up to Seneca one weekend to play a concert at the high school, and they wouldn't even recognize her until she came out onstage when her boyfriend, the lead singer, said he wanted to introduce the woman he loved, and the inspiration for all his music, and they would kiss, and Amanda would be in the front and see her, and she'd tell Melanie, and then minutes later everyone in the audience would know. . . .

Virginia was thinking about how a boy in a band would probably think it was cool, the way she cut herself, but she wouldn't tell him right away, though, and then she realized how good it would feel, that what she really needed to feel better was to do it some more, and she was suddenly aware of anxiety so present and physical that it felt like someone had blown up a balloon inside of her and it was pushing out in all directions, and if she didn't cut herself soon, she was going to explode. If she cut herself she could bleed off some air, and take a breath, because no matter how much air she sucked in now, she couldn't get it all the way into her lungs. She stopped at the side of the road, closed her eyes, tried to let her heart slow down.

Shallow breaths, that worked. There. She felt a little better when she opened her eyes again . . . but how could it be getting dark already? How long had she been walking?

"Oh," she said out loud, when she realized where she was, where she had been headed all along. Of course. She looked around, up and down Route 9. There were no cars anywhere. She turned off the road and into the woods, looking for Walker. He'd been right all along. Amanda wasn't her friend. She never was. Walker had said she shouldn't trust her. She should have listened to him.

Virginia was not surprised as what had been a clear and sunshiny day turned suddenly foggy, or that late afternoon was morphed into night, wouldn't have been even if she'd noticed it. What Virginia was experiencing wasn't a dimming of light, or a fog materializing, obscuring the spaces between herself and everything around her—tree trunks thick and rough, prickly bushes brushing her knees, spotted with glossy black berries, each a hard bitter dose of poison, grasses dying and yellow under branches fallen to the ground— though somebody else might have. To Virginia, it was more like something vital was draining from the world. Outlines dissolved, distinctions between one thing and another faded. She felt herself growing less specific; and the more she felt like just a shape moving in the gray mist, the less the accumulated details of her life seemed particularly hers, the less pressure she felt weighing down on her. Those things, they were just things that happened to somebody, and it was somebody she did not care about that much at all.

Ahead, that's where she'd find him. She saw the fire glowing, the figures around it. She walked toward them.

1971

Despite the fire blazing only a few feet away, Ellen shivered as the fog crept in, moist and cold against her skin, tightening the circle it formed around them. They'd been sitting for—she didn't have any idea, she realized. It might have been minutes, it could have been hours. She'd been somewhere else in her head; she'd jumped ahead to after they'd done whatever they were doing, followed wherever Mike was leading, and things had changed, the world was getting better, and they were all celebrating. The war was over, and Mike was gone.

But he was still there, across the fire from her, eyes closed and face serene, like a mystic.

Behind him, she saw a shadow take form in the nebulous gray haze, growing darker and more solid. Her eyes slid back to Mike's face, and she jerked, startled, when she saw his eyes were now open and he was looking at her.

"Say hello to Virginia," he said, and from behind him a young girl stumbled into their circle.

Everybody turned to look at the girl, a chunky teen in odd clothes, eyes downcast as she turned to face Mike.

"Okay," she said, "I'm here. I give up. You can do what you wanted to do to me."

"Not me, Virginia." He stood up. "All of us." He waved his hand around at the five hippies sitting around the circle, all of them staring up at her, looking stoned and stupid. "You're very important to us. You should know that. You will be the thing that holds us together; the thing that will make us strong enough to do great things, Virginia. And after that, I have a special assignment for you, so you can get even with everybody."

"Whatever," Virginia said. "What should I do?"

"Nothing any of the rest of us won't be doing too, darlin'. I just need you to start by taking off your clothes."

She hesitated, suddenly shy, stood there unmoving.

"People," Mike said, "help her."

The hippies stood up and started undressing her, the men a bit more eagerly than the women.

Peter didn't hear about what happened in the cafeteria, or even that Virginia's plans for Saturday night had gone awry, until last-period study hall, when he sat next to Trish. After school, they went to the buses together looking for Virginia, because Peter was more than a little worried about how she was going to react to being socially humiliated and cast out again, but she wasn't on her bus. After asking around, they found out she hadn't been in her last couple of classes, either.

Trish was supposed to be home because Sarah wasn't ever supposed to be in the house by herself, so she tried not to leave her there alone more than a couple of hours, and she always got home before her mother did. By the time they had finished making out good-bye against a wall outside, everybody was mostly gone. After she left, Peter spotted Buddy's car in the parking lot and found him sitting there with the door open, one foot out on the ground. When Peter came up behind him, Buddy had a pen in his hand, an open notebook on his lap. Peter said, "Hey," and Buddy quickly shut his notebook and tossed it into the passenger-side foot well, where it joined a variety of trash.

"'Sup?" Buddy said.

"Ah, I was looking around for my sister. She wasn't on her bus."

"She was looking for you too."

"She was?"

"Yeah, before."

"Before when?"

"Before, I don't know, couple periods ago. After lunch. I think she might have cut and left."

"Dude, you think you could give me a ride? See if she's walking home? She can be a pain in the ass, but I should see if I can find her."

"I don't mind. She's okay," Buddy said, surprising Peter. "You'll have to give me a couple of bucks for gas, though," he added, back to form.

Peter wanted to roll his eyes at that, but restrained himself.

"Sure," he said, and walked around to the other side of the car and got in. Buddy started up the car and pushed an Iron Maiden cassette he'd snatched up off the floor by Peter's feet into the cassette player as he turned out of the parking lot.

"You like Iron Maiden?"

"They're okay," Peter said, although he didn't think of them as "serious" rock and roll. "I like Zeppelin way better."

"I got *Two* down there somewheres," Buddy said, gesturing toward Peter's feet. Peter started stirring the mess, pulling out cassettes, looking for it, while keeping an eye out the window.

Coming up High Street, slowly heading their way, was an old but nearly spotless Cadillac driven by an elderly woman, her hair stiffly shaped and freshly blued; she looked like she might be on her way home from a weekly hairdressing appointment, the high point of her week, next to church. She drove slowly and cautiously, both hands on the steering wheel, craning and straining up and forward over it, hoping to bring the road a foot closer and clearer. Buddy waited until he was right next to her and then he hit the horn.

The Caddy's windows were closed, so they couldn't tell what sound she made, but she threw her hands up into the air and her mouth was wide open, and Peter heard the sound of glass breaking as she swerved into a parked car and smashed her headlight.

"Dja see that?" Buddy barked, and started laughing hard. He hit the gas to race away, and it was a minute before he stopped chuckling to himself and noticed that Peter had picked up his notebook and had it open in his lap.

"Hey!" He reached over with his right hand and grabbed it. "Fuck you think you're doing?"

"Nothing. Sorry," Peter said and went back to digging around for the tape. He found it this time on the first try, and swapped cassettes.

"Ah, fuck it," Buddy said, and tossed the notebook back to Peter, who was leaning out the window, looking. "Here. Maybe you can help me. You're supposed to be smart, right?"

"I guess," Peter said, and opened the notebook up to what Buddy had been writing when he'd interrupted him; he looked back and forth, out the window and back to the notebook, to make sure he didn't miss Virginia on the way.

"I gotta pass everything this year. I got left back once, and my stepfucker, I mean stepfather, says he's gonna make me enlist if I fuck up again." Buddy reached over and turned the volume way up, and the opening guitar riff of "Whole Lotta Love" tore from the speakers, hacking a path through the car's interior for Robert Plant's vocals to follow.

"Oh, shit. Really? That sucks," Peter said, and meant it. He couldn't imagine getting into a situation like that.

People in the 1800s were cruel to animals, Peter read. *They shot horses all the time, and drowned cats in sacks. Even though they went to church and believed in God more, we're better than they are, because we don't hurt animals for no good reason. Now there are cruelty laws to not hurt animals, but you can't go to jail.*

"I think you can, actually," Peter said, now back to scanning Route 9. "Go to jail for hurting an animal, I mean. I saw this article, somebody posted a link on MySpace once. A guy left his dog in a cage for like a week, and it starved to death. The guy got sentenced to, I forget, a year or something."

"The fucking bastard," Buddy said, looking grim and shaking his head. "They should give him, like, the firing squad. But that's good. Right? I can add that because it's part of the subject. Can you write that in?"

"I don't know, dude," Peter said. "Maybe I could go over it with you after you write the whole thing."

Buddy turned and looked at him. "That is the whole thing, man. Can you make it longer?"

"Hey, this is my house coming up," Peter said, which served the secondary purpose of changing the subject.

"Guess we didn't find her," Buddy said, pulling over to the shoulder. "Maybe she's already home."

"Yeah, I guess. Well, okay, thanks for the ride."

Buddy held out his hand, flat, palm up. Peter started to slap him good-bye but realized what he wanted, so he took his wallet from his back pocket and extracted two of the six singles that were in there, and passed them over.

"Thanks," Buddy said, slipping the money into his pocket.

"See you tomorrow," Peter said and got out.

"Not if I see you first."

Buddy spun the car from a standstill into an over-powered, dirt-flinging U-turn, and roared off back toward town.

"Virginia?" Peter called out as he entered the house. He checked the first floor and then went upstairs; she wasn't in her room, either, but he noticed it was cleaner than he remembered, and it smelled appreciably better, too. Or maybe it was just the contrast, because the rest of the house was starting to look a bit dusty and disordered.

Downstairs again, he looked out the window into the backyard, and though she wasn't there, he started to feel a growing anxiety tied to a suspicion of where she was. By the time he was outside and headed toward the woods, his suspicion felt more like a certainty, and he walked faster and faster until he broke into a run, shouting "Ginny! Virginia!" all the time.

Racing between trees, trying to remember the way, he looked ahead for the clearing he'd been to; in the dimming light of late afternoon, it was hard to tell one stretch of trees from another. But there, on his left, he saw a flash of something pale on the ground in the distance. He headed that way, breaking through the trees into open ground, but the closer he got to the figure he saw lying in the grass, close to where the fire had been, the more slowly he approached.

"Vrginia?" he said hesitantly, from a few feet away. "Ginny?"

And then he was right there, and there was no mistaking his sister, but the shock of seeing her laid out naked like that prevented him from taking her in as a whole. His brain just threw up its hands for a moment, went off-line, and let him stand there looking at his naked sister as a shape, an assortment of parts, a white form against the dying autumn grass.

When he came back, when he felt himself again in a scene in which he was a participant, what he was focused on was a stick poking out from under her back. It must hurt, he thought, and knelt to pull it out from under her. He put his hand on her hip to shift her weight off of it, and the feel of her skin, cool and soft, made it very real. Her breasts shifted when he moved her, like fluid, almost, and he couldn't help but look, and then his eyes ran down to the thatch of hair growing from between her legs. He'd never imagined . . . but that was it, he didn't imagine her like this at all and it embarrassed him and fascinated and repelled him at the same time. Moreover, the tracery of cuts and scars that covered her body, her belly, her breasts, like cracks running everywhere through shattered glass, the fresh cuts a filigree of bloodwork up and down her arms and legs, sparked to life a flutter of panic in him. He wanted to help her, bandage her, get clothes on her, but then he wondered how she could even wear clothes against skin that savaged; every touch must hurt.

"Ginny!" he said, and she opened her eyes, looked at him, but didn't move or say anything.

"Are you okay?" he asked, though the answer was obvious, the question absurd. She was not okay. She was very far from okay, and there was nobody else around to help make it okay. "Come on, we have to get you home. To a doctor. We have to—"

She stood up abruptly and Peter fell back to the ground from where he'd been crouching over her, jerking back without thinking, to avoid making contact with her naked skin. "There's nothing wrong with me," she said, and started walking away. "Everybody always thinks there's something wrong with me, but there isn't."

Peter hurried after.

"But . . . what are you doing out here? Where are your clothes?"

"Like you're so perfect," Virginia said.

"What?"

"Shut up."

"Virginia, you're freaking me out, okay? What the fuck were you doing out here? Did you see . . . that guy?"

It had gotten darker, a twilight lowering over the woods, and when Virginia stopped and turned to face him, her pale white skin stood out from everything around it, the marks all over her now indistinct; she looked like a wraith, and an adult woman. There was nothing about her that seemed like his little sister.

"Peter, you have your friends and I have mine, and you know what? Mine are much cooler than yours, so you don't have to pay anybody to hang out with me. I'm not some charity case, and people are going to be sorry that they treated me like one." She spun around and continued back toward the house, Peter right behind. Branches and brambles swiped at his sister's bare skin as he followed her.

"Ginny, that was just, it was like a joke, the money. There was nothing wrong with it, it was like a play-date, or a blind date or something. We knew you'd like each other, and we were right, right? Listen, at least take my shirt, okay?" He'd unbuttoned it and held it out to her.

She grabbed it from him and threw it up above them, to hang from a low branch of the nearest tree.

"I like how it looks up there."

"Virginia, what's wrong with you?"

"Nothing's wrong with me. I'm just fine. And I know some guys who agree with me. They think I'm hot. They like me."

"What guys are you talking about?"

"Guys. Cool grown-up guys. Not kids."

"Did somebody do something to you in the woods? Did somebody . . ."

"You can't even say it, can you? You can't say 'fuck.' You're probably not even doing it with your precious Trish, are you? Ha. That's right, I did it. And not just with one guy, either."

Peter didn't know what to say, just continued after her out of the woods and across the backyard to the house. Virginia stopped with her hand on the back door.

"I know, Peter. Why don't you come to my room later, and you can fuck me, too. I'll show you what to do. Then you'll know what to do with Trish." She stepped toward him, and he took a step back. She laughed, and reached out and grabbed his hand and pulled it against her breast. "You want to, don't you?"

Peter pulled his hand back as if burned. "I don't," he

said, weakly, feeling guilty of the charge just by being accused of it.

"Right. I can tell how much you don't want to, loser." She smiled and turned and went into the house.

The phone ringing in the kitchen was what yanked Peter out of his momentary overload; he rushed through to the kitchen to answer.

"Peter?"

"Mom. Hi."

"Is something wrong? You sound upset."

"Mom, I . . . " *I what? I was just feeling up my sister when you called? Or no, this is better, how about, your daughter has apparently been having sex with strange men in the woods? Who might or might not be ghosts?* " . . . I, no, I'm not upset. It's just Virginia's acting . . . all weird again."

"But you told me she was getting back to her old self, and she was so excited when she told me about her new friends!"

"She was, it's just that, I don't know—"

"I'm 'she,' right?" From behind him. He turned and saw his sister standing in the doorway, dressed now. "I can talk to Mom for myself, thanks." She crossed the room and took the phone from him.

"Hi, Mom. I don't know what Peter was saying, but you don't have to worry about me. I'm doing really well, and I have friends here now."

"That's good, honey, I'm glad to hear it. Is Peter okay?"

She looked over at her brother.

"Well, he's retarded, but you and Dad are used to that, right?"

In New York, Julia laughed, relieved. That was the Ginny she knew.

"Honey, I called to say I can't come up this weekend. I'm sorry. The project I'm—"

"That's okay, Mom. We understand."

"I really miss you, though."

"I know, Mom." She looked over at Peter. "Peter does, too, so don't worry."

"Tell your dad for me, okay?"

"Okay. Bye."

The smile that had been on Virginia's face as she spoke to her mother disappeared, and she handed the phone to Peter before she left the room.

"Mom?" Peter said to the dial tone, before he hung up.

Loud banging woke Peter up. Before he knew what was going on, he glanced at the alarm clock: 3:30. "What?" he said, aiming it at the door. The banging continued. Peter hauled himself out of bed and walked to the door to his room, yanked it open to find nobody there, and realized that wasn't where the sounds were coming from. He followed his ears this time instead of his assumptions, and it led him to the door to the veranda on the back of the house. His sister's room was at the other end.

"Virginia, what do you want? That's you, right?"

"Who else would it be? Let me in."

"Why? What are you doing out there?"

"Just let me in, okay? It's cold out here."

"Tell me what you're doing first." Peter was nervous, and it sounded in his voice. "Okay? Then I'll open the door."

"What do you think I'm doing?" she said in a suddenly honeyed tone. "I'm coming to visit my big brother."

"Do you have any clothes on, Ginny? Because if

you don't, go back to your room and put something on if you want to come in."

"Peter, I'm not a slut. I have clothes on."

Peter relaxed about fifteen percent and opened the door.

She pushed past him, and sat herself down on the bed. It was dark, but he could still see her. She didn't have any clothes on.

"I lied. But fess up, you don't really mind, do you? Look at me, am I really so horrible to look at?"

Peter looked at the whole situation, and there was nothing about it that wasn't horrible. He'd somehow fucked up helping his sister out socially, and that had somehow, he was sure, led to her doing some guys in the woods, and that had somehow turned her into some kind of . . . he didn't even know what. The phrase that came to his mind, one he'd encountered in a book at some point, was "brazen hussy." That's what she was acting like. And that had led to her forcing her way into his room, naked, in the middle of the night, and he did not want to think about what she had in mind.

But he also *looked* at her, in the moonlight filling the room, and as much as his eyes shied away, she wasn't bad to look at. In shades of gray, he couldn't see the cuts and scars at all. She wasn't the boy-slim girl she'd been, and she wasn't even the blobby fat girl she'd turned into. Her body had matured, reconfigured some, and leaning back on the bed, heavy breasts thrust forward, her legs not completely together, she had the body of a promising woman, and it wasn't horrible to look at; in fact, he was having a hard time not looking. He'd gotten Trish's shirt off a couple of times now, and he couldn't think of anything he'd rather see than her, but he'd never seen a girl completely naked, and not a girl with a woman's full body like Virginia's.

He felt a movement in his boxers and looked away, horrified.

"Peter, Walker said we should do it."

"Okay, that's it!" he said, and grabbed up the blanket from his bed and wrapped it around her.

"Stop," she yelped.

He pulled her up, covered now, and started pushing her toward the veranda door.

"*Pe*ter! Stop it! Don't be a jerk!" She swung out at him, but he grabbed her arm and stopped her.

"You're going back to your room, and you're never going to come in here like that again."

She fought him, but he was stronger, and he dragged and pushed her back to her open door, and in.

She stood there, poised to fight back, and then shrugged off the blanket and threw it at him. He caught it, and it hung down to the floor. "You're just too scared to do it," she said.

"Virginia, you jerk. Brother and sister, remember? You know how there's a list of things we don't do together and the *only thing on it is have sex*?" He slammed the door shut, feeling a great relief to have her naked self on the other side of it.

"But, come on, you are scared, right?"

Peter almost fell over his own feet, tangled in the blanket, turning to face the voice behind him.

Leaning back against the railing was the craggy-faced, long-haired guy. Walker. Okay, the ghost.

"Get out of here. Keep away from my sister. Leave us alone."

"Peter, Peter, Peter. I am so disappointed in you. A healthy young boy like yourself, first I send you a delicious little visitor every night, don't ask anything from you in return, and when I introduce you, you reject her.

"And now, look at you, your sister is so ripe and ready, the girl is just dripping with fuck-me juice, and I've got her throwing herself at you. You know how many boys fantasize about this? And, Peter, no fruit is ever sweeter than forbidden fruit. Believe me, this is the thing I know best. Now stop being a frightened little boy and get back in there. Enjoy yourself. Show little Ginny what you can do."

Peter would probably not have become so insensibly angry if the words he was hearing weren't stirring something inside himself, or perhaps it was purely protectiveness, a rage of protectiveness, but whatever it was, the anger released itself in forward motion and he hurled himself at the smirking long-haired figure on the railing, who was not, of course, there by the time Peter would have made contact. Peter managed to stop himself before he went over, but it was close.

Peter looked around. He was gone.

Peter tried his sister's door, but she'd locked it. He picked up his blanket, and went back to his room, where he locked his own door before he went back to bed. He didn't start to fall asleep until daylight.

18

The next day, Peter rode the bus to school with his sister and kept a wary eye on her. She ignored him; she seemed self-contained, somehow. At school as she disappeared from sight in the hallway, she wasn't interacting with anybody, but she wasn't withdrawing into herself, either. And in her footsteps, it seemed to him, there was just a hint of an unfamiliar anger about her, too.

At lunchtime, Peter hooked up with Trish behind the annex. Taking her by the hand, he led her away from the others, around the corner. She came willingly, but she resisted when he leaned in to kiss her, turning her head away and pushing him back.

"Peter, I have to tell you something. Amanda told me some stuff, about your dad."

"Huh?"

"She didn't tell me before, why they didn't pick up your sister," she said, hesitantly. She clearly didn't like telling him this. "It was your father. He scared them all. She said that he, like, wasn't wearing anything, and he was, like, showing them his, y'know, his dick." She couldn't even look at him as she finished.

If Peter had taken a moment to think before he spoke, things might have gone differently, but the feel-

ings that flooded his body upon hearing Trish's words
precluded any thought. It was all part of the same
thing, what she'd just said, his sister's behavior last
night, and his response—did he want to do it with his
sister? He saw her naked body in his memory and in
that second he wanted to disappear from the earth—
and the sticky, oozing couplings of the nighttime visits, and it all filled him with shame and self-disgust,
and he couldn't live with it; he couldn't bear the feeling, or the suspicion that Trish could see through him
to the way he was at that moment seeing himself.

And so he reverted to the default tactic of men and
teens when confronted with the damning: deny, deny,
deny.

"What? No way. My father wouldn't do that.
Amanda must be lying." But he knew that it was true
before the words had left his mouth.

Trish hadn't been accusing Peter of anything, didn't
hold him even a tiny bit responsible. At sixteen, her
first circle of connection was to Peter and her friends,
not her family, and she just assumed the same thing
was true of him, that it was us against them, not family against family, and so she hadn't associated Phil's
behavior with his son in any more than a circumstan-
tial way. She was telling him out of an impulse toward
commiseration, out of sympathy for Peter, for having
such a fucked-up father. Her openness to Peter's situation, the sympathy and tenderness she felt toward him
at that moment, made his response feel almost violent.

"Peter! She wouldn't do that. Why would she make
that up?"

"I don't know. She's a kid. Who knows why kids do
anything?"

Peter felt himself falling forward; he'd chosen the

wrong response, taken this thing in the wrong direction, and he knew he was wrong, and his brain was trying to figure out how to reverse, back up to where it
started, but it was getting worse. It was almost a relief
when Buddy came around the corner, drawn by their
raised voices, and said to Crisp, who followed, "Isn't
that sweet? They're having their first fight."

"Shut up, Buddy, okay?" Trish said, and walked
away from the bunch of them.

No, wait, I'm sorry, I'm wrong, come back, Peter
wanted to shout after her, but in front of the other guys
the words couldn't make it past the conceptual stage.

"Chicks," Crisp said, shaking his head.

"Yeah, right?" Buddy said.

Peter ignored them, started off after Trish.

"Dude, fuck her," Buddy said. "She'll get over it,
whatever you were fighting about. Come with us,
we're cutting the rest of the day."

"Dude, I got a lot going on," Peter said. "I don't
know."

"Okay. I guess we'll just have to do all the crank
ourselves."

"What?" Peter said, the chaotic track that had been
loudly playing in his head skipping to this sharp, clear
single note, as if someone had hit fast-forward.

"Crisp went by his father's place last night," Buddy
said. "Give 'm some," he directed Crisp. "Poor guy's
got pussy problems. Needs a treat."

Crisp reached into his pocket and pulled out a bullet, a small, plastic, projectile-shaped powdered-drug
delivery system, and held it out to Peter, who did not
hesitate. He snatched it up from Crisp's hand, but
stopped, realizing he didn't know how to work the
thing.

"Here," Buddy said, and took it from him. He showed him how to twist it while turning it over to load a charge. He held it up to his nose and snorted, hard. "See," he said, after sniffing, and passed it back to Peter.

Peter mimicked the motion and took a hit, and immediately felt his head clearing. "Ahh." He held the bullet out to Crisp.

"Take another," Crisp said. "You got catching up to do."

"Dude," Peter said, realizing that so much was just out of his hands as he shook another hit into place, "where we going?"

Nowhere, it turned out, they went nowhere in particular, drove from one regular hangout to another until it was dark, sharing two sixes and a pack of Marlboros among them to accompany the crank. But the speed in their blood made it feel like they were going somewhere, doing something, having an adventure. It felt like something of significance might happen at any moment, and they should move faster and faster to get there sooner, and the more he felt that way, the more distance Peter felt from the tarry morass of issues that awaited him when he stopped. Really, though, he was just taking the long way home.

Or would have been, anyway, if they hadn't seen Weaver drive off the college campus in his mother's Toyota and head off toward Route 14 down the far side of the lake. He pulled out right in front of them, ignoring a stop sign to do so, and they followed him, honking, but instead of pulling over and stopping so they could confer, he continued driving, swerving dangerously across the two-way road.

A few miles past town, Buddy managed to pull up next to him, because Weaver was driving at not much more than a walking pace. Weaver looked over and recognized them with a goofy and very un-Weaver-like grin. Through the open window he told Crisp, riding shotgun, to tell Buddy to pull over.

"I can hear you fine, Weaver. You gotta pull over first."

"Oh, yeah," he said, but instead of pulling onto the shoulder, he crept forward a few more yards and stopped the car in the middle of the road.

Buddy shook his head, and pulled up past him and swung over onto the shoulder. The three of them were out of the car and over to Weaver in seconds. Crisp leaned in the driver-side window.

"Must be something good," he said to Weaver, who gripped the steering wheel tightly and peered ahead of him down the road, not completely sure he wasn't moving.

"Oh, yeah," Weaver said, "it's good. It's kick-ass."

"Listen," Buddy said, pulling open the driver's-side door, "why don't you slide over? Lemme park ya, and then we can compare drugs, okay?"

When they'd gotten Weaver safely off the road, they all climbed into his car. Crisp and Buddy tossed away their cigarettes first; there was no smoking in the Toyota.

"Okay, so what you got?" Crisp said, handing the bullet of crystal meth to Weaver.

Weaver turned it over in his hands, looked at it. "What I got . . . I scored some acid, is what I got. Blotter." He took a hit of the crank.

"Cool," Crisp said.

"How much?" Buddy asked.

"Uh . . . " Weaver had forgotten what he'd paid. He'd forgotten the transaction completely. "I don't know. Nothing. Pay me nothing. You can pay me double nothing, Crisp. And you can just owe me," he said to Buddy.

Weaver had the stuff in his wallet. He took it out and passed a hit to each of them. Peter looked at the little square of thick matte paper. Printed on it was a tiny line drawing of Kenny, from *South Park*, in his snorkel jacket.

Crisp popped his into his mouth and announced, "Oh my god, I ate Kenny." Buddy ate his, too.

"I don't know," Peter said, holding the thing between his fingers and looking at it. He'd never even seen acid before, and even though he'd laughed at the scare stories about LSD he'd grown up with, he always assumed there was some truth to them.

"Ah, don't be such a pussy. It's just like doing a lot of pot and crank, but you see cool shit," Buddy said, helping himself to another hit of crank as a chaser.

"Yeah," Weaver said. "It's intense. Acid is like . . . it's the Cadillac Escalade of drugs."

"Yeah?" Crisp said. "Then what's pot? Like, the F-150 of drugs?"

"Could be," Weaver said. "And crank is the Corvette. No, the Jaguar of drugs."

"No, see," Buddy said, interrupting, "crank's like a muscle car. A Corvette, that'd be some classy drug, like cocaine."

While the three boys demonstrated an ability to work with analogy that had been nowhere in evidence when they had taken their PSATs, Peter looked at the hit of blotter for a final time and then put it on his tongue.

*   *   *

Sitting in her room with Walker, fuming, hurt, tremendously unhappy, wanting to make somebody hurt as much as she did, wanting to make *everybody* hurt as much as she did, but more than that even, wanting to make herself numb, Virginia listened closely as he told her what he wanted her to do. She even took notes when it got more complicated.

Where to find the grenades in the basement, what plastic explosive was, how to place it and how to set a fuse. How to sneak into school at night after dark, when it was all locked up, and where to put the stuff to kill the most kids.

It was complicated, but it was what they both wanted, and she was going to get it right.

1971

Nobody had said anything when Ellen left, but Mike had watched her walk away. Even Alex had remained focused on the girl who had walked into their circle from out of the fog, Keith at that moment on top of her, stripped naked, too. All the men had taken their place on top of her in turn, while the women had marked her, slicing into her skin in patterns that ran down her arms and legs like blood lace, all of it at Mike's direction.

It was too much for Ellen; she couldn't go along with it, and she couldn't stop them, either, so finally the only thing she could do was leave. By walking away from that scene she was walking away from Alex, she knew it and it broke her heart, but if Alex could be involved in this, she wasn't who she thought she was. She knew that in leaving she was giving Alex to Mike, and that before the night was over he would have her in ways that made her shudder to think about.

Ellen stumbled through the fog back to the house, still lightly tripping, afraid she was lost more than once, but she got there, and when she did, she didn't go inside, just got in her car and drove back to her dorm. It felt like she hadn't left the house, these people, for weeks, like she hadn't slept in all that time. As she drove, trees loomed up and over from the side of the road, reaching for her sometimes, and she'd hit the gas, taking quick panicked breaths until she could look in the rearview mirror and see that it had in fact been just a tree. The headlights seemed overly bright when she first got into the car, and later they seemed much too dim, but that, she realized, was because she was back in town, under streetlights, and she was shortly safely parked, in her bed alone in her dorm, wanting Alex but seeing her out in the woods taking a knife to that girl.

The girl never objected, though she made many sounds; it wasn't against her will. She gave her body to the men, and offered her skin up to the knife, but it still was too much for Ellen. Doing things to themselves, each other, that was one thing. But this . . . Ellen fell asleep with the scene playing over and over in her head, the look on the girl's face. At first, she was expressionless, resigned. By the time Keith had climbed on top of her, after Paul and Seth, though, she was smiling, but it was a smile that didn't seem to have anything to do with what was happening to her. Her body was pushed and pounded, and she was cut again and again, and the smile never changed. That smile . . . it scared her as much as anything she'd seen that night.

Ellen didn't see anybody from Oneida House on campus for the next few days, and when she called out

there, the phone rang and rang, until the day she called
and got a recording saying the phone had been discon-
nected. She almost drove out to see Alex then, and she
probably would have the next day if Alex hadn't
shown up herself.

Ellen was sitting outside Denton Hall, reading class
work under a tree, and didn't even hear Alex sit down.
She looked up from a book and there she was, sitting
next to her, looking out over the quad. She didn't look
good. Her hair hadn't been washed and the green
T-shirt she wore wasn't just dirty—like her jeans and
the hooded sweatshirt she wore over it, it was grimy.
There were lines on her face, healing cuts, shallow
ones, that made Ellen wince just to see them. They
made Alex look old.

After looking at her for a moment, Ellen looked
away over the quad, too.

"I wanted you to know I'm going to be okay. I won't
be seeing you again. We're going to disappear after.
Go underground."

"After what?"

Alex didn't answer. She shifted her body uncomfortably, and a foul smell came off her, the smell of an
unwashed body, but it wasn't the smell of the body that
Ellen had held and tasted and smelled. It was a more
offensive, more aggressive smell. A male smell.

"You're sleeping with him," Ellen said, a statement
of fact.

"It's not like that, El. I am, yeah. And not just him.
But it's for a reason. It's to make our bonds to each
other stronger than our own selfishness. We're a revolutionary cadre, and what I want isn't important. My
desires are the least important thing in the world.
Working together, achieving our goals, that's impor-

tant. We're making a better world. And if he says the way to do that is to fuck Seth, or him, or some stranger, then that's what I do." She hesitated, then said, less forcefully, "I'm glad you left before all that."

Ellen put off thinking about it. It wasn't something she could take in right now. "Do you have to go, Alex?" she asked, trying a last time. "My parents, they've got a summer house, we could—"

"Do me a favor?" Alex said. "Don't be any closer to the stage than this when the speeches start at commencement, okay?"

Ellen looked down at the other end of the quad, where they were already erecting the stage where all of the faculty and administration would sit, along with the guest speaker, Governor Rockefeller, as the seniors each made their way up to the podium to receive their diplomas.

It took her a second.

"But, *Alex*—"

"Promise me."

"But you can't do this, I know you, you—"

"I'm trusting you, Ellen. This is your part of it, okay? You wanted to be part of what I was doing, and your part is to promise me this one thing."

Ellen looked at Alex's face, and knew she couldn't move her.

"Yeah, okay."

Alex stood up, and Ellen did, too. Alex took her face in her hands and kissed her, and then she walked away.

19

Peter didn't go to school that next day, and probably wouldn't have even if he'd woken up before eleven. Since embracing the traditional teen values of his new crowd, he'd had a handful of drug and alcohol hangovers, but with a body so young and clean—like a water filter that hasn't yet had to contend with all that many impurities flowing through it—they had done nothing more than slow him down a little in the morning and leave him with a slight headache that went away after a cup of coffee and a shower.

The acid, though . . .

It felt as if the acid had picked him up and shook him, kicked him over a hill and dragged him back again. Or maybe it was the acid combined with the rest of the drugs he'd consumed last night. Whatever it was, he'd opened his eyes when the alarm went off at 7:30, didn't move a muscle, took inventory—his thoughts bobbing along his brain waves like flotsam on a turbulent sea; his body feeling muffled and immobilized, as if embedded in a cocoon of spiderweb cotton candy—and, realizing he could go back to sleep simply by closing his eyes again and sinking, he did.

When he woke later, he felt better, good, in fact,

energized. He jumped out of bed, stretched, and felt an ache in his back and shoulder muscles, and remembered climbing with Buddy and Weaver to the top of the water tower, pulling himself up the narrow ladder arm over arm, feeling like they were the Fellowship of the Ring or something, like they were on some great quest full of significance, until the three of them stood precariously on the narrow lip of a catwalk running all the way around the weather-beaten dome. From up there the lights of the town had seemed so bright and pretty, almost unworldly, and the landscape—lake and town and woods—was suddenly loose from where it belonged, it didn't have a context, and that's when it began to look like a model made of toy parts; when he pointed it out to the others, they thought so, too, and decided they weren't going to put up with it, living in somebody's toy landscape all this time, and they'd stay up there until it was real again, but they lost track of that completely when they'd decided to piss on Crisp, who lay, passed out, on the hood of Weaver's car, fifty feet below. They had all been sloppily unsuccessful due to the wind, and Weaver suggested they go down and drink more beer so they could try again, which struck them as brilliant, but they sort of lost track of their plans and never did climb back up.

They'd eventually made it home; or at least Peter had. For all he knew they might have eaten some more acid, and were out there tripping, still.

Altogether, Peter thought, a pretty good drug. In the end, he still preferred crystal meth, you could go about your life if you had to, but there was something to be said for variety. He'd probably do it again first chance he got.

He went downstairs to make some breakfast. He was starving, he realized.

It looked like there wasn't a clean dish in the kitchen, there were so many piled up in the sink: dishes, cups, forks and knives and spoons. The floor was a little gritty, and sticky in places, too, as he walked to the cabinet where the cereal was. He found a box of Special K about half full. He was out of luck on the milk; the two percent had just enough in the bottom of the carton to smell bad.

Peter ate his cereal dry out of the box while the coffee dripped, and then sorted through the dishes in the sink, stacking them to rinse and put into the dishwasher, but the dishwasher, it turned out, had to be emptied first, so he decided to put the whole thing off for later, or leave it for . . .

Peter hadn't seen Molly for a while, he realized. What was up with that? Eating cereal out of the box, he took a walk through the other rooms on the first floor of the house—all of them falling into greater or lesser disarray. The dining room table was stacked with papers, the living room badly needed a dusting, and there were shoes and things sticking out from under the couch.

Huh.

Nobody said anything about Molly taking time off. He'd have to ask his father what was going on later, that evening. In fact, he also had to ask his father to sign a note excusing him from school that day, which wasn't really something he was looking forward to. He stopped in front of the door to his father's study. Or maybe he didn't have to ask his father for a note. He opened the door and walked in.

The room was dark, the window facing the lake almost completely obscured by the low branches of a tree just outside the house. Surely he could forge his father's signature if he had something to copy; even if he'd never done it before, it was something other kids mastered in junior high. Peter turned on the light. It was an even bigger mess in here than in the rest of the house. Books all over the floor, papers scattered on top of them and underneath them. He could barely walk to the desk.

Peter and Virginia had been taught not to go into their father's workspace since they were little kids; it was one of the forbidden things. That didn't mean they never did so. Both together and alone, they had been unable to resist peeking into and exploring the place their father disappeared into, the room that claimed more of his attention than they'd ever received. What was in there that drew him? they couldn't help wondering. Whatever it was, they never spotted it. Their father's study turned out to be the most lifeless and boring space imaginable. His papers, his books, his journals, all of them concerned with things that couldn't be less interesting.

Still, it remained a forbidden space, and Peter felt like a little kid sneaking in there now. At his father's desk, Peter started sifting through papers, journals, manila folders, looking for anything with his father's signature on it, when he found himself staring at a very old newspaper, each page protected by a sealed plastic covering, a newspaper he recognized. It was the hard copy, the paper version, of the article his father had shown him online in his office, about Joseph Smith in Seneca. It was old and yellowed and crumbling at the edges.

What Peter hadn't seen online was the daguerreo-
type picture right below the article. Peter recognized
Joseph Smith, having seen dozens of depictions of him
before, and the paper identified the other two men as J.
Greene and G. Walker, but he didn't need to read the
names to recognize the long-haired man standing next
to Joseph Smith. It was the freak from the woods or his
twin brother.

Peter moved the paper aside and found a folder underneath, marked *Oneida House*. Inside he found pages
and pages of typescript, but on top was a computer
printout of an old-timey picture, but this one was a photograph, one of those formal Civil War–looking por-
traits. If Peter wasn't mistaken, it was shot against the
background of the lake, right outside in his backyard.
Two men, standing shoulder to shoulder in uncomfortable looking suits. Phil had circled one of them with a
red marker, and written *Noyes* next to his head. The
other man was identified as *Walker?* Peter recognized
him, too. His father was right. It was the same guy.

Under that was a real photograph, an old Polaroid
snapshot, and there was no question who it was. He sat
at a candlelit table, the periphery of the picture dark,
and he was looking right at the photographer. There
were two young women to his right, maybe a little
older than Peter, and a piece of a person past them. The
way they were dressed, he'd guess it was taken during
the sixties. The girl on the far right, with the dark hair,
she looked a little familiar, but Peter couldn't place
her. The blond girl next to Walker . . . it was the girl
from the woods. The honk of a horn outside made him
jerk, and he stepped back into a pile of books, knocking it over.

The car horn honked again, a long blare this time,

and Peter got out the front door in time to see Trish getting out of the driver's-side door of Buddy's car, in the middle of shouting.

". . . such an asshole, Buddy!"

"Hey," Buddy said, getting out of the shotgun seat, "fuck you. I let you drive and everything. Gimme a break."

"I don't care, Buddy," Trish said, and slammed the door.

"Hey, Peter!" Buddy shouted. "Trish wanted to drive out here to say she's sorry."

"I didn't say that!" she said, hands curling into small fists when she turned to him.

Peter walked down the porch steps.

"Hey," he said, feeling a little sheepish about how he had reacted to her yesterday.

Trish walked toward him. "I didn't come to apologize because—"

Peter cut her off. "No, that's okay, you don't have to, you didn't do anything wrong. I should apologize." He reached out and took her hand when she got to him. "I shouldn't have said that. You're . . . " He sighed, and had to start over before he could say it. "I know you're right about my dad. He's been acting really weird for a while."

"Aw," Buddy said, as he walked up to them, and reached out and rubbed both their heads, tousling their hair. They both reached up automatically to swat his hands away. "Look at you guys, all making up. I'm gonna cry." He walked past them and up the three steps in two long strides, and asked over his shoulder as he went in the front door, "Got any beer?" before continuing into the house.

"C'mon," Peter said, and they followed him in,

stopping behind him where he stood in the doorway to the kitchen.

"Y'know, Coulter, for some fancy professor's house, this place is pretty gross."

Trish squeezed Peter's hand. "It does smell a little," she said, apologetically.

"Ah, yeah, I know, things have been pretty fucked up around here. I think our housekeeper must have quit or something."

"Housekeeper?" Buddy said. "You got a butler, too?"

Peter ignored him, and went to pour himself a cup of the now-brewed coffee. "Want some?"

Trish took a cup, but Buddy passed, and finding the fridge devoid of beer, searched the kitchen until he found an unopened bottle of Scotch high up in the back of one of the cabinets.

"You mind?" he said, sitting down at the kitchen table with them.

"Help yourself. Good luck finding a clean glass, though."

"I look like I have a butler?" Buddy said, and cracked the seal and proceeded to drink from the bottle, a solid swig to start, then sipping at it after that. "So, what's up with your father?" he asked. "Your girlfriend was telling me on the way over. He got a thing for little girls?"

"No! Or, I don't know, maybe. Everybody's acting all fucked up here. My father, my sister, and . . ."

"And what?" Trish asked.

"And, god, this sounds so stupid, but, okay, I think this house . . . the woods, I don't know . . . something. I think Buddy was right."

Trish looked at him quizzically, not understanding.

"I think . . . I think there are ghosts here."

"Ha!" Buddy said, and slammed his hand down flat on the table, making Trish's coffee slop over. "I fucking *told you*!"

"Yeah, you did, and I think they've done something to my father and my sister."

"And not you?" Buddy asked.

Peter's face grew warm, and he could tell his cheeks were red, as he thought of his encounter in the woods, the late-night visits; they'd stopped, but still . . . . "They tried, I don't know, I've seen them a lot of times, but they leave me alone now. But Virginia's like another person all of a sudden, and my father, he barely talks anymore, and sometimes, the way he looks at my sister, it creeps me out."

"Oh, baby," Trish said, and put her hand to his face. "Why didn't you tell me? You should have said something."

"I don't know, I just couldn't. It was too . . . weird."

"So, what kinda ghosts?" Buddy asked. "I've heard things, but nobody ever says exactly."

"Well," Peter said, and pushed out the photograph he'd found, which he'd carried into the kitchen and laid on the table, "this guy for one."

Buddy pulled the picture toward him and examined it.

"Doesn't look like a ghost," Buddy said. "More like Jesus, or some hippie . . . .Who's this babe? Looks kind of familiar." He put his finger on the dark-haired girl to the left.

"Lemme see," Trish said, and snatched the picture out from under Buddy's hand.

"I know who that is," she said after a moment, and put the picture down on the table. She waited with a smile on her face, made them ask.

"Well?" Peter said.

"That's our history teacher. That's Ms. Bourne."

"No way!" Buddy said, and grabbed the picture back and stared at it again. "Nah, look at her, she's skinny, and really cute—"

Peter took the picture from him and looked again.

"Like fifty years ago, you dumb ass," Trish said to Buddy.

"Could be," Peter said. "I can sort of see it."

"I'm telling you, that's her."

"So what's she doing with your ghost?"

"I don't know," Peter said, "but I think I'm going to ask her."

They got back to the school around four, after most of the kids were gone. Peter had walked them out to the clearing in the woods, where they didn't see anybody, but found the still-hot embers of a dying fire, which was disconcerting enough. He told them as much as he could about what had been going on, and when he started getting a little freaked out and choked up talking about the way his sister was acting, even Buddy was sort of sympathetic, drawing him out with questions about what had happened and what exactly she'd said. He didn't know what had happened to Virginia in the woods, but from what she'd said and what he'd seen, it made him shudder every time he thought about it.

Ms. Bourne was in her classroom on the third floor, putting books into a shoulder bag, when Peter knocked on the open door.

"Oh, hi, kids. What can I do for you? I was just leaving. Is it something that can wait until tomorrow?"

"We'll just be a minute, Ms. Bourne. I have to show you something."

"Okay, what is it?" She hefted her bag up onto her shoulder as they walked toward her.

Trish held out the picture.

Ms. Bourne looked them each in the eyes questioningly before she took it. She held the picture up to look at it, and as soon as her eyes focused, it seemed, she let out a sound and half dropped, half flung the picture from her. Before they could move, she reached down to pick the picture up again, dropping her bag as she did so.

"Are you okay?" Peter asked, genuinely concerned.

She ignored him and stared at the picture, and tears formed in her eyes.

"That's you, right?" Trish said.

Ms. Bourne nodded her head, but didn't take her eyes off the picture. "I need to sit down," she said, and stepped back to her desk and pulled out the chair to sit.

Peter turned to Buddy, to ask him if he could go get some water for Ms. Bourne, but he wasn't there.

"Listen, though, Ms. Bourne. That guy, the guy in the picture, remember I asked you about ghosts? That guy, I see him at my house."

She looked up at him. "That's not possible," she said. "This was thirty-five years ago."

"Yeah, well, I can't help that," Peter said. "I keep seeing him. And some others. And I think he might have done stuff to my sister."

Their teacher held out the photo, pointed to the blond girl seated on the other side of Walker. "Her, too?"

"Uh, yeah," he said, looking away, his cheeks flushing. "I see her, too."

Ellen Bourne just sat at her desk, shaking her head. "It can't be Alex," she said. "No, it can't be."

                      *   *   *
1971

It was only a matter of time. Ellen was going to
narc. She knew it as soon as Alex walked away. She
wrestled with herself for days, weighing her loyalty to
Alex and her passing belief in the cause she'd heard
espoused against the lives of who knows how many innocent people, but she always knew that in the end she
couldn't let them go through with it. What took her so
long, really, was convincing herself that this was what
Alex really would have wanted, no matter what she
had said, that someday Alex would thank her, and it
would be okay.

They heard the day before, the day before the night
they were going to sneak onto campus like guerrillas
and plant the Semtex under the stage, wired to a timer
to go off at the height of the proceedings. They'd already been tripping nonstop for a couple of days by
then, though, so people might have wondered how
successful their foray would have been, might even
have suspected they would all have died in the process.

By the time word got back to them, Ellen had been
down at the state police building in Canandaigua for almost twenty-four hours, since she'd gone to campus se-
curity and told them what was up. They had made her
wait while they searched the stage and the buildings all
around, and they'd called the governor's people and can-
celed his trip, and called state police headquarters, who
sent two detectives to pick her up, and the cops called
in Rochester's one FBI agent, too. Agent Matthew
Scoresby had always known that when he finally got his

hands on one of these radicals, it would be on a campus, but he'd always figured on Cornell.

She thought she'd be done after she'd made sure nobody'd get hurt, but she realized after how naive that was. They weren't letting her go anywhere until she told them where to find everybody. So there she'd sat in a cell for an entire night and a day. The cops mostly treated her like somebody's daughter, but the FBI guy wasn't letting her go anywhere until she gave him names.

Once word got out that somebody had been planning to plant explosives at graduation, every student at Harcourt College assumed the plan had been hatched at Oneida House, and most of the faculty thought so, too. Somebody finally thought to call state police headquarters and mention that, and the state troopers were on their way out there when Agent Scoresby got word, so he brought Ellen with him in the back of his car to show him the way, hoping to get there before somebody else made all the arrests.

"Take another," Mike said, and passed around some more hits of acid.

He had to help Amy and Seth, hold it out and stick it in their mouths, they were so out of it by then, tripping for days, nights passing into days, staying awake only by adding black beauties, high-grade speed, to the mix every few hours. They were sitting on the floor of the living room now, all of them, the curtains drawn, each off in their own pocket universe, their own version of reality, realities that only coincided when brought together through the guidance of the solid, sober, rock-steady Mike.

Their informant, an associate professor of religion, having come and warned them they were about to be seriously busted, had left a while ago, but it was hard to say how long.

"Okay, people, are you all ready? It is time for us to disappear," Mike told them. "I'm going to need you to do what I tell you if we're going to slip away and get underground."

Five dazed, glazed sets of eyes stared up at him as he stood among them.

"We gonna blow something up now?" Seth asked.

"Nah, man," Mike said, and reached out to help him up. "That's over, not gonna happen. New plans. C'mon, everybody up, let's go. We have a boat to catch."

Alex stood up, a little more awareness in her eyes than anybody else's. "Boat? What do you mean?"

"You'll see, darlin'. Just trust me. Have faith in me. I've got it all taken care of."

He eventually got them all on their feet and out of the house, into the late evening outside and down to the pier. Docilely, they followed him out to the end of the pier, and one by one they stepped down into the rowboat, gently rocking in the water below. A cloud of tiny insects surrounded their heads instantly as they lowered themselves into their seats.

Mike stood above them, Seth and Paul and Keith and Amy, each of them focused on something: Amy on the water, dipping her hand in over the side of the boat, watching the droplets fall when she raised it up; Keith on Amy; Seth and Paul just looking up at Mike on the dock, the setting sun haloed behind his head.

Alex looked ahead of her, couldn't see the boat from where she stood, just Mike ushering her over the edge of the pier, and she started to freak a little. "C'mon," Mike said, and held out his hand to her.

"No," Alex said, and took a step back. "I don't want to."

"Why not, darlin'? You trust me, don't you?"

"Yeah."

"So, c'mon, get in. You're in the boat or out of it, and you gotta be in it to take this trip, Alex, darlin'. We can't do it without you."

Hesitantly, she stepped toward him; in her doubt she wasn't the determined feminist revolutionary she had styled herself for years now, she was what she was, a child, and she was doing what the grown-up told her to. She peered down over the side and saw her friends sitting safely in the boat.

"That's right, we're all going together." He held out his hand and she took it and he firmly led her to the edge of the pier, where she stepped down into the little boat with the others. Mike untied the rope that fastened it there and hopped in after her.

It was near an hour later and full dark before Mike stopped rowing, his cell of five traveling with him, caught up in the appearance of the slowly revealing stars, the sound of the oars splashing in the lake, the glitter of starlight on the rippled water their passing left behind. Keith and Amy were humming something together, their hands resting on each other's chests; they hummed to the rhythm of their heartbeats. Seth and Paul were living in a world almost entirely visual, watching the trails of the oars, the splintering gray grain of the wood, the way the water in the bottom of the boat sloshed slowly back and forth.

Alex, though, Alex, she never did feel at ease, not once, all the way out. She held something back, some hard little kernel of self behind all the drugs; the observing part, the critical part, the part that had always

watched her, the part she could never turn off. It had
watched her all the time she was growing up, all the
time she'd put into making herself who she'd become,
a strong, engaged, political being; it watched, always
ready to remind her that she was just some girl, and
people only listened to her because she was pretty.

But it was that same part now that kept her aware
that things were not right. That same implacable and
unforgiving eye saw the situation and knew that it did
not make sense. They weren't heading to the opposite
shore, and they weren't headed south down this one;
Mike was rowing out past the shelf thirty feet down
that ringed the shore. He was rowing them out past the
drop-off to the deepest part of Seneca Lake, the deepest lake in western New York.

The kids on campus liked to say the lake was bottomless, but they liked to say that sharks turned up
sometimes, too, having traveled through some complex
of canals and underground waterways all the way from
the ocean. They liked to say a lot of things, but it wasn't
bottomless at all. Compared to, say, the Mariana
Trench, six miles deep, it was nothing, just a wading
pool, but it was still six hundred feet straight down, six
hundred feet of water, and if you were a person in a tiny
boat in the dark night, and there was nothing under you
but water for six hundred dark feet, it might as well be
six miles. Enough was as good as a feast, and you'd
drown before you sank a tenth of the way down.

Alex's thoughts wouldn't stay straight, they
wouldn't focus, but they were starting to hum with
fear, a fear of the nothing below, beneath the thin skin
of wood, all that water, and you couldn't breathe in
any of it, she almost couldn't breathe now from the
fear, and the acid picked it up and amplified it, dis-

torted it, echoed the fear around and around her head, growing louder and larger and more unbounded all the time, until all she was was fear, fear contained in a body animated solely by fear, and she curled up on her side in the bottom of the boat, their feet all around her, and cried, while the dirty sloshing water soaked her shirt and jeans and hair.

Mike had picked up Keith and Amy's tune, and hummed to himself as he rowed.

Alex didn't know they had stopped until she felt the weight shift in the boat, and she looked up and saw Keith stepping over the side. She looked around. Amy was already gone. *"No!"* she screamed, at the same time scrolling back in her mind, rewinding, hearing what Mike was saying.

"I'll be back for you," Mike told them all. "Wait for me here, that's right, get out and I'll come back for you when it's time, when things are ready. Stay here until I need you, and I'll come back and get you when the time is right."

Alex stood up and made a grab for Seth as he went over. "No, stop, don't!" She missed, and then turned the other way to reach for Paul, threw herself over the seat to grab him, but she was too late again, he was gone with a huge splash, and now she was on her knees in the bottom of the boat, leaning over the side reaching for Paul, who had just surfaced, looked around himself, dog-paddled to stay afloat. There were Keith and Amy, a little way off, clinging together, but they were going under like that, so they had to let go of each other or sink, and they started paddling, too, and there was Seth a little closer, choking on water, his wiry bush of hair sodden and weighted down.

Alex felt Mike's arm around her waist. He had

crouched down next to her, and she turned and looked into his face and he smiled at her. "Are you still committed, Alex? Do you still have faith that we can change the world?"

She started to struggle, to get away from him, but he tightened his grip around her waist as he spoke. "Are you still ready to follow me? Because you have to get out and wait here until I come back."

She was pushing at him now, trying to get out of his grip, pounding him with her fists, but there was nothing she could do. He was too strong. He lifted her up, her center of balance moving forward, from her hips, to her waist, to her shoulders, and now he flipped her over into the water. She made a grab for the side of the boat, but all she did was scrape the skin off her knuckles and then she was underwater, couldn't see, couldn't breathe, the bulk of the rowboat beside her and nothing below. She dragged herself up hand over hand through the water, pulling herself up toward the air, and then she was another bobbing head, gasping in the night air, dark water all around her, her friends all lost, all suspended between Mike's words—he'd be back for them, he'd said so, and they were committed, they had faith in him—and the understanding that he'd left them there to drown, nothing beneath them but nothing, that knowledge crushing them, pushing them down into it, as fear ran through them all.

She heard the splash of the oars in the water, and saw the rowboat start moving away, and she struck out after it, throwing her arms up and over and down, three strokes, five, but the boat was farther away each time she looked. It was hopeless, the shore so far away, nothing but black water in every direction, and then she looked back toward her friends, moving toward each other as they started to slip down, taking longer to come up each time, and she turned around to join them, pain starting to burn in her shoulders, and as she watched them go under, one by one, she realized it was all her fault, she had called him here, she had been tempted by the strength and knowledge and power he promised, and when she invited him in she had killed them all.

Ellen could see the red and blue lights flashing through the trees from the road, before they turned in to Oneida House. When they drove down the driveway in the brown sedan, they had to park behind two state troopers' cars, the four guys already up on the porch, standing around Mike.

Scoresby told her to wait in the car, but after she'd watched them stand around the porch from the back-seat for ten minutes, she let herself out and walked up to join them. Mike was looking her way and saw her coming before any of the cops.

"Ellen! Good to see you again, darlin'. Where you been keeping yourself?"

Ellen started to go up the porch stairs past them, to look for Alex inside. Scoresby stopped her. "Where you think you're going?"

"Inside, to find my friends."

"There's nobody inside, honey," one of the troopers said. "We've been all over the place."

"Where are they?" she demanded of Mike.

"Who's that, Ellen?"

"Where is Alex, Mike?"

"Beats me. I just got here. Everybody was gone."

Ellen turned to Scoresby, agitated, determined. "He did it"—she pointed at Mike—"he talked all of them into it. He brought all the stuff with him and he made them do it." She turned on Mike. "Where are they? Where's Alex? Did you do something to them?"

"I don't know what she's talking about, Officers. I was invited here for dinner by a very attractive young woman, Alex, I believe her name was. I think she had plans for me, if you know what I mean"—and he winked at the cops, so Ellen could see—"but the place was empty when I got here."

Ellen threw herself at him, fists balled up, but Scoresby and one of the troopers grabbed her before she could touch him.

"Just calm down, little lady," the trooper said, "and we'll sort everything out." He looked at Scoresby. "You can put her in the back of my car for now."

Mike winked at her as Scoresby led her away. "See you later, little lady," he said.

They never found any of them, and when they found the trunk Ellen told them to look for, the one she knew was in the house, filled with guns and grenades and Semtex plastic explosives, it was empty. In the end the only thing they could charge him with was trespassing on college property, and they didn't bother.

Ellen stayed in town all summer, calling everyone in the college administration she could reach, the state police, even the governor's office a few times, trying to keep them looking. They went through the woods for miles around the house, even dragged the lake as far out as they could before it got too deep for their nets, but nothing ever turned up. By the time school started again in the fall everybody but Ellen was ready to put it behind them—who knows with these kids, they could have hitched out west, and nobody'd find them until they wanted to be found—and the college closed down the house because nobody wanted to live there now, anyway.

20

". . . I got a job waiting tables, and kept looking, going out to the woods all the time, and when I saved some money I hired a detective, but he never turned up anything either. I went back to school after a while, and tried to forget about it all, but I just couldn't get myself to move away from here, just in case Alex ever came back.

"I used to call her parents every year around Christmas to see if they'd heard from her, but they weren't very friendly after the first couple of years, and then they changed their number. Now, I just try not to think about it." Ellen looked at the kids. "I guess that's not an option anymore, is it?"

"What about the guy, Walker?" Peter asked.

Ellen looked calm, but you couldn't miss the anger right below the surface. "I used to see him around, in the woods, when I'd be out looking for them, and sometimes there'd be lights on in the house, and I'd look, and nobody would be there, but I was sure it was him. The last time I saw him was the next summer. I drove out and parked by the house, and he was sitting out on the pier, looking out at the lake.

"I walked out there, and told him I wasn't going to

give up looking until I found Alex or her body, and that I wasn't scared of him, even though I was. He said, 'We all have to have faith in something, darlin',' and then he walked off into the woods. That was it. I went back to the house a few more times, but I didn't see him again, or anyone else. I assumed he'd just moved on. But you've seen him?"

"Not me," Trish said. "Peter. And his sister, and his sister's been acting really weird about it, too."

"He'd have to be almost sixty by now," Ellen said. "Are you sure you recognize him from the picture?"

"He doesn't look any different, Ms. Bourne. Just like in the picture."

"But, he can't. That's impossible. It must be somebody else."

"I don't think so," Peter said, and he handed her the two other pictures he'd brought with him. The printout of John Noyes, and the newspaper article about Joseph Smith.

Ellen looked from one to the other, took it in, figured it out, and a shudder ran through her, but it seemed to be shaking her together, putting all her pieces back in place. When she looked back up at Peter and Trish, she seemed calmer than she'd been since they first showed her the pictures.

"The question isn't 'Are you paranoid?'" she said; Peter recognized the saying and finished for her. "The question is 'Are you paranoid enough?'"

While Trish and Peter were learning from Ellen Bourne what had passed at Oneida House thirty-five years earlier, Buddy was headed there to investigate what was going on in the here and now.

It's not like he wanted to take advantage of a

friend's little sister, and for all his stupid, lumbering macho nature, he'd never force himself on a woman . . . well, maybe if she was passed out on roofies or something, because that didn't really take any force . . . but he'd only do that if it was somebody he knew, and he didn't think she'd mind. But a stranger? No way would he ever do that to a stranger.

But after hearing Peter talk about Virginia and the way she'd been acting, well, fuck, if she's giving it away, it's not his fault if he happens to be standing there when she does. It's not like he'd be making her do something she wasn't doing anyway. He wasn't doing anything wrong at all. Hell, Peter'd probably thank him. Way better she do it with a, you know, a friend of the family, than some strange guys in the woods. And Buddy always had liked them sort of chunky.

In the basement of her house, Virginia wiggled herself deeper into the hole in the wall behind the boiler. She'd burned herself on the forearm, and again on her hip, getting past it, and she knew she'd burn herself again getting out, but she was determined. It was dark in there and the flashlight was weak, and as she pulled herself on her belly through the dirt and the dust, she could see things skittering in the periphery of the light, and she had to remind herself not to get scared. She rubbed at her eyes with the back of her hand, but that only got more grit in them, so she just stopped and blinked until the tears flowing out and down her cheeks made it a little better. She continued forward, and finally she saw the khaki duffel bag that Walker had told her would be there.

Carefully, she reached out, snaked her hand between

the two-by-fours that separated her from the bag and just barely managed to grasp a corner of it. She tried to pull it toward her, but it was heavy, as if it were full of rocks. She crept forward, her pants dragged down lower on her hips, the cold, damp floor against her belly, and got a better grip. She rolled onto her side and pulled. The bag inched toward her.

Be very careful, he'd told her. She understood it was full of things that could explode, and in a way she didn't care, but she wanted to do what Walker asked, and she didn't want to just die. She wanted everybody else to die, too.

Slowly, she dragged the bag close enough to reach out and open the zipper, and she started removing, one by one, the things he'd told her to get. The grenades looked just like grenades in cartoons, but the other stuff looked just like modeling clay, except it was sweaty. She took pounds of it, piece after piece, and a half dozen grenades. There were guns in there, too, but Walker told her to leave those, so she did.

Carefully, she put it all in the backpack she'd dragged in with her, and she started out and almost forgot the fuses, but she went back and found those, too. Backing out of the hole took even longer than crawling in, but she had a real purpose now and discovered that she could be more patient than she'd ever thought.

Outside, it was getting dark as Buddy pulled up to Peter's house, and it didn't look like there were any lights on, but he parked in front anyway, thought he'd look around for her. He was startled as he approached the porch and realized somebody was sitting on the steps.

"Dude, who's that? Coulter, is that you?"

"Dude, not even close," the guy said and stood up.

Tall and thin, long dark hair.

Buddy pointed. Even in the fading light he recognized the guy from the pictures. "Fuck. I know who you are . . . you're that guy!"

"I am," Walker said, smiling and nodding. "I'm that guy. I know who you are, too."

"The fuck you do," Buddy said.

"The fuck I don't," Walker said, and began descending the porch stairs.

"I'm not scared of you," Buddy said, backing away, the thing he'd always said when he was scared of someone.

"You shouldn't be, Buddy," Walker said, approaching him.

"How do you know my name?"

"Does it matter, dude? You come sniffing around here after some underage pussy, a guy is just about to offer to help you get some, you care how I know your name?"

Buddy, cautiously, "No. I guess not."

"Here, hit this," Walker said, and held out a joint, which Buddy hadn't noticed in his hand before. Tentative, Buddy took it, took a hit without taking his eyes off of Walker.

"Good shit, huh?"

It was. Buddy felt a head rush almost before he'd even finished exhaling. "Whoa." He stumbled back a step, and Walker reached out and put a hand on his shoulder to steady him.

"Thanks, dude," Buddy said, automatically.

Hand still on Buddy's shoulder, Walker began to guide him away from the porch.

"C'mon, got some women I want to introduce you to."

"Hey!" Buddy said, and pulled away from him. He turned and started toward the porch stairs again.

"Dude, there's nobody home. C'mon with me, I got some juicy babes just waiting for you in the woods."

Buddy looked at the guy through narrowed eyes as he took another hit, one foot on the first stair.

"Nah," he said, deciding.

"Really, you don't want to go in there, Buddy. She's not for you. I've got some prime meat, just what you're looking for."

Buddy took the burning end of the joint between two fingers and squeezed it until it was out, then dropped it into the cigarette pack in his shirt pocket.

"No, thanks," he said, and started up the stairs.

"You can't go in there!" Walker said, raising his voice. "She has things to do."

"Yeah," Buddy said, his fear of the guy completely gone, seeing him like this. "She's gonna do me."

Buddy turned his back on Walker and walked to the front door. He knocked, and when there was no answer, he let himself in.

Upstairs, in his bedroom, Phil had been floating in and out of consciousness for hours, feverish but increasingly lucid. He thought about the book he was going to write, the one that would change everything people knew about the world, and imagined the glory and the acclaim that it would bring to him.

But first, he knew, he must get right with God. He'd learned his lesson. He wouldn't make that mistake again. He'd wait until he heard from Walker that he was done with the girl, and then he would make her suffer, the way God wanted, before he killed her.

When he heard the knock on the door downstairs he

roused himself, brushing at his chest as he got up, flinching at the pain, but unable to keep his hands away from what felt like hundreds of little itches, all over his chest. He walked to the door, one hand scratching at the flayed portions of his skin, breaking through newly formed scab to the raw flesh below.

He unlocked and opened his door, listened carefully. Somebody had come in.

In the light from the hallway, he looked at his fingers, at the maggots he'd turned up, some squashed, some still squirming.

He wiped his fingers off on his leg, realized he was wearing nothing, and quickly went to the closet and drew on a pair of pants and a shirt before returning to the door, opened just enough for him to listen.

"Right here," Peter said, and Ellen pulled her car onto the shoulder of the road. "If we walk down here, I can find the place I saw her."

Trish, sitting in the backseat, said, "It's gonna be dark really soon. Are you sure you know where you're going?"

"No," Peter said, and got out of the car, pulling the seat forward so Trish could step out, too. "I'm not."

"Oh," Trish said. There wasn't anything else to say.

Ellen Bourne hadn't wanted to wait until tomorrow to come look for the ghost of her love. She'd spent thirty-five years suspended, in a way, her feelings for Alex placed right *here*, just far enough away that she didn't feel them, but close enough that she never forgot they were there. If she could make contact, even if it were only with her spirit, then she didn't want to wait another minute.

It was a clear night and the moon was out, and the

first hundred yards or so through the spectral white boles of a stand of birches, all bare of leaves now, was easy enough, but they soon found the light dimming, and moments later they were walking into a fog, rolled in out of nowhere, and walked closer together, the three of them, hands on the trunks of trees as they passed. It was more a sense of open space than the sight of it that told Peter they'd found the clearing, and it wasn't hard to find the spot where the fire had been, because a fire glowed there now.

Peter shuddered, tried to laugh it off in front of the two women, finally gave in and just said, "Spooky."

They approached the fire through ever-thicker fog, until they were in a cave of open space within it. Red glowed all around them from the fire at their feet.

"Right here?" Ellen asked.

"Yeah. She wasn't alone, though. That guy was there, too."

"I know all about him," Ellen said and sat herself down, prepared to wait as long as it took.

"Well . . . ," Trish said.

"You can go," Ellen said.

"I don't want to leave you alone out here," Peter said, although he wanted to leave even more than Trish did.

Ellen looked at him, furrowed her brow. "I've been alone with this for a long time, young man. I certainly don't need your help now," she said, but not harshly.

"Okay. Our house is that way," Peter said and pointed north. "When you're . . . done."

But Ellen wasn't paying any attention to them anymore. She was looking into the fire and concentrating on Alex, trying to call her there by thinking about her as hard as she could.

*   *   *

"Hey, V.," Buddy said, startling Virginia, who thought she was alone in the house. She'd come up from the basement carrying her backpack carefully, her face and clothes black with grime.

"What are you doing here?" she asked, and then noticed a spider that clung to her shoulder, and brushed it off. "Who let you in? Is Peter here?"

"Nah, the door was open. I just came to see how you were doin'. You looked like you were having a hard time the other day." Even covered in dirt, the girl looked ripe.

Virginia looked at him, not knowing whether to trust him or not. Well, it didn't matter, because she had things to do.

"I'm busy," she said. "Go away."

"Oh, don't be so harsh," Buddy said, and remembered the joint in his pocket. "I got some reefer if you want to get high."

"I don't do drugs," she said.

"Ah, c'mon. Reefer's not drugs. Everybody smokes pot."

"Well, I don't, and I don't want to hang out with any of Peter's loser friends."

"Don't think of me that way. I'm just this dude from your school. Don't you want to make some friends of your own?"

She walked closer to him, cautiously.

"You got your car here?"

"Yeah! You want a ride somewhere? We could just take a ride around the lake, if you want."

"I gotta go to the school."

"Hey, no problem," he said, not questioning why she'd want to go to school at night. He held out his hands. "Here, gimme your backpack, I'll carry it for you."

She swung away, alarmed. "Don't touch that," she said a little shrilly.

"Relax, I don't need to carry your backpack, okay?"

Buddy turned and walked toward the door, stopped when he got there. "You coming or what?"

"Yeah, okay," she said, and followed him.

Upstairs, Phil, listening in, felt something very much like panic. He knew why that boy was here, even if Virginia was too stupid to figure it out. He had waited, following the conversation, scratching idly at his chest under his shirt, assuming that Virginia would turn the boy out, tell him to get lost, but then she'd agreed to go with him.

The little tramp. She was going to throw away her virginity on that thug, and then where did that leave him? No virgin sacrifice, that's where. No virgin, and no opportunity to put his house in order. He could torture and kill the girl afterward, he'd be glad to, but he knew that wouldn't be good enough.

He'd have to stop her, preserve her virginity. Surely he could do that. He was the girl's father, after all. He opened the door and headed down the stairs, unaware, as the fathers of teenage girls so often are, that the only place his daughter's virginity still existed was in his imagination.

In the woods Ellen sat by the fire, eyes closed, thinking loudly, almost shouting in her head, calling out to Alex. She knew she was here now, she had no doubt. All that time that she couldn't leave Seneca, this was why. It was because Alex was still here too, and now she'd see her, talk to her, once again.

Across the fire she heard a stirring and she opened her eyes.

Graham "Microgram" Walker sat there, smiling. "Boo," he said.

She closed her eyes and returned to her meditation, her prayer.

"She's mine now, you know. She's been mine ever since. She chose me, not you, and she'll forever be mine."

Ellen opened her eyes. "You tricked her," she said, spitting the words out. "She was just a kid. We were all just kids. We didn't know what we were doing. You took advantage of her."

Mike laughed. "I suppose you could see it that way. Doesn't matter though. Choices were made. Nobody said it was going to be fair."

Next to him, a form took shape, a pale light glowing, ethereal.

"Alex?" Ellen asked.

On the other side of Mike, another shape began to form, a larger figure, male. "Keith?"

Slowly, on either side of Mike, people she hadn't seen since 1971 materialized, watching her, silent, waiting for her to speak.

From the porch, Phil shouted, "Wait!" and ran toward them.

Buddy stood with his hand on the open door of his car. Virginia had just gotten to the other side.

Phil stopped a few feet from Buddy. It wasn't that far, no more than twenty yards, but in his current state, the sprint had left him panting. His face was pale, his hair sticking out, sweat was running down from his forehead.

"Dude, sit down before you have a fuckin' stroke," Buddy said, genuinely alarmed.

"I will not sit down. And you're not taking my daughter's virginity."

"Da-ad!" Even charged with nihilistic purpose, even with the prospect of her own death clearly ahead of her, Virginia could be embarrassed by her father.

"Come with me," he told her. "Now."

"Dad, I have important things to do. Can you just go back in the house?"

"You're coming with me. I won't have you leaving with him."

"Dad, stop, okay? You're messing everything up. Just leave me alone."

"That's enough," he said and stepped around the front of the car toward her. "There are some things that I need to do to you, and I can't do them if you let this lout have sex with you."

"Yo, old man. That sounds a little fucked up, you know?" Buddy said.

"This is no concern of yours, boy. Get in your car and get out of here."

Phil stepped closer to Virginia and snatched at her, but she stepped back, out of his reach.

"Yeah? Make me," Buddy said. "Why don't you just leave her alone?" He opened the back door and took the baseball bat from the backseat.

"What have you got there?" Phil said, alarmed.

"You wanna find out?" Buddy said and started around the car toward Phil.

"This is ridiculous. This is my daughter. You're no one. She's mine to do with as I please." On the last word, he lunged for her again and got a handful of hair.

"*Ow!*" Virginia screamed, and almost dropped the backpack she'd been cradling in her arms.

"*Hey!* What's going on?" Peter shouted as he came around the front of the house with Trish. It was too dark by now for him to see from that far away.

Peter walked over toward the car, Trish alongside him, until he stood near Buddy.

"Dude," Buddy said, just loud enough for them to hear, "your old man's seriously losing it."

"Peter," Phil said, "tell your friend to leave. He shouldn't be here."

"What are you doing here, anyway?" Peter asked. "You ditched us."

"Oh, that," Buddy said. "I had to come here to, uh . . . *Your father*, man, check him out! I think he has some, like, seriously twisted plans for little V."

Peter didn't need to be convinced. He turned to his father, started walking around the car, Buddy following him, Trish behind them both.

"Dad? Do you see what you're doing? Don't you think you should let go of Ginny?"

"Why," Phil said, backing away, off the driveway and onto the lawn, "so you and she can rut like animals under my roof?"

"Ewwww!" Virginia and Trish said at the same time.

He had his arm around her neck now, and was backing up down the lawn, toward the water.

Buddy stepped forward, bat in hand.

"Here, Coulter, let me take care of this."

"*No!*" Virginia said, very aware of what she was carrying in her bag.

"Aw, I wasn't really gonna hurt him," Buddy said, although he had started looking forward to the prospect of doing just that, since it was sure starting to look like he wasn't getting laid tonight.

"Dad, this is just weird, okay? You have to let Virginia go."

Phil didn't say anything, just glared at them, from one to the other, and then suddenly turned, grabbing Virginia by the arm. He ran for the rowboat that rested onshore next to the pier, pulling her behind him. Virginia yelped in surprise.

At the boat, the boys getting closer, Phil threw Virginia in over the side and pushed the boat off into the water. Virginia hit the bottom of the boat violently, and in the backpack she carried, surrounded by half-pound bricks of Semtex explosive, in the handle of a Vietnam-era hand grenade, a rusted pin weakened from the impact.

Ellen looked around the fire, from one lost, familiar face to another. There were Keith and Amy, still right next to each other, inseparable. There were Seth and Paul, both of them looking at her quizzically. But mostly Ellen looked at Alex, an apparition, but an apparition as lovely as she had been in life. Ellen's eyes brimmed with tears at the sight of her.

But now, instead of just lust and love and admiration, Ellen felt something new, something that surprised her, although it shouldn't have. After decades of teaching teenagers, seeing their energy and folly and knowing that as often as they went wrong, they wanted to go right, she felt protective of them all, too. She felt like gathering them all up in her arms and telling them it was all right, they could come home, they were forgiven their mistakes, it wasn't their fault. And when she looked at Alex she felt like she was looking at her child

as much as her lover, a child gone astray wandering in
the dark, a child who needed to be led back to the light.
She had loved her, but there was no way around it.
They'd never been anything more than children.

"You don't have to follow him anymore, Alex. Any
of you. He lied and he tricked you. He took the best
part of you and twisted it into something hurtful, and
he made you turn it on yourselves. Let go now. Leave
him. He didn't want to make a better world, he just
wanted to hurt this one. That's what he does. That's
what he's always done, and you can walk away from
him. You can be free of him and go wherever it is you
belong."

Still they looked at her, the five once-proud young
rebels, reduced in death to stooges, appendages,
flunky wraiths, doing the bidding of the thing that had
killed them.

"Dad, what are you doing? Stop!"

The boat was far enough out that they couldn't see
the two of them in the dark anymore, but Virginia's
voice carried clearly across the water.

"Dad, please! You're hurting me!"

Peter had run out to the end of the pier to get closer,
and Buddy had been right behind him, and the whole
thing creaked under their weight. Peter turned to
Buddy, an unspoken plea, and Buddy, lout though he
was, felt bad that he couldn't help.

"Sorry, dude. I don't swim."

They could hear Virginia sobbing now, and then,
"Peter! Help me!"

Peter took one more look, back to where Trish stood
on shore, took off his jacket and let it fall, then stepped
his sneakers off. Buddy held out the bat he still carried.

Peter shook his head, turned and dove into the blackness.

They weren't that far out, but Peter was no Olympian, and at first he made more noise than progress, and for twenty feet or so, the lake grass and weeds that grew up to the surface kept tangling him up. But he was getting closer, and the boat wasn't moving, and after a few minutes of stroking, he reached it.

Peter tried to be silent as he came up to the boat, but he must not have been as quiet as he thought, because when he looked up his father was standing above him holding an oar like a golf club.

Phil swung the oar at Peter's head, and if he'd been in better shape he might have cracked his son's skull wide open, but Peter moved faster and ducked down, so that the blade of the oar, slowed by the water, just glanced off his head. It hurt, but did no real damage.

Peter grabbed at the oar as it went back up, and yanked, and his father lost his balance almost immediately, but instead of being pulled out of the boat, he managed to fall backward into it, landing on Virginia.

"Ginny, jump out!" Peter yelled, but Virginia couldn't jump or even crawl with her father's weight across her legs. She put her hands up on the bench seat behind her, and tried to leverage herself out, but her father rolled over and grabbed for her again.

"*Cut it out!*" she shouted through gritted teeth.

Peter pulled himself around to the stern of the rowboat, closer to where Ginny was, and tried to lift himself up to where he could get a grip on her and pull her into the water away from their father.

In the woods, the fog thickened and ebbed, reflected red and yellow as the fire guttered and flared, and

Ellen kept talking. She told Alex how much she missed her and what they might have been together; she told Keith and Amy of the life they might have had, and Paul and Seth, too, a whole world waiting for all of them, bigger and more interesting than they had imagined in their little campus universe.

And all the time, Mike sat there smiling and certain.

They were both surprised when all five figures suddenly extinguished themselves. Just disappeared.

Virginia reached out for her brother, pulled away from their father.

Peter managed to push himself up out of the water, lean over the side and into the boat. The edge of the wood pushed hard into his stomach. He gripped his sister under the arms. "Come on," he said, watching their father begin to lift himself and reach for her.

"Damn you, boy!" Phil shouted. "You're *grounded*!"

Peter twisted his body around like a fish flopping on a hook at the same time that Virginia pushed with her feet, and she tumbled over him out of the boat and landed with a great splash in the water, Peter still holding on to the side with one hand.

"Virginia! Get back in here! I'm your father! Do as you're told!" Phil leaned way over the side and swiped at her, and the boat tilted all the way over, almost capsizing.

Peter let go and the boat rocked back, throwing Phil into the bottom of the boat again, and then suddenly Peter and his sister weren't alone in the water.

In the woods, they sat there, the two of them, silent, both of them knowing something was about to happen, but neither of them knowing what, neither knowing who would prevail.

Peter would have screamed if his mouth hadn't immediately filled with water as he felt himself being pulled down under, felt hands on him, touching him all over, and it might have even felt good, if he wasn't drowning. Through the dark water he could see motion and shapes off to his left, and he knew his sister was being pulled down under, too.

I'm sorry, Ginny, he thought. I tried.

Down, deeper and deeper, and he could see the woman's face in front of him, Alex his teacher had called her, and there was somebody else with her, both pulling him down. He felt Alex's hands on his face, and even in the dark cold water, her face was so close to his that he could make out her smile, and it was like all those dreams of sex and drowning all over again, and she brought her lips to his, and he thought his last thought: I never got to do it with Trish.

Up above, when Phil fell back, the lurch of the boat had slammed the backpack into the side, and the rusted pin that held the handle of the grenade in place through all those years—through Jimi Hendrix and the Grateful Dead, through Joni Mitchell and Bob Dylan, through the Ramones and Talking Heads and Pavement, Sonic Youth, Liz Phair and the Strokes—the rusted pin that had lasted for all that time finally gave out and crumbled to dust. Three seconds later the grenade exploded, setting off the four and a half pounds of Semtex and five more grenades in the backpack.

Blood might be thicker than water, but Peter and

Virginia's father was blasted into a fine mist of blood and bone and flesh that was quite a bit less dense than the water into which it settled over the next few minutes, floating down like floss.

Thirty feet below the explosion, deep in the cold water, Peter was just conscious enough to register the blast, and just deep enough to be entirely cushioned, protected from any harm. Seconds later, he and his sister were being lifted, sped upward by many hands to the surface, where they emerged gasping, coughing out water and drawing in great lungfuls of air and, however inadvertently, a fair amount of their father, something they happily never realized.

Together, they began swimming toward shore.

By the fire, they both heard the explosion.

"Damn," Mike said, and shook his head. "I was so sure."

"You mean it's over?" Ellen asked.

"Yep, that's it. You win. Alex and the rest, I'll never see them again."

"What happens to them now?"

"Fucked if I know. I just work here."

"So, what? That's it? You just go away?"

"Are you kiddin', darlin'? I never go away." Mike stood up and smiled, brushed off his jeans, and vanished into the fog.

21

Trish had gone into the house to get blankets, and now Peter and Virginia sat on the hood of Buddy's Camaro, all huddled up.

"You okay, Ginny?" Peter asked, after sitting in silence for a long time.

"I don't know," she said. Then after a minute, she added, "Our dad's dead." There was a little sob in her voice.

"Yeah, he is." Peter didn't want to say anything to upset Virginia any more than she was, but he didn't think it was that big a loss. Okay, he couldn't help it. "He was kind of an asshole, in case you didn't notice," he said.

"Yeah," Ginny said, nodding. "He wasn't a very good father."

"No, he wasn't," Peter said, shaking his head.

"He never did anything with us," Ginny said.

"Yeah, all he cared about was his work, like we weren't important to him."

"Yeah," Ginny said. "He never paid any attention to us."

Buddy, who'd been leaning against the car smoking a cigarette, spoke up.

"Well, V., he was sure paying some attention to you at the end there."

Peter froze, not sure how Virginia was going to respond, but when he heard her snort of laughter, he relaxed.

"So, Ginny, what do you think we should do?"

"I want my mom." She looked over at him. "Can we please go back to Brooklyn now, Peter?"

Peter looked away. No way he wanted to go back to Brooklyn.

"You know, Mom didn't like him much, either."

"Yeah, so? What's your point?"

"I'm pretty sure she'd move up here now."

Ginny got angry. "I don't care what you do and I don't care what she does. I'm going back to Brooklyn. It *sucks* here." She slid off the hood of the car, let the blanket fall to the ground.

As she stomped by Buddy on her way to the house, he grabbed her arm. "Hey, why you gotta be like that? You can have a pretty good time here, you know?"

Virginia swung around, her fist in the air, ready to let Buddy have it, when something stopped her. She'd never noticed before, but Buddy had really pretty brown eyes. She became aware of an odd feeling in her stomach, but it wasn't unpleasant. She lowered her fist, and Buddy let go of her arm. They looked at each other.

"Whatever," she said, and then continued on toward the house.

"Ginny?" Peter called after her.

She stopped and turned on the porch.

"I guess we don't have to go back to Brooklyn right this minute," she said.

ABOUT THE AUTHOR

Howard Mittelmark is a writer and editor. He lives in New York City and on echonyc.com.

To correspond or find out more, visit howardmittelmark.com.